THE CLUB BY THE SEA

TAYLOR MARTIN

STM PUBLISHING

Copyright © 2024 by Taylor Martin.

All rights reserved.

No portion of this book may be reproduced in any form without written permission from the publisher or author, except as permitted by U.S. copyright law.

FOREWORD

I've always been drawn to the idea of a good story. Believe it or not, storytelling is all around us. We read the stories of our peers' lives each day as we scroll through social media. We see stories in marketing campaigns across the globe. We listen to stories through songs by our favorite artists. We watch stories through films. We frame the stories of our lives and display them on the walls of our homes. I've worn many hats in my lifetime, but storyteller is the most consistent one—the one I return to at the end of the day.

My debut novel, *The Club by the Sea*, is a story I dreamed up after listening endlessly to music one night. A particular song on Taylor Swift's album *Evermore* sparked the concept for what I originally thought would make a cool music video. Unfortunately, I have no connections to the legendary Taylor Swift. So, the idea of turning it into a book became the next big thing. With this imaginary concept and inspiration from Baz Luhrmann's film *Elvis*, I got to work.

This book is dedicated to my fifth-grade teacher, Mrs. Mulholland, who truly sparked my love for storytelling and writing. She believed in my work at such a young age, and I've carried that with me throughout my entire education. Early on, I knew that if I ever had the opportunity to publish a book, it would be dedicated to her. Wherever you are, Mrs.

Mulholland, I did it. Your impact on my life as a student has stayed with me throughout my entire career.

I have so many others to thank for making this happen, and you can read more about that toward the back of the book.

This story was once just a figment of my imagination, and now you are holding it in your hands. For that alone, I cannot thank you enough. So, without further ado, allow me to take you into the world of Clark James. Welcome to the *Sea House*.

-Taylor Martin

CHAPTER 1

Present Day

He leaned his athletic frame against the floor-to-ceiling window to get a better view of the sea, resting his right arm slightly above his freshly slicked-back blonde hair. Between the glare from the sun and the thick film of dust, Neal Smith was having a hard time seeing the commercial listing's panoramic views. Using the end of his crisp, white sleeve as a dust rag, he cleaned off a small spot on the glass. Behind him, he could hear Miranda, one of his project managers, reviewing the property specs.

"Aren't the views just stunning? Once those windows are cleaned, you'll be able to see the potential of this space," Miranda said as she continued walking through the massive empty room. Her black stilettos pinged on the old, creaky, hardwood floors as she swiftly moved about the former nightclub. Her voice and movements echoed throughout the expansive space.

"I'm telling you, when we complete this renovation, people will be talking about Smith Developmental for days. Weeks even." Miranda gesticulated dramatically, her red-painted fingernails flashing as the sunlight hit them.

Neal turned to Miranda, his hands on his hips as the sunlight beamed against his back. "The views are breathtaking, and I can definitely see the potential of the space, but what's its story? How long has it been vacant?"

"Almost 10 years now. The place has definitely seen better days. It was built in 1940 and was a swanky jazz club for nearly three decades. It was tremendously damaged during a fire in the '60s. After that, the building was purchased by new owners who attempted to restore the property but never really got it off the ground. They held onto it for a good bit until it became known as a high school party joint."

Miranda's disgust with the current condition of the space was evident as she pointed to the oversized graffiti on the walls. Neal took it all in. Typical teenage vandalism. "Brock loves Sharon," "For a good time, give Chris Morton a call." A fair share of oversized penises peppered with sexual vulgarities.

Neal's eyes slowly scanned the entire space noting the old booth seating and few mahogany tables that served as remnants of the past. "So, it's a ritzy jazz club, and then after it's mostly destroyed by a fire it becomes a place for teenagers to pop molly and hook up? Very Monterey," said Neal. "What can you find on this jazz club? Any photos?"

Miranda opened her rose gold MacBook Pro and turned it around for Neal to see. "Of course I've done my research. I had to visit the Monterey courthouse to find these photos. From the looks of it, it used to be all the rage. The place where anybody who was anybody could attend lavish dinners and shows. It's mostly known for showcasing the famous jazz singer Clark James. People from all over the world came to see him perform. Marilyn Monroe, Frank Sinatra, and James Dean were just some of the famous patrons of the club."

Quickly clicking through the old black-and-white photos of the space, Neal saw what the property used to be. And Miranda was right. It was evident that the vacant, run-down venue was once one of the coolest jazz clubs in the country. Photos showed candlelit tables surrounded by people dressed to the nines, champagne toasts, and dancing. And then, the one and only Clark James.

Curious, Neal zoomed in on the photo of the iconic jazz singer. He was young, with a sharp jawline and dark, short hair that curled perfectly in place against his forehead. Clark appeared to be in his twenties and was wearing a white dinner jacket with a black-and-white polka-dotted handkerchief in the front pocket. The famous crooner was leaned back with his arms wide open as if he was about to take a bow. The spotlight beamed behind him, casting him in silhouette.

"I've not heard much of this James character, but then again, I'm not familiar with the jazz world. It looks like he was a heartthrob, though. Any idea where he is now? Would be cool to have him come back to this space if we revitalize it."

"What do you mean, *if*?" Miranda asked, shutting the laptop.

"Oh come on, Miranda. You know this project is going to cost a lot of money. Possibly our biggest expense yet."

Miranda shoved her laptop into her oversized Louis Vuitton bag. She continued, avoiding Neal's concerns.

"So, that's the interesting thing. I can't find much on Clark James after the fire. It's like the guy vanished. There is no death certificate or really much of anything tying back to him. All I can find are old photos of him from his time at the jazz club. And then the occasional online vinyl shop that sells his old records. He's not even on Spotify or other streaming platforms."

Neal wiped his forehead. The humidity was starting to get to him, as the California morning temperatures continued to rise. Any minute now, his slicked-back hair would become curly.

"Very interesting. Let's see if we can find more photos and articles from the building's heyday. And then let me think on it."

"Neal, we don't need to sit on this one. You've been saying for months that you're ready for the next big thing. Something that's groundbreaking. A break from condos and downtown lofts. And here it finally is!"

Neal adjusted the engraved cufflinks that showcased his initials, twirling them in his calloused fingers.

"That's very true."

It was apparent to Miranda that Neal was deep in thought, a million miles away from where they stood. "And it's closer to home, which you've also been saying you wanted," she continued.

Neal snapped back to reality, giving a quick nod. "And that's also true."

"Neal, I'm telling you, we breathe life back into this space and people are gonna love it. Plus, it's historic. You know how people eat that up."

Neal smiled, revealing his perfectly straightened teeth. "They do love historic, don't they?"

Miranda crossed her arms against her fitted pink blazer. "So, you're in?"

"If we can turn this back into the gem it once was and stay under five million dollars, yes," Neal replied, checking the time on his iPhone.

"We can discuss the budget more on Monday. I like it better when you think things through, so give it some more thought over the weekend," said Miranda.

"The budget has been thought through, Miranda. Keep it under five million, preferably under three, if at all possible. Let's get the utilities rolled over into our name. And please, let's get the AC going," Neal said, walking past Miranda toward the front door.

Miranda took notes on her iPhone as they made their way out the front door of the vacant building. "Will do. I can have the utilities transferred to our name today. Is there anything else you need me to do before you head out for the weekend?"

Neal pulled the Range Rover keys out of his pocket and pressed the remote start button. "That should be it. Let's get the contractors and architects here by the middle of next week. I think we can make this all happen before summer if we start soon. But for now, I have to get to the airport or my nana will kill me. She hates when I'm late."

"Ahh, that's right! This is the weekend! Nana and Grandad are coming to town. What do you have planned for them?"

Neal quickly got into the driver's side, shut the door, and rolled down the window. "Tonight, we're going to have dinner at my house, and tomorrow we'll drive up the coast. We'll probably take the Bronco and explore. The last time my grandparents were in Big Sur, they were newlyweds, so it will be fun for them to experience the coast again."

Miranda grinned. "Well, I think that's absolutely adorable. Tell Nana and Grandad I said hello. You need to bring them here. I'm sure they'd love to see your next big project."

"Yeah, that's a good idea. You have a good weekend, Miranda." Neal began to roll up the window.

"Neal, one more thing. Be prepared for them to ask questions about Josie. After all, you're still wearing the cufflinks she bought you for your birthday."

Neal's eyes darted down to his wrists and then back to Miranda.

"Doesn't mean a thing, Miranda. I can wear cufflinks if I want to wear them."

"Hmm. Yeah, okay. Let me know if there's anything else I can do for you. If not, I'll see you next week!"

Neal quickly thanked Miranda and sped out of the gravel parking lot while checking the clock in the dash. Ten minutes behind schedule. If he was lucky, he could beat the rush hour traffic in time to get to the Monterey airport.

CHAPTER 2

While on his way to the airport, Neal thought more about the rundown nightclub. It was in terrible shape, yet when he'd stepped into the space, he instantly felt its potential. Just seeing the few old photos of the nightclub from Miranda's laptop promised that. At the same time, he knew something was different about this project than anything he had done in the past.

Perhaps it was the value of bringing a new experience to Monterey. Since moving to Big Sur from Los Angeles, Neal was eager to find projects closer to home. Most of his development projects took place in LA or surrounding areas of southern California. Neal felt it was time to do something in his new community instead of six hours away.

As Neal's GPS arrival time continued to elapse, he started to wonder if this project was more personal than just adding value to the neighborhood. Nearly a month had passed since he and Josie, his girlfriend of a year, had decided to call it quits. Neal recognized old habits and knew he often used his work to provide an escape from reality. In fact, it was the main reason why Josie decided not to move from LA to Monterey with Neal.

Too stubborn to let go of his pride, Neal continued with the move to Big Sur anyway, turning the home that he and Josie were supposed to share into his own paradise. Distracted by his thoughts, Neal didn't realize he was close to the airport until his iPhone started ringing. The screen in the middle of the dash flashed his nana's contact photo.

"Hi, Nana! Have you and Grandad landed?" Neal closed the Range Rover's sunroof.

"Hi, Sweetie. Yes, we've landed. But you know your grandfather. I argued and argued with him that we did not need to check our bags, but he insisted it would be easier on us if we did. Well, guess what? We're here at the baggage claim and they have yet to bring our luggage off the plane. Are you waiting for us outside?"

Phew. Good. I've got a few minutes, Neal thought.

"I'm almost there. Don't worry though. They're pretty quick with luggage. It'll be all right. You're back in the Golden State. Life is easier here, especially in Big Sur."

Neal could hear the buzzer of the baggage carousel in the background.

"Ha! Yeah, right. Ooh, here we go! Listen, Honey, our bags are finally arriving. Your grandfather–"

Neal could barely make out what Nana was saying. He imagined her dropping the phone below her chin while talking with Grandad.

"Neal, are you there? I'm back. Your grandfather is off to the bathroom. I mean, really? He can't wait five minutes? Anyway, as soon as he's back, we'll grab our suitcases and be out to find you."

Grandad's bathroom habits scored Neal the perfect amount of time.

"Sounds good, Nana. I'm pulling up to the terminal now. I'm in the black Range Rover. I'll be standing outside."

"Oh, the Range Rover. Well, look at you, Mr. Hollywood. We'll see you in just a sec."

Neal ended the call and eagerly waited on his grandparents. Originally from California, they moved to the Southeast after retiring. After many claims of LA not being the same as it once was and tired of the rising cost of living, they settled in a house in East Tennessee, just outside Knoxville.

They moved right before Neal graduated from high school. During summer and college breaks, Neal would occasionally fly to Tennessee to visit them. But once Neal started making money and moving up the corporate ladder his schedule became harder to accommodate, and it became easier for Nana and Grandad to fly out to California for visits. Courtesy of Neal, of course. It had been more than two years since Nana and Grandad had last been to California, though.

And since then Neal had moved from Los Angeles into the mountains of Monterey. The house he bought was something he and Josie loved the second they toured the property. The four-bedroom, three-bathroom Spanish-style home overlooked the sea and hills of Big Sur. It was the perfect sanctuary for relaxation and peace, something he desperately began to crave while living in Los Angeles. Josie loved LA and wasn't quite committed to moving at first. But when she saw the house and the views she thought it would be a good change for them.

However, when Neal continued to prioritize work over their relationship, tensions grew. In the final week before closing on the Monterey home, Josie caught Neal by surprise when she revealed she didn't think their relationship was going to work out.

Nana and Grandad had made their way outside the airport, eagerly waving at Neal. Nana wore light blue jeans and a simple navy blouse along with gray suede Birkenstock sandals. Her straightened salt-and-pepper hair was shorter than when Neal last saw her, coming to just below her chin. In contrast, Grandad's brown hair had been thinning for the last few years. The few remaining strands laid across his glistening head. Wearing his signature casual look of khaki cargo shorts and a navy moisture-wicking t-shirt, Grandad followed closely behind Nana, pulling their matching black hardshell suitcases.

"Neal! Hi, Sweet Pea!" Nana beamed, eagerly waving her hand high above her head.

The common greeting from his Nana. No matter what age or success, Neal was always going to be nicknamed "Sweet Pea." Neal hugged Nana first, following up with a quick side hug with Grandad.

"Welcome back! How was your flight? Let's get those suitcases in the back," Neal said as he reached into Nana's wide-armed embrace.

As he and his grandmother hugged, Neal could feel pressed against his chest the beaded chain which held Nana's red reading glasses. Her signature scent, a perfume by Estée Lauder with a name he could never recall, filled the space between them.

"Look at you, Handsome!" Nana gently touched Neal's shoulder. Before getting out of the car, he had thrown on his light blue linen blazer that went perfectly with his custom tailored khaki dress pants. The blue blazer brought out the color of his eyes, and when the light hit just right you couldn't tell if they were green or blue.

"Thank you, Nana," Neal said, turning his head as Nana planted a big red kiss on his cheek.

She gently licked her thumb and brushed it across Neal's face, removing the lipstick residue.

"Well, the flight was okay. Your grandfather slept the entire time. But all I kept thinking about was how much longer it would be until we saw our Sweet Pea. And oh my!"

Nana gawked at Neal's platinum black Range Rover. Neal smiled, pressing the tailgate button, making it gently lower to a close. Grandad opened the backseat door, gesturing for Nana to get in.

"Neal, this car is very, very, very nice. When did you get this?" She marveled as she rubbed the tan leather seats.

"Thanks. I'm not sure. Maybe about six months ago. I needed something to drive to properties, and this does this job. Grandad, you still got the Vette?"

The Vette was the nickname for the 2018 Corvette that Grandad one day bought on a whim. Grandad had always had expensive taste and a love for cars. And it drove Nana crazy.

Grandad buckled his seatbelt across his plump belly. "We still have it. I occasionally take it for a spin. You know how fast that sucker goes?"

Nana huffed and rolled her eyes. "Oh please. The car stays in the garage more than it's actually on the road."

Grandad looked at Neal. "Don't listen to all that. I drive it once a month. Goes from zero to 90 miles per hour within seconds, you know!"

Neal laughed, "Sounds safe, Grandad. Real safe!"

"Hey, can I smoke a cigar in your car? You mind?" Without waiting for a response, Grandad began unwrapping a cigar from its packaging. He loved a cigar, especially since he "quit" smoking three years ago.

Used to Grandad's habits, Neal rolled down the passenger window and cranked up the tunes. Through the occasional sing-along to oldies and Grandad's smoke breaks, they continued to catch up during the commute to Neal's house.

Nana moved to the middle seat in the back of the Range Rover so she could see both Neal and Grandad.

"Hey, Neal? Have you talked to Josie at all?" she asked as the Rolling Stones

"You Can't Always Get What You Want" faded out.

Hesitating to answer, Neal darted his eyes to the rearview mirror to see Nana focusing on him.

"Uh, not that much."

Nana rested her elbow on her knees, propping her head on her hand.

"Really? That's too bad. You know, we really liked her."

Neal continued to look straight ahead at the interstate.

"Yeah, I know. But I guess it doesn't always work out, does it?"

"She hasn't seen the house at all since you moved in?"

Neal shook his head. "No. We've barely spoken since the night she decided she was staying in LA."

Grandad chimed in. "Well, why don't you call her? Tell her to come over and see the place. Invite her over for dinner."

Neal chuckled. "Because we've broken up, Grandad. We don't do dinner together anymore."

"Well, you can still make amends, Sweet Pea," suggested Nana from the backseat.

"Exactly! It wouldn't hurt, you know?" Grandad aimed to get his point across.

Neal flicked on his turn signal as he began to exit the highway.

"All right, enough about me and Josie, okay? Let's talk about something more fun. Like our plans for this weekend!" Neal was doing his best to change the subject.

Nana looked up from her iPhone. She'd successfully updated her Facebook status to "Arrived in sunny California."

"Oh, yes! Tell us what you have planned for this weekend!"

"I thought tomorrow we could drive up and down the coast. I want to show you all this new property I'm developing. I think you both will really love it."

Nana and Grandad smiled in unison.

"We would love to. You know we always love seeing your next project. What's this one going to be?" asked Grandad.

"I'm thinking this one is going to be my biggest and best yet. We're renovating a run-down venue that overlooks the sea. It's going to be incredible once we restore it."

Neal looked in the rearview mirror to see Nana's reaction. She had moved back to the right side of the backseat, now leaning against the armrest, looking out the window. She was admiring all of the coastline's glory.

"Sounds exciting!" she said as she focused her eyes on the view.

California's current political climate and cost of living had turned Nana and Grandad away from the state. Although they were no longer the biggest fans of the West Coast, Neal was glad to have his grandparents back in town for the next few days.

CHAPTER 3

The next morning, Neal woke up to the scent of bacon and coffee wafting through the house. It was 8:00 on Saturday and Nana was already up and cooking breakfast, something Neal rarely did. He needed to get a workout in before the California heat started to set in, but the aroma of a home-cooked breakfast was calling his name. All normalities and rules went out the window when Nana and Grandad were in town.

Before heading to the kitchen, Neal checked his phone notifications. Three emails from Miranda. The subject line of the first? *Dirt on the Jazz Singer*. Neal clicked to open the email.

Hi Neal,

I was able to find more info on the jazz singer. Besides being a total hottie, Clark James was the jazz sensation of the West Coast. People traveled from all over the world to come to the club to watch his shows. I was able to find some old audio snippets of his live performances on YouTube. Attached are the files.

Cheers,

Miranda

Neal clicked on the audio file attachment. The 35-second clip was that of Clark James belting out a note followed by a rousing saxophone solo. The audience roared with applause and screams. Not too shabby, thought Neal.

Returning to his inbox, Neal clicked on the second email from Miranda. The subject line read: *Jazz Club Photos*.

Me again.

Okay. This place was phenomenal. Packed seats, amazing food and drinks. Live dance parties on the terrace overlooking the sea. My goodness. We have to bring this back. Think people still appreciate jazz?

Cheers,

Miranda

Neal browsed through the attached photos. Miranda was definitely right. The vintage pictures looked like something out of a movie. Photos of Clark James singing on stage with his band. Photos of couples dancing on the terrace. And then one photo in particular that stood out to Neal, that of a young lady wearing a black dress with her hair pinned back. She was laughing while holding a glass of champagne and leaning into Clark James. The lady looked awfully familiar to Neal.

As he began to walk down the steps to the kitchen, Neal clicked on the final email from Miranda. The subject line: *TIME TRAVEL*

Okay, last one, I SWEAR.

It might be the rosé I'm drinking, but I'm seeing articles claiming that Clark James was some sort of time traveler. That's apparently why he never aged.

Crazy stories, I'm sure. But I thought it was interesting since it was brought up numerous times during my search. Maybe we can find this guy and he can tell us the secret to everlasting youth.

Anyway, enjoy your weekend.

Miranda

Neal swiped out of his email. Hmm. Time travel. Yeah, okay, he thought. Just as he was putting his phone away, he walked into the kitchen to find Nana and Grandad putting the finishing touches on breakfast.

Grandad was still in his gray plush robe, a Grandad morning staple, and was drinking his cup of coffee while Nana finished up the breakfast potatoes.

"Good morning, Sweet Pea. How'd you sleep? Coffee is ready and I'm just finishing up the potatoes. You like your eggs scrambled, right?"

Neal smiled at Nana and filled his cup with coffee. "Morning! Yes to the scrambled eggs. I slept great. I should be asking you all. How did you guys sleep?"

"I slept like a rock. What kind of mattress did you get for that guest bed? My Lord, I fell asleep as soon as I laid down," said Grandad as he took a sip of his coffee.

"Oh, I know. Your grandfather snored all night long. Your new space is very comfortable and cozy. Quiet. I think Josie would really love it."

Neal rolled his eyes as he poured creamer into his coffee.

"Nana, please. Not first thing in the morning. Can we not talk about Josie as soon as I wake up?"

Nana looked up from cooking breakfast. "Okay, I'm sorry. I really should stop, shouldn't I?" she said while adjusting her glasses on the bridge of her nose.

"Thanks. But yes, I like it out here. LA was fun, but I needed somewhere to relax. Where I could collect my thoughts and breathe at night. Big Sur has always been that place for me, so I thought why not call it home." Neal made his way to the kitchen table beside Grandad.

"You're right about that. We used to love to roam the coast. I've always loved it. Before I met your grandfather, I spent a lot of time in Monterey. And after we married, we would occasionally spend the

THE CLUB BY THE SEA

weekend somewhere along the coast. It's a beautiful place," said Nana as she placed plates of food on the table.

Neal, Nana, and Grandad began to dig into the breakfast spread. While mapping out their day, Neal decided to fill in his grandparents on the jazz club renovation.

"I can't wait to show you all this space today. You know, back in the '40s this place was the coolest spot around."

Neal looked at his grandparents. Grandad smiled and said, "Is that so? What was it?"

Neal continued, "Well, it used to be a jazz club where you could eat dinner and watch world-class performances. But I think it was mostly known as the place where Clark James would sing."

Nana cleared her throat. "Oh my goodness! This coffee is so hot. Burned my entire throat just now."

Neal and Grandad glanced at Nana, both surprised by her reaction.

"Clark James. I remember hearing his music on the radio. People really did love that guy. I wasn't much of a jazz fan, so I didn't really get it. But I always heard of people raving about his shows," said Grandad.

"Yeah, I've heard a few snippets of some of his live performances. I don't know much about jazz either, but from the clips I've listened to, it sounded like a very fun time. I can only imagine what it was like."

Nana got up and began removing empty plates from the table.

"Well, I am sure it was a grand time. And we can't wait to see the space. I don't really remember much about Clark James, either. He was–"

Grandad interrupted Nana. "What do you mean you don't remember Clark James?! You loved his music. You were always humming his songs when we were dating. I couldn't get you to stop."

Standing at the sink, Nana turned and began washing the breakfast dishes.

"Well, that's right. I did love his music. He had a great voice. But I barely remember it now. I wasn't one of those crazy girls who showed up to every show and fawned over him, I'll tell you that."

"Nana, you don't have to wash the dishes. We can load them into the dishwasher later."

Nana shook her head, "Oh, nonsense. Dishwashers don't scrub as well as I do. Anyway, Clark James, he…I…okay, yes, I liked his music, but that's it. Nothing more."

Neal and Grandad swapped glances. Grandad rolled his eyes.

"Babes, it's fine to say that you were a fan. He was a teenage heart-throb. No big deal. But you know, I always wondered what happened to the guy. It's like he just vanished one day."

Continuing her cleaning spree, Nana began to wipe off the glistening white quartz countertop. Neal pulled out his phone.

"Yeah, I actually got some emails from Miranda and she said sort of the same thing. There's a lot of speculation about the guy. Crazy stuff like he was a time traveler."

Nana froze, sponge in hand.

"You know what? I think it's time we start getting ready for our day. Less chit-chat and more exploring! We need to get out there and enjoy this beautiful California sunshine. Hello Vitamin D, am I right?!"

With that, Nana marched out of the kitchen, leaving Neal and Grandad looking at each other.

"California puts her in a lively mood sometimes. She'll be fine. Let's get the Bronco out and seize the day, what do ya say? Hey, you mind if I smoke a cigar on your back patio real quick?" asked Grandad.

Neal nodded and let Grandad continue onto the patio to enjoy his third cigar of the morning.

"Be ready to leave the house at 11:00, Grandad," Neal called after him.

CHAPTER 4

Neal, Nana, and Grandad set out at 11:15. Before the temperatures got even hotter, Neal thought it would be best to see the jazz club at the beginning of their Big Sur tour. And it was only a short 10-minute drive from his house, making it the closest project he had ever renovated.

"Let's stop at the club first. Yesterday, it was pretty toasty in there without the air conditioning on. I'm hoping Miranda has the utilities in our name and that we have them up and running, but it's been years since the A/C has been operational, so who knows," said Neal as they continued down the curvy road.

"You guys are going to love the place though. It's this beautiful building with floor-to-ceiling windows that overlook the ocean. There's a huge terrace off to the side of the building that would be the perfect spot for outdoor dining and a bar. It really has so much potential."

Nana nodded her head and forced a smile. Grandad cranked up Bruce Springsteen's "Dancing in the Dark."

Just as Neal and Grandad were about to belt out the final chorus, Neal pulled into the gravel parking lot of the jazz club. "Here we are…the historic jazz club," said Neal as he shifted into park.

Seeing it in earlier daylight made Neal realize just how much work was in store for this renovation. The building's faded gray facade had accumulated years of thick, green grime. Many spots looked completely rotted. The old rickety windows had been spray painted over a few too many times over the years. Most of the windows were missing shutters, leaving behind only the thick outline of the ones that once were attached. It was clear extensive parking lot reconstruction would need to take place.

"Never mind the condition of the property! Check out these views!" Grandad said as he opened the car door for Nana. She nodded and stood in place, taking in the expansive scenery.

"Yeah, it's not in the best condition right now, but everything will be redone. Let's go inside, shall we?" Neal led the way toward the club's entrance.

"The property sustained extensive damage during a fire and it was somewhat repaired by former owners. But they weren't able to ever really do anything with the place. It kind of became a hangout where high school kids came to party until we purchased it."

Neal pushed open the large arched mahogany doors and led Nana and Grandad into the dark space. The dusty pendant lights began to buzz as Neal flipped each light switch, revealing the entire space's glory.

"Great artwork. Nothing like teenagers confessing their love to each other through spray paint," joked Grandad.

Nana gingerly walked to the large windows that overlooked the sea. "These views take me back to my younger days. It's like I'm 20 and seeing Big Sur for the first time all over again." Nana faced the windows and began to faintly hum a tune unfamiliar to Neal.

Pulling out his iPhone from his back pocket, Neal began showing his grandfather the photos of the jazz club during its heyday. "Grandad, I can't believe you lived here and never went to this club."

The elder man put on his reading glasses and admired the photos, "Well, like I said, jazz wasn't really my thing. I remember people coming here and loving it, but I was more into surfing the waves and hitting up the beach bars."

Neal paused his scroll. "Here he is. The infamous Clark James. He performed on that stage right over there many, many times," said Neal, pointing. "And there are crazy rumors about the man. Tales of him being a time traveler, disappearing and never being seen again. I want to find him just to learn more about his time here."

Nana stopped humming. "Neal, are you sure you want to take on this project? I know you're a pro at this, but my goodness. It needs so much work and the upkeep...I can't imagine it being cheap to run."

Neal looked up from his phone. "I think it will be all right, Nana. The repairs aren't even that bad compared to some of the other properties we've developed. And I don't know, something about this place speaks to me. It's all so interesting."

Neal swiped to the photo of Clark James standing with the young lady in a black dress. "Grandad, check out this photo. Some chick with Clark James. There's no telling what crazy things he got into with fans here." Neal handed his phone to his grandfather, who brought it close to his face as he peered over his reading glasses.

"Wait a second..." Zooming in on the photo of the woman, Grandad paused. He examined the photo, his eyes moving from the phone to the back of Nana's head.

"My God, Babes. This lady in the photo looks just like you at that age."

Nana quickly turned from the window.. "Oh, come on, Daniel. That would be crazy. I–I never met Clark James."

Neal snatched the phone from Grandad's hands.

"Nana, I thought this photo looked familiar. It's you...isn't it? You're the woman in the photo?!" Neal rushed over to Nana, holding the phone out for her to see.

"Hmph. You both are being crazy. This is crazy! All of this. Being in this building. Hearing you both talk about Clark James. Saying that I'm this mysterious woman in a photo?! Are you even hearing yourselves?"

Jerking the phone from Neal's hand, Nana glanced at the photo.

"That's enough!"

Nana let out a sigh and then paused. She held the phone close to her chest and gazed down at the black-and-white image. When she looked back to Neal and Grandad, there were tears in her eyes.

"This is just too much. I–I don't even know what to say."

Grandad took off his glasses. "Babes, what are you saying? What's wrong?"

He inched closer to Nana and Neal followed.

"Okay, it's true. The things you've read about this jazz club and what it used to be are true. I know that because..."

Neal and Grandad stood completely still, staring at Nana. They seemed frozen in time.

"I know this because, well, the woman in the photo *is* me. And I did, in fact, know Clark James."

Neal chuckled. "No shit! Nana, you've been holding out all these years?! You knew Clark James?"

Grandad cleared his throat. "Yeah, I'm confused, Milly. You knew Clark James? You've never mentioned him. In fact, you insisted earlier this morning that you never even met the man."

THE CLUB BY THE SEA

Nana adjusted the strap of her black leather purse on her shoulder. "Daniel, I know. It's very complicated, and it's a long story. I haven't told anyone. In all honesty, I didn't think I'd have to."

She quickly walked to the door that led to the terrace, pausing at the gated entrance. Slowly turning toward Neal and Grandad, she dropped her purse at her feet.

"Take a seat, boys. I will tell you the story of my time with Clark James."

Grandad sighed. "Unbelievable."

"Okay, just listen. Neal, get those two chairs over there by the stage."

Neal grabbed two sun-bleached wooden chairs that were covered in a thick film of dust and brought them to the center of the room. Grandad grabbed a third and motioned for Nana to take a seat.

Nana sat, folded her hands in her lap, and took a deep breath. "Okay," she exhaled. "Our story begins in 1945."

CHAPTER 5
Paris, 1945

"**H**IT IT!"

The trumpets blared and the saxophones followed. The music was too fierce to stop the club patrons from moving in their seats. One by one, table by table, the live music swept everyone off their feet and onto the dance floor.

The bass picked up and the lead singer, Alfie Dupont, let out an energetic scream. "BONJOUR, PARIS! TONIGHT...WE CELEBRATE! AND WE DANCE!"

The crowd screamed and became one with the beat of the music. Rob dropped Alexandria's hands to light a cigarette. After a quick inhale, he grabbed her by the waist and pulled her in. "Good golly, I'm going to miss you and all of this!"

Alexandria pulled Rob's face close to hers and went in for a kiss.

"All right, love birds. Knock it off! We only have 48 hours left in Paris. Let's make the most of it!" shouted Kent.

Rob and Kent were just a few of the many American soldiers in the French jazz club that night. Both GIs served together in Paris, quickly becoming friends over their shared love of music. Rob had a background in playing the piano and singing, while Kent just loved listening to records. The war had been declared officially over and some American troops were to return back to the US any day now. Until then, Rob and Kent had some celebrating to do.

While stationed in Paris, Rob and Kent bonded during their frequent visits to nightclubs and the rush of live music, dancing, booze, and women. The war messed with their heads and the nightclubs offered a sense of escape. During one drunken night out, the two stumbled into Alexandria and Colleen as they were leaving a dive bar. After that night, the four of them turned partying at Parisian nightclubs into a frequent weekend activity.

Rob shouted over the blasting saxophone. "HEY, KENT! LET'S GO GET ANOTHER DRINK!"

Kent nodded his head. "Ladies, may we get you anything?"

Alexandria and Colleen shook their heads, beginning to dance with each other. "Hurry back!"

Rob and Kent ran off to the bar and ordered two old fashioneds.

"To us...and to Paris!" Kent clinked his glass against Rob's.

"I don't know, man. Are you ready to go back to the States?" asked Rob as he undid the top button of his shirt. The dancing and booze were starting to warm him up.

"I am. Paris is a spectacular city, but I want to get back home. I'm ready to see my mom and pop, hug my brothers and sisters."

"I understand that. But Paris has something over me. *This* place has something over me," laughed Rob, gesturing to the activity around them.

"I should be doing *this*! Singing, dancing. Singing JAZZ!"

Kent laughed. "Jazz? You're good, man. I've heard you sing a few times, but I don't know if you're *that good*. You think you can captivate a crowd like that gentleman up there?!" He motioned toward Alfie Dupont, who was standing center stage.

"Sure, I can!" Rob laughed as he took a sip of his old fashioned.

Kent smirked. "Oh yeah? Well, we only have a few nights left in Paris. Prove it. Go up there and join Alfie on stage."

"Psht. You're bananas."

Kent smirked. "That's what I thought. You're not going to be a jazz singer, man."

Rob threw his drink back and let out a sigh. "You know what? Watch me!"

Rob passed his empty glass off to Kent and made a run for the stage, quickly leaping to join Alfie Dupont at the mic. Rob was known to be a regular at the club. He'd even ad-libbed a few times from the crowd. But never had Alfie asked Kent to join him on stage.

"Well, well, well, ladies and gentlemen. It seems we have an American soldier who wishes to perform for us this evening."

The crowd cheered in unison. Kent had made his way back to the dance floor with Alexandria and Colleen. The three of them looked up to the stage in disbelief.

"Well, GI, ready to sing your heart out?" laughed Aflie.

Rob bashfully nodded, running his fingers through his short, black hair.

"Let's do a little "Boogie Blues." You know that one? We'll give the audience something to sway to."

Rob inched closer to the mic and nodded.

"Join me on the chorus. Ready? One...two...three!"

Alfie began singing. "Don't the moon look lonesome tonight?"

The crowd began to collectively swoon while looking up at the stage. The spotlight then shifted to Rob, and Alfie handed him the mic. It was now or never.

Rob cleared his throat and slowly began.

"Would You like to go to the country?"

Alfie let out a gasp. "KEEP GOING!"

"Baby, can't take you, ooh."

The entire room erupted into applause.

"Ladies and gentlemen, the GI can sing! Alfie pulled Rob in for a hug.

The crowd screamed, and Rob felt the energy throughout his entire body. He didn't want to ever shake this feeling. This was the life he was meant to live. And he would do anything to make it happen.

CHAPTER 6

New Orleans, 1945

Rob had been back in the United States for three weeks now. So much in his life had drastically changed over the past few years, let alone the past few weeks. He went into war not having any experience with warfare and weapons. He had never even ventured beyond the border of Tennessee, his home state. But Rob felt joining the war effort was his ticket to freedom, his way of getting out of his parents' house and avoiding the responsibilities of farming. Growing up in a rural area during the Great Depression, Rob knew this was not the life he wanted. Seeing his parents struggle to make ends meet was all the motivation he needed to get out.

He wasn't prepared for what life would be like at war. But is anyone really prepared for that? The horrific scenes of the past years were constantly replaying in Rob's mind. From the endless nights of military planes jetting above them to the echoing sounds of buildings being destroyed by bombs. And then there were the number of casualties Rob had witnessed, once barely surviving a bombing incident along the outskirts of Paris. The impact was so forceful that it knocked his helmet completely off his head, forcing him to the ground. He oftentimes thought he could still feel the ground as his body plunged toward the pavement. The only thing that seemed to stop the intrusive thoughts were the jazz club and the memory of singing live on stage with Alfie Dupont during one of his final nights in Paris.

Rob returned to America knowing what he had to do. He needed to sing jazz. While in Europe, Ken had shared with him the stories of New Orleans, the Louisiana city bathed in French culture. Sure, their jazz clubs weren't like those in Paris, but they were close enough. Instead of settling back home in Tennessee, Rob headed straight for New Orleans.

With the little money he had, Rob was able to pay weekly for a hotel room on the outskirts of the city. He began bartending and waiting tables at Vivian's, a jazz club located on Bourbon Street. There was one small obstacle to Rob's burgeoning jazz stardom, though. Vivian's entertainment lineup was fully booked. As much as he begged and pleaded to the club owner, Miss Vivian herself, Rob was denied a performance spot.

"The stage is reserved for professional musicians only," Miss Vivian said. "Not military veterans with little experience."

One early morning after the club had closed for the night, Rob took a break during his cleaning duties. The lights were still dimmed and the scent of liquor wafted off the sticky planked floors. Rob was the only person in the empty club, and he made his way onto the stage where the grand piano stood.

Taking a seat on the squeaky stool, he pushed back the fallboard and glanced around the room. Nobody but him in the dark space. Running his fingers along the ivory keys, he closed his eyes. Through muscle memory, he began to play the tunes he remembered so well from his childhood. He slowly began singing the lyrics. He continued, both his playing and singing growing stronger, more powerful.

Miss Vivian's apartment sat above the club, and the sound of the piano awoke her that night. Rolling over in bed, she removed her silk sleeping mask and flicked on the table lamp beside her bed.

"Goodness gracious! Who's playing that piano at this hour? The club has been closed for a while."

She flung the covers off herself. Throwing on her thick robe, Miss Vivian made her way down the steps of the apartment into the nightclub. From the back of the room, she was hidden from sight in the dark room. She leaned against the back wall as she watched Rob belt out the familiar tune.

"Well, I'll be damned. Soldier boy can play the piano," she whispered to herself.

As the final note reverberated, Miss Vivian slowly began to clap.

Hearing the faint sounds echo through the dark nightclub, Rob jumped up from the stool. "Hey, who's there?!"

The clapping continued to get louder as Miss Vivian approached the stage.

"Robbie, baby. You have a nice voice. And you sure can play them keys," she said.

Bundled up in her fuzzy black robe and with her hair in curlers, Rob found her a sight to behold.

He smiled. "Oh, Miss Vivian! I didn't know you were here. Thank you so much!"

She pulled her robe tightly against her body.

"Well, how could I miss it? You woke me up, dammit!"

Rob moved toward the front of the stage. "I–I am so sorry to wake you. But does this mean I have a spot in the performance lineup now?"

Miss Vivian cocked her head to the side. "You're good, but not that good. The lineup is full, Robbie."

"Oh, come on. Please?!" Rob begged.

Miss Vivian made her way toward the back of the club. "It's full, Robbie. Now get back to work. The place reeks of piss."

Over the next several weeks, Rob tried every time he worked to convince Miss Vivian to add him to the club's lineup. He showered her with her favorite cocktails when she attended shows. He continued playing songs as he closed the club and while she slept. Sometimes that made it worse, though, and he knew it was too much when Miss Vivian would bang her thick wooden cane on the floor to let Rob know she'd had enough.

One night, after serving Miss Vivian a few too many of her favorite cocktails, Rob went for it again.

"Please, Miss Vivian. Just let me sing. Give me a chance.."

Miss Vivian took a puff of her cigarette. "Robbie, baby. How many times do I have to tell you? The lineup is full. We don't have any room left for another act."

"Just listen to me sing one song. One song. That's it. I'll never sing again after that." Rob was begging now.

Miss Vivian rolled her eyes. "Oh, I've heard you. I've heard you every single night for the past month straight. Interuptin' my beauty sleep."

Rob flashed a charming smile. "But that first night you admitted I was good. You still agree?"

Miss Vivian lit another cigarette. She took a long drag, held her breath, and slowly exhaled, smirking.

"Why do you want to be a singer so badly, baby?" she asked.

Making his way to the stage, Rob turned and faced Miss Vivian.

"I don't know, Miss Vivian. I just know that when I was in Paris I'd never felt more alive than I did up on that stage."

"Robbie, baby, everyone wants to be a star. What makes you think you're different?"

"My work ethic. I have what it takes. I know I'll do whatever it takes. And I've written a few songs. Just let me sing one for you." Rob approached the piano.

Miss Vivian had no choice. Another musical ambush by Rob was clearly in motion.

Rob's fingers began to dance along the piano keys.

"High up in the sky…the little stars climb," he belted out as he played along.

Giving it all he had, Rob continued to perform for Miss Vivian, closing his eyes and letting the song completely take over his body.

After belting out the final note, he opened his eyes to see the remaining closing staff of the NOLA Jazz Room frozen in place. Miss Vivian leaned back in her chair as she rubbed the miniature skull set atop her cane.

"Robbie, baby! You *can* sing." She stood and hobbled toward the stage.

Rob beamed with pride. "So…I got a spot?"

"Hush, child. The lineup is still full."

Rob dropped his head and slid off the piano bench, slumping to the floor.

"But I have an idea."

"Oh? And what's that?" Rob asked, perking up.

"Like I said, the lineup here is full. But I got a sweet friend who is looking for new talent at his jazz club. And you would be the perfect fit there."

Rob liked the sound of this and jumped off the stage, landing right beside Miss Vivian.

"I'm in! Where is it? Bourbon Street? Jackson Square? Royal Street?"

Miss Vivian held her frail hand up in the air.

"Shh! You talk too much. Baby, it's not in New Orleans. This jazz club is out West. In the land of the angels. California."

She placed another cigarette between her darkened lips. "It's called the Sea House, and it overlooks the beautiful ocean and canyons of Big Sur. I just know you would fit in there."

Rob hadn't dreamed of ever going to California. He doubted he had enough money to travel there.

"I don't know, Miss Vivian. I barely was able to afford the trip to New Orleans. California is a long way away. And what if I get there and your friend doesn't want me to sing?"

She struck a match, lighting the cigarette, and let the thick fog of smoke surround her face.

"Baby, he will want you to sing. You're just the type he's looking for. He's looking for the next big thing. Someone he can..." She took another puff and quickly exhaled. "Someone he can make into a superstar."

Rob laughed. "A *superstar*? Miss Viv?! You think I can be a superstar?!"

Miss Vivian rolled her eyes, "No, I didn't say that. But when you *do* become a superstar, you better not forget me and my little jazz room. Tell you what, baby. I'm going to buy you a train ticket to California."

Rob couldn't believe it. "Miss Vivian, are you sure? You don't have to do that for me."

"No, I don't. But I want to. And like I said, the owner of the club is an old friend. I can have you on a train to California by tomorrow evening."

Rob hurried over to Miss Vivian, forcefully hugging her. "THANK YOU, MISS VIVIAN. This means so much to–"

She pushed him off of her.

"Rob, get out of here before I change my mind. Pack your bags. Be at the train station tomorrow evening at 5:30. I'll let my friend know you're coming."

She began to walk toward the door of the club. Before exiting, she turned and looked at the young man. "And Rob, baby, are you sure that you want this?"

"Oh yes, I'm sure! I want it so badly, Miss Vivian. I would do anything!"

Miss Vivian let out a snarky laugh. "Anything? You want it that badly, huh?"

Rob nodded his head.

Rubbing the mini skull on the top of her cane, Miss Vivian flashed a smile at Rob, revealing that she was missing a few teeth. "You will fit right in at the Sea House, baby. Yes, you are just his type."

Rob smiled. "Just whose type, Miss Viv?"

"Mr. Lawrence, of course. You're exactly who he's looking for."

CHAPTER 7
BIG SUR, CALIFORNIA, 1945

Miss Vivian fulfilled her promise, providing Rob with a one-way train ticket to California along with an additional small cash bonus for a hotel stay and taxi ride once he arrived. After a multi-day train ride, Rob was eager to step onto solid ground in Monterey, California.

Arriving in the early evening, Rob checked the time on his pocket watch, a keepsake he purchased from one of the street markets in Paris. 5:30. Plenty of time to get a cab out to Big Sur where he could then make his appearance at the Sea House. Rob waved down a taxi and threw his small suitcase of belongings into the trunk.

The cab ride was mostly filled with silence, and it was well into their journey that the taxi driver started talking.

"So, where you from, Mister?" The driver peered into the rear view mirror.

Rob looked away from the window toward the front of the cab. "I've been a little bit everywhere over the last few years. Today, I'm from New Orleans."

The cab driver kept his eyes on the winding road. "Ah, I see. And you know the Sea House?"

Rob returned to looking out the window, taking in the view of the crystal blue waters below the cliffs. "I'm going to sing at the Sea House! I'm hoping to land a spot in their lineup."

"You're a musician? The Sea House has a reputation for showcasing some of the greatest artists in the country. My wife and I love going there for date nights every now and then."

"Well, I want to be a musician. That's what took me to New Orleans and now brought me to California," said Rob.

As he said this, the cab pulled up to the Sea House. The parking lot was filled with cars, overflowing alongside the curvy road leading up to the club. A giant neon sign with an occasional flicker beamed "THE SEA HOUSE."

"Here we are, sir. And it looks like it's already a full house tonight. The place fills up quickly!"

A gentleman in an all-black ensemble complete with a vest and bow tie opened the taxi door. "Hello, sir. Welcome to the Sea House. It's our pleasure to have you here with us today."

A velvet green carpet created a runway to the entrance of the club. Large terracotta planters each filled with a lemon tree sat on either side of the arched mahogany doorway. This was by far the grandest jazz club Rob had seen.

He paid the driver and stepped out of the taxi. Soft jazz music filled the air. He grabbed his suitcase from the trunk and made his way toward the Sea House.

As he entered the club, Rob was greeted at the host stand by two women in black dresses. A tall, slender woman wearing bright red lipstick and her auburn hair pulled back into a bun smiled at Rob as he approached.

"Good evening, sir. What name is your reservation under?"

Rob put down his suitcase. "Oh, I don't have a reservation. My name is Rob–"

The other woman, shorter and a bit older, looked up from the clipboard she was holding. Her gray roots peeked through her slicked-back hair, which had also been pulled into a bun. Adjusting her glasses on the bridge of her nose, she forced a quick smile.

"With no reservation, we will have to put you on the terrace for now. Once a seat in the house opens, we will be happy to move you inside, sir."

Rob smiled, "Oh, that's completely fine. I was actually hoping to speak with the owner. He's expecting me."

The younger lady spoke. "Oh, you know, Mr. Lawrence?"

Rob nodded. "Uh, yes. I believe so. You see, I'm here because I want to sing in your lineup. And I was told that the owner, uh, Mr. Lawrence, would like me and let me perform."

The women swapped glances and burst into laughter. "Oh, sir! You cannot be serious? Our jazz performers are some of the best in the country. We don't let just anyone walk in and take the stage. I'm afraid you've shown up at the wrong time. Auditions are only during closed hours, and as you can see, we are open and busy.

Rob pulled at the collar of his shirt, nervously. "I understand. But maybe one of you ladies could get Mr. Lawrence for me, and I could just talk to him?"

"Sir, Mr. Lawrence is busy right now. The best we can do is seat you on the terrace. Whenever a table becomes available, we will be more than happy to seat you in the house."

Rob nodded. "Ah, I see. So, the terrace it is."

"Perfect. Please follow me right this way." The lady with the red lips gestured toward the terrace, menus in hand.

Rob followed the woman through the spacious dining room. Candlelit tables filled the area, a giant stage obviously the room's focal point. Although it was still early in the evening, the majority of tables were filled with people in fashionable attire.

Although Rob was wearing dress pants and a white button-down shirt, he immediately felt slightly underdressed. Most of the men in the room were wearing party jackets and ties. As Rob stepped out onto the terrace, he noticed a group of people at a table in the center of the room close to the stage.

Sitting at the middle of the table was a man dressed to the nines: black blazer with a red pocket square, black shirt, black dress pants, and black leather shoes. His hair was slicked back and he had a perfectly curled mustache. The man lit a cigar and said to those at the table, "Anywho, this show tonight will be her last. Of course, we're sad to see Bonnie Frank go, but it's time for a new era."

The entourage of people at the man's table gazed adoringly at him and seemed to hang onto every word he uttered, toasting their glasses of champagne to seemingly everything he said. Rob continued to observe from the terrace. *That's what I want*, he thought. *For people to admire my every move.*

"Here we are, sir. This is our signature dinner menu and then this is our selection of wines and cocktails. Your waiter tonight on the terrace will be Joey. He should be with you momentarily." The young hostess forced a smile.

"Thank you, ma'am. Hey, if I may ask, who is that sitting at the table in front of the stage?"

The woman glanced toward the table and then back to Rob. "Sir, that is Mr. Lawrence, the owner of this establishment. The man you claim is expecting to see you."

Embarrassed by his ignorance, Rob nodded and thanked the hostess, who turned and returned to her post at the stand. Within moments, a waiter wearing black dress pants, a crisp white button-down shirt, and a pressed black apron arrived at the table. He was short and slender with tanned skin. His short black hair shined from the grease that kept it slicked to the side. His thin black mustache perfectly lined his upper lip.

"Good evening, sir. Welcome to the Sea House. My name is Joey, and I will be serving you tonight. Would you like to start with a beverage this evening, sir?"

Rob needed something to help loosen his nerves. He glanced at the cocktail menu.

"Hmm…I believe I'll stick with what I know. I'll take an old fashioned."

"Excellent choice. Our old fashioned is the best drink on the menu. Any food to begin your evening? Might I suggest Oysters Rockefeller?"

The thought of eating raw oysters made Rob's stomach churn. "No thank you, Joey. Just the old fashioned will work for now. I'm hoping to get a seat inside soon."

Joey grabbed the menu and smiled, "Yes, I understand. Although, it might be a while until a table inside becomes available. Tonight is the final show of our star entertainer, Bonnie Frank. It's going to be a full house."

"Where is she going? Is she moving to a new venue?"

"Unfortunately, sir, I'm unable to answer that. I only know this is her final performance at the Sea House."

Rob nodded and thanked the young man. As Joey walked off to get the drink order, Rob began to realize that it might be harder than he thought to get in at the Sea House. It seemed to be a very uptight establishment.

Joey returned with the old fashioned. "Here you are, sir. Have you had a moment to look over the menu? Would you like to order anything to eat?"

Noticing the prices, Rob knew he would have to order something small in order to have enough left over for a hotel room. "I believe I will go with a Caesar salad for now. Thank you, Joey."

Joey wrote down Rob's order and looked up from his notepad. "Fantastic choice, sir. Oh, and one more thing. If you're wondering when the best time to talk to Mr. Lawrence is, it's once the dance floor has opened for the night. I overheard that you were wanting to speak to him."

"Oh...yes. Thank you. I would really like to meet him and speak with him this evening. Any advice?"

Joey anxiously tapped his foot.

"Your best chance of talking to him is after he opens his third bottle of champagne. He is currently on his first bottle. Do not approach him when he is at the table with his friends. Nothing irritates him more than when he is interrupted at his table."

Rob nodded while glancing over at Mr. Lawrence's table. Joey continued talking. "And like I mentioned, your best chance of getting him to listen is once he's on the dance floor. He's more pleasant to deal with after he's got some booze in him."

Rob thanked Joey, who scurried off to help other patrons. Rob's salad arrived just as the show was beginning.

The spotlights hummed as they were turned on and pointed toward the stage. The orchestra began to play, each second the music getting faster and louder, until the room went completely dark and all you could see on the stage was a woman's silhouette.

"Good evening, ladies and gentlemen!"

The crowd roared.

"I have just one question for you. Are you all ready to celebrate life with me tonight?"

More thunderous applause.

"HIT IT, BOYS!"

With that, the orchestra began to play, and the spotlights focused on the famous Bonnie Frank. Her short, silver sequined gown glistened in the stage lights as she sashayed along the stage with her long brown hair pulled half-up, revealing a face full of dramatic makeup.

"Blue skies, smiling at me..."

The singer gracefully danced along with the orchestra's rhythm. Rob could see why the Sea House was packed full of people. Bonnie Frank had a way of capturing everyone's attention. Even the people who weren't fortunate enough to score a table inside were mesmerized while watching from the terrace.

Rob's eyes bounced back and forth from the stage to Mr. Lawrence's table. Champagne bottle number two had just been popped. The people at Lawrence's table seemed to be living in an entirely different world. Lighting cigars and cigarettes in between bites of caviar, throwing back champagne and wine, and applauding periodically at the show. This was the person Rob wanted to be one day. It's as if he was seeing his future self.

"Hmph. Sir, you must stop staring."

Snapped back to reality, Rob looked up from the table to see Joey standing over him holding another old fashioned. "Oh, I–I didn't see you there." Rob could feel his face flush.

"I thought you might want another old fashioned." Joey sat the drink on the table and took a seat on the banquette beside Rob. "So, what exactly brings you to the Sea House? Why do you want to talk to Lawrence so badly?"

Rob took a sip of his drink, grimacing at how strong this one was. He cleared his throat to alleviate the burn from the alcohol. "I'm a jazz singer. I'm trying to get in the lineup."

"Oh, another one." Joey used his hand to wipe imaginary crumbs from the table. "You're one of many. We see people come in daily saying they're a singer. Who knew so many people were into jazz? What makes you different from all the others?"

Rob put his napkin on the table. "I've learned from some of the best. While serving in the war, I was stationed in Paris. My buddies and I would go to the jazz clubs there any chance we could get."

"Ah, now, that might put you on Lawrence's list. He likes people who have something different about them. He wants people he can invest in, turn into his next project. People with no ties. Do you have a family?" asked Joey.

"Yeah. I mean, I got a mom and pop back home. But I'm not married or anything. I actually haven't spoken to my family since returning to the States." Rob took another swig of the old fashioned.

"Oh, so you're a broken war veteran. That makes you even more perfect for Lawrence," scoffed Joey.

"Broken? I don't know if I would go that far. I mean, I've seen some horrendous things, but I'm not broken. I've just experienced different things in life."

Joey held up his hands. "Sir, I'm kidding. What's your name, anyway?"

"It's Rob." He extended his hand across the table, formally introducing himself to Joey.

The waiter firmly shook Rob's hand, "Well, nice to put a name to the face. And would you look at that? The third bottle of champagne has just been popped."

Rob glanced over at Mr. Lawrence's table. "Should I go now? What do you think? How do I look?

Joey laughed. "Easy, man. You need to give it just a few more minutes. Like I said, it needs to be when he's on the dance floor. It's almost time. He and his little crew are about to start the party."

"Ah, I see. They do this every night?"

"Just about. Life at the Sea House is different. It's as if time doesn't exist. The parties are endless, the shows are grand, and the views are unforgettable."

"You sell it so well. And what about working here? How's that?"

Joey stood up and pushed the chair back under the table. "It's one of the best jobs in Big Sur. You work here and you're taken care of. And if you get on Mr. Lawrence's good side...well, you're set for life."

Rob nodded and glanced over at Lawrence's table.

"Interesting."

Grabbing Rob's empty salad bowl, Joey nodded toward the dining room. "And would you look at that? The dance floor has just opened. Now's your chance, Sport."

Rob looked over at the dining room and saw the mass movement of dancing bodies in front of the stage. He noticed Mr. Lawrence dancing with one of the women from his table. This was going to be his way in. He needed to find someone who he could swing around the dance floor.

Scanning the terrace, he noticed a woman with wavy blonde hair standing alone, looking to the sea beyond the cliff. She wore a royal blue dress and sipped on a glass of red wine. Rob stood up from the table and quickly ran his hands through his short, curled hair. He began to walk toward the woman in blue.

"Beautiful view, right?" He made his way to the woman, who glanced over at him and took a sip of her wine.

"Oh, absolutely. There's nothing quite like Big Sur."

Rob stood beside her and pointed to the ocean. "Ah! If you look very closely, you can see dolphins."

The lady leaned forward, searching for the dolphins. "Ah! YES! There they are! Marvelous!"

"Say, what brings you to Big Sur?" asked Rob.

"Oh, I'm an actress in LA. Just spending the weekend here. It's a nice little getaway."

"An actress! I thought you looked familiar. What picture have I seen you in?!"

The woman blushed. "Well, you probably don't really recognize me. I've not had any leading roles. I've only been in a few films as an extra. But I'm currently in the acting school at Universal Studios. I'll get that role someday."

"Ah, I don't doubt that, Miss..."

The woman put her wine glass down on the stone pillar beside her. "Ah, so sorry. My name is Emma. Emma Grace. And who might I have the pleasure of speaking with?"

"Rob. Rob Matthews," he said as he shook her hand. "Say, Emma Grace, would you care to join me for a dance?"

Emma glanced over her shoulder toward the dining room. "Oh, I don't know. I'm not much for dancing. I'm more of a stick-to-the-terrace type of gal."

"Are you sure? Just one dance?" Rob gestured toward Emma.

Emma grabbed her wine glass and gulped down the last few drops of red wine. "Well, okay. But don't get upset if I step all over your feet!"

Rob chuckled and offered his arm to Emma. "Oh, I'm sure it will be all right, Miss Emma."

Rob and Emma made their way into the dimly lit dining room, weaving their way through the crowded dance floor. Holding Emma's hand, Rob guided them into place just a few feet from Mr. Lawrence.

Bonnie Frank stood beside the piano and began to sing the first few lyrics of a popular ballad. Rob grabbed Emma's right hand and gently placed his other hand at the small of her back. The two of them began swaying in unison to the music.

"So, Rob, what brings you to Big Sur?"

"Jazz. I am a singer!" said Rob.

Emma's eyes widened. "A singer! Where do you sing?"

Rob held Emma's arm high, giving her a twirl.

"Hopefully right there on that stage."

Emma chuckled, flirtatiously.. "Ah, lucky me, I guess. Dancing with the Sea House's next big star!"

Rob pulled her in close. "A guy can dream, right?"

In his periphery, Rob noticed Mr. Lawrence now dancing with a different woman, someone not at his table when Rob arrived at the club. The ballad had just ended and Bonnie Frank was now singing a more upbeat song. This was his chance.

"Emma, I think it's time to cut a rug! Show me your best dance moves!"

Emma laughed and covered her face with her hands. "I told you I'm not much of a dancer, Rob."

Rob laughed and shimmied his torso towards Emma, making her laugh even harder. Emma dropped her hands and did her best to shimmy back.

"There we go! What about this one?!" Rob began to shuffle backward while waving his arms.

Emma continued to laugh as Rob kept shuffling backward until-oomph-he knocked into Mr. Lawrence, causing him to spill his glass of bourbon.

"Oh my goodness. I am so sorry, sir." Rob placed his hand on Mr. Lawrence's shoulder.

Mr. Lawrence appeared to be unbothered. "Hey! No problem. There's plenty more bourbon to go around this evening."

Rob nodded and inched a little closer to the dapper man. "I know, sir, but I should've paid more attention. I apologize. My name is Rob," he said, extending his hand to Mr. Lawrence.

"Lawrence. Jay Lawrence," he said as he firmly shook Rob's hand.

"Well, Mr. Lawrence, please let me buy you another drink to make up for my clumsiness."

Mr. Lawrence shook his head. "Nonsense. No need to buy me another drink. I own the place. How about I get you and your lady a drink?"

Rob motioned for the young woman he'd met only moments earlier to come closer.

"Emma, come on over. This is Mr. Lawrence, the owner of the Sea House. Mr. Lawrence, this is Emma Grace. I'm sure you recognize her from a movie or two."

Emma blushed, tucking her blonde hair behind her ears. "Well, hello, Miss Emma Grace. I do believe I've seen your beautiful face around before."

"Well, thank you, sir. I certainly enjoy my evenings at your establishment. I come here often."

"How grand! Let's get you two a drink!" said Lawrence as he gestured toward his table.

"Come on. Please have a seat at my table. Let me grab someone. JOEY! JOEY, OVER HERE!"

He motioned for the waiter who was helping patrons on the terrace. Joey shuffled over, his posture straightening as he approached the table.

"Yes, Mr. Lawrence. What can I get for you?"

"Joey, this young man was dancing his ass off and bumped right into me." Mr. Lawrence chuckled as he grabbed Rob's bicep.

"Ah, is that so?" Joey looked over at Rob and arched his eyebrows.

"Just couldn't help himself! The music was too much! Say, get us two glasses of bourbon, straight. And for his beautiful lady, a..."

Emma cleared her throat. "Oh, I'll take a glass of red, please."

Joey nodded and hurried off to get the drinks.

"So, Rob, I don't believe I've seen you around here before. Is this your first time at the Sea House?"

Rob nodded. "Yes, sir. I just arrived today, actually. From Louisiana."

Joey arrived with their drinks and began passing them out, first handing Mr. Lawrence his glass of bourbon.

The man took a sip, his face lighting up. "Ah, Louisiana. Fantastic place. I've been there many times. The city of New Orleans inspired me to open this establishment."

"Well, coincidentally, sir, I used to sing at a jazz club in New Orleans. Miss Vivian's. Perhaps you've heard of it?"

Mr. Lawrence guffawed. "VIVIAN! Hell, I know her! Great friend of mine. We go way back. Anyone who's friends with Vivian is a friend of mine."

Rob smiled and held up his glass to salute Mr. Lawrence. "Well, cheers to Vivian and to friendship."

Lawrence chuckled and clinked glasses with Rob.

"Hear, hear!"

Rob took a big gulp of liquid courage and went for it.

"So, this is Bonnie Frank's last show, huh? What's next for the Sea House, if you don't mind me asking?"

Lawrence glanced up at the stage. "Yeah, she's giving it her all tonight. Best damn show of her life, honestly. But yes, we're moving on. Looking for something new. We've got a few prospects lined up, but you know, Rob, we're still looking."

Rob feigned surprise. "You know, I just happen to be a singer. I would be honored to be a part of your performing lineup. It would be incredible to sing here every night."

Lawrence finished his glass of bourbon. "Tell you what, Rob. Let me hear what you got. Stop by tomorrow morning at 11. I'll give you a shot."

Rob grinned "Oh, thank you so much, sir. I cannot thank you–"

Mr. Lawrence stood up and buttoned his jacket, holding up his other hand. "Look. I like you, Rob. I can tell you've got star quality. Tomorrow morning you can show me what you've got. I'm heading out for the night. I've had all the bourbon and fun I can stand for one night."

Rob stood and shook Mr. Lawrence's hand. "Yes, sir. I understand completely. Thank you! I'll see you tomorrow at 11. I won't be late."

Lawrence laughed and began to walk away. "See you then, kid. And Miss Emma Grace, it was nice seeing you again."

Emma gushed and thanked Mr. Lawrence. Rob looked at Emma, the two exchanging glances as Mr. Lawrence walked away. Rob's plan had proved successful. He was in with Mr. Lawrence. It was time for him to thank Emma for her unwitted role in his plan and to get some rest before his big audition..

"Well, Emma. Thank you for dancing with me tonight. I think it's best if I head out for the evening. It's getting pretty late, and as you just heard, I have a big audition tomorrow."

Emma stood and moved closer to Rob. "You're smooth, Rob. I watched how that all unfolded. Congratulations."

She inched closer until her face was just a few inches from Rob's. "Try not to forget about me when you're a big star, okay?"

Rob smiled and grabbed Emma's hand. "Emma, how can I forget you?"

Emma blushed and leaned in to whisper in Rob's ear. "You don't have to. The night doesn't have to end, you know?"

Rob smiled. "Ah, where to then?"

Emma took Rob's hand, leading him toward the door.

"My place."

CHAPTER 8

Briiiiing.....Briiiiing....Briiiiing!

The alarm clock pierced Rob's dream, forcing him to bury his face in his pillow.

"UGH...turn it off! Ugh–the time...what time–" Rob quickly sat up, triggering a rush of blood to his head. "Jesus!" Rubbing his forehead, Rob grabbed the alarm clock and noticed the time. 10:00 am. "Shit. Shit. Shit."

Rob dropped the alarm clock onto the nightstand and began frantically searching the room for his clothes. He located a single black sock and pulled it on. Dashing to the other side of the bed in which Emma was soundly sleeping, he snatched up his pants.

"Shirt...shirt...where's my damn shirt?"

Rob tiptoed around the room, trying not to wake Emma. "Ah, there." He grabbed it from the lampshade near Emma's head. As he threw his shirt over his shoulders, he began to recall the moments from the previous evening. The multiple glasses of bourbon. Coming back to Emma's bungalow. The multiple glasses of wine. Feverishly making their way through the entire house before settling into Emma's room.

What a night. But Rob's head was throbbing, and he thirsted for water to cure the hangover that was starting to kick in. Picking his belt from amongst Emma's pile of clothes on the floor, Rob tightened it around his waist. Emma began to stir, letting out a little sigh.

"Going so soon?" She shifted under the covers. Rob turned toward her. "I–I overslept. Last night was great, Emma. But I have my audition at the Sea House in less than an hour."

Emma's head appeared from under the covers and she slowly rubbed her eyes. "Ah, that's right. The Sea House's next starring act. You're going to do great."

Running his hands through his hair, Rob dashed over to Emma. "Thank you. You, Emma, are a beauty." He kissed her on the cheek and ran out the door.

Rushing down the hallway into the cozy living room, he grabbed his watch from the arm of the chair at the front door. "BYE, EMMA GRACE!" He shouted as he slammed the door behind him.

Standing at the curb, Rob waved his hands at a cab that was slowly approaching Emma's house. Rob pulled open the yellow car door, throwing his body into the backseat of the cab.

"Morning! To the Sea House. Make it fast. I only have 30 minutes."

The cab driver glanced in the rearview mirror. "Yes, sir. I'll do my best." And with that the car began the windy ascension through the palm-tree-lined streets of Monterey, giving Rob the perfect amount of time to fully awaken.

CHAPTER 9

"Sir...we're here." Grabbing the last bit of cash from his wallet, he handed it to the driver while getting out of the car.

"Thank you, sir. Have a nice day."

Rob paused at the green-carpeted entrance to the Sea House and looked at the front door. He ran one hand through his hair and did a quick breath check, breathing into his other hand to try and catch a whiff. His oversleeping hadn't allowed time to freshen up. Exhaling, he pushed the front door open and entered the Sea House.

The place felt different during the day, almost as if it was meant to come alive in the evening. No hostess was there to greet him this time and most of the lights were off in the club's foyer. Checking his watch, Rob noted the time. 10:58. Not too shabby for a hungover man. He walked into the large banquet room where he'd danced just hours before.

Every light was on in the banquet room and, for the most part, the space had been cleaned. There was hardly any evidence of last night's celebration. Toward the front of the room, Joey was putting fresh white tablecloths on the round dining tables.

Dressed casually in blue jeans and a white t-shirt, Joey tossed a tablecloth onto Lawrence's table. As the tablecloth ballooned in the air, he noticed Rob making his way toward the front of the room.

"Well, look who it is!" said Joey as he smoothed the tablecloth's wrinkles.

Rob let out a laugh. "Joey! My man! How are you?"

"I'm well. How are you feeling? That's the real question."

Rob let out a sigh. "Hmm...not my best. I'm hungover and desperately in need of a glass of water and a bottle of aspirin."

"Yeah, I would say so. Those old fashioneds will do that to you. Not to mention, you're still in your clothes from last night," laughed Joey.

Rob's cheeks flushed with heat. "Yeah, I, uh, had a few too many and maybe had a little sleepover last night."

Joey grabbed four wine glasses off a cart beside him, strategically placing them on the table.

"Oh yeah? What a way to ring in your first night in California. You left your suitcase here last night too. Just sitting out on the terrace."

"Oh shit. You're right. I got caught up in the moment last night and completely forgot it."

Joey moved to the next table to continue the table-setting routine. "No worries. I brought it inside and put it behind the bar. Let me go grab it for you."

Joey patted Rob on the back as he walked past him, making his way toward the bar.

Within a few short minutes, Joey returned with Rob's suitcase and a glass of water. "You're radiating booze. Figured you could use this."

Rob thanked him and tossed back the entire glass of water like a shot. "Ahh. I needed that. Thank you so much, Joey."

"No problem. All ready to sing?" Joey asked, nodding toward the stage. Rob glanced over at the stage and then back to Joey. "I guess so. Wish I hadn't drank so much last night, but here we are."

"Gentlemen, good morning!" Mr. Lawrence's voice echoed through the dining hall. Turning around, Rob saw that Mr. Lawrence had made his way into the room from the entrance at the back of the stage and was now standing just above them.

"Good morning, sir. How are you doing this morning?" Rob straightened and stood a bit taller.

"Well, Rob, I'm feeling pretty good. How are you? Judging by your attire, I'd say you've probably felt better."

Rob forced a laugh. "Yes, sir. I have definitely felt better. Nonetheless, I'm excited to sing for you today."

Mr. Lawrence took a seat on the edge of the stage. "Let me ask you something, Rob. Do you have a place to stay? You left your suitcase here last night."

Rob wiped tiny beads of sweat from his forehead. "I, uh, do not yet, sir. I spent last night with my friend. I might've gotten a little too carried away and forgotten my suitcase here when we left."

"Ah, yes. Miss Emma Grace. She's your friend, right?" Mr. Lawrence chuckled as he struck a match to light his cigar.

"Yes, Emma Grace."

"I remember seeing you two dancing last night. That's the power of a beautiful woman, right? They can put us in a trance." He took a puff of his cigar.

Rob nodded. "Yes, they certainly can."

Mr. Lawrence jumped from the stage, landing on his feet right beside Rob.

"Well, tell me, Rob, do you get distracted easily?"

He inched closer to Rob, the cigar smoke consuming the space between them.

"Are you going to let sweet Emma Grace distract you? The party scene, is it all going to be a bit too much for you?"

Rob's hands began to grow cold, a familiar side effect of his anxiety. He stuffed his hands in his pockets and cleared his throat. "No, sir. I work hard. Last night was just a one-time thing."

Mr. Lawrence took a long drag of his cigar, the sizzle of the ash filling the awkward silence.

"Well, that's good. I'd like to hear you sing now." Exhaling the cigar smoke, Lawrence strutted to his usual table.

"Right. Yes," Rob said as he quickly climbed onto the stage. Walking up to the single mic stand, he exhaled.

"Test...testing..."

Tapping the microphone, Rob nodded toward Mr. Lawrence's table. "All right, I'll be singing a song called 'Night and Day'...acapella."

Pouring himself a glass of water from the pitcher on his table, Mr. Lawrence nodded. "Go ahead."

The words spilled from Rob's mouth, filling the empty banquet hall. "Night and day ...why is it so?"

With each line, Rob felt the power in his chest build. Fortunately for him, the hangover wasn't completely holding him back. Each word flowed from his mouth, deep and low with vibrato. Closing his eyes and getting lost in the lyrics, he leaned back, pulling the mic stand with him.

"Day and night ...night and day..." he belted out the final note, holding it for what felt like a minute. His voice reverberated off the dining room walls. When he opened his eyes, he noticed that Joey was no longer setting the tables. Instead, he was staring directly at the stage, fully locked in Clark's attention.

Mr. Lawrence popped his hands on the table and stood up, clearing his throat.

"You. Robbie."

A sly grin spread across his face as he pointed his index finger toward Rob. He let out a chuckle.

"You got it. And I'm going to make you a star."

Rob exhaled the breath he hadn't realized he was holding. Laughing, he eagerly made his way to the edge of the stage.

"Ah, Mr. Lawrence. Thank you! Thank you so much!"

"Come on down here, my boy. Let's talk."

Rob jumped off the stage, landing right beside Mr. Lawrence.

"So...when do I start? Tonight?"

Mr. Lawrence laughed. "Tonight? No. There's no show tonight. And we need to work out some details, Rob."

Rob eagerly nodded. "Of course, sir."

"Let's start with your living situation. You need a place to live, Rob." Mr. Lawrence placed his right hand on Rob's shoulder.

"Right, I do. At the moment, I'm tight on funds, but I will find a place with my first paycheck."

"Nonsense. Come with me. I want to show you the living quarters," said Mr. Lawrence as he led Rob to the dining room entryway.

Rob followed him outside through the main entrance of the club, and they made a quick right from the doorway down a narrow pebble pathway. The walkway went past the club and the parking lot, winding down a small grassy hill overlooking the sea.

Rob followed along, taking in the views while trying to process all that was happening. Noting the scent of salt from the ocean in the morning air, Rob walked behind Mr. Lawrence until they arrived at a small wooden cottage sitting at the end of the path. The simple shaker-sided building was painted dark blue with a terracotta roof and featured a small porch overlooking the ocean. Tall trees loomed over the back of the cottage, providing the perfect amount of shade.

"This is the headliner's cottage, a special place we provide for the main acts of the Sea House." Mr. Lawrence looked back at Rob. "Shall we go in?"

Rob nodded, his excitement evident to his host.

Mr. Lawrence opened the arched door at the side of the cottage, leading the way into the tiny kitchen. "It's not much. One bedroom, one bath. A simple kitchen and a living room. But not many people have views like this in Big Sur. It's private and the perfect place to unwind after a night of singing to a full house."

Rob laughed. "A full house?! I like the sound of that. This is perfect, Mr. Lawrence. How much is the rent?"

Mr. Lawrence walked into the living room. "Ha! Rent? There isn't rent for our main act."

Rob moved his gaze from the kitchen to Mr. Lawrence. "Really? I don't mind paying rent, sir."

Leading the way back outside, Lawrence opened the arched door by the kitchen. "Nonsense. It's just one of the many perks of being the headliner at the Sea House."

"Ah, I see. So, what are the other perks of the gig?" Rob asked.

Mr. Lawrence rolled up his sleeves as the California humidity was beginning to kick in. "Tell you what. Why don't you get some rest, take a shower. Clean up. You look like shit. We can meet for dinner tonight at the club at 6 o'clock."

Rob nodded. "Yeah, that sounds good to me." Mr. Lawrence began to walk down the pebble path back to the Sea House. "We'll go over all of the details and the contract then, Sport."

CHAPTER 10

After a bit of shut eye and a shower, Rob felt like a new man. The hangover from the previous night's decisions was gone and he was feeling ecstatic for his dinner with Mr. Lawrence. After all, just 24 hours before, he'd arrived in Big Sur with no job or place to stay. Things were strangely beginning to fall into place.

Rob pulled on his brown plaid sportcoat, a jacket that had been passed down through many generations in his family, and began the trek up the pebble stone path to the Sea House, arriving exactly at 6 o'clock. The same two women from the night before greeted him at the hostess stand, only this time with a little more enthusiasm.

"Welcome back, sir! We're excited to have you join us here at the Sea House," said the hostess with the red-lipstick smile. "Please come this way. Mr. Lawrence is eagerly waiting for you to join his table."

Now, that's more like it. A nice change of attitude, Rob thought. He followed the hostess into the ballroom where Mr. Lawrence was waiting at his usual table. "Ah, Rob, you made it!" He jumped out of the booth to shake Rob's hand. "And you look like a new man now. Take a seat! Thank you, Lauren, for bringing our newest headliner to the table."

Rob took his place in the booth and thanked the hostess, whose name he knew he'd remember.

Mr. Lawrence shuffled a large stack of papers that were laying on the table. "I was just going over your contract before you arrived. Shall we discuss more of the details?"

Rob took a sip from the glass of water in front of him. "Absolutely!"

"Great. First thing. Rob, I mean it when I say that I'm going to make you a star. If you listen to me and trust me as your advisor and friend, you'll have people flocking from all over the country to see you. How does that sound?"

Rob chuckled. "That sounds amazing. I'm all ears, Mr. Lawrence."

Lawrence took a sip of his wine. "Good, good, good! So, first thing, you need a new name. Rob isn't star material. We need something powerful, something unforgettable."

Rob stared blankly at Mr. Lawrence. "Oh, I, uh...I'm not sure about that one. I've always just gone by the name my parents gave me at birth."

"Well, no worries. I took the liberty of creating some names for you. Which of these do you like best?" Pulling out his glasses, Mr. Lawrence took a look at the contract. "Ah, let's see. We have Stone Maverick, Brock West, Clark James, Dean–"

"That one. I like that one," Rob said while pointing at the contract.

"Clark James. You like that one?"

Rob nodded. "Well, it's official, ladies and gentlemen. Clark James." Mr. Lawrence chuckled as he drew a big circle around the name.

Rob laughed. "It's going to take some time to get used to, but I like it!"

Mr. Lawrence flipped over to the next page of the contract. "All right, now. We need to discuss the terms. Some of these are negotiable while others are pretty set in stone."

Rob took another sip of water and nodded at Mr. Lawrence.

"First, the living quarters. In exchange for your talent we will provide you a place to stay, food and beverages, and living necessities. Wardrobe, hairstyles, whatever. Basically, if you want it or need it, we will make it happen for you."

Rob nodded.

"Second, the pay. You have the potential to be the highest-earning employee here. We'll start by paying you forty dollars a week. The more people come in to see you, the more you'll get paid. So, you should want to have the house packed for every show."

"Wow! Forty dollars a week? That's the most I've ever made, sir. And there's potential for more?"

Mr. Lawrence smiled. "Way more. Plus, we're covering your living expenses, so there's no need to spend all your money. In fact, I'm more than happy to operate as your personal banker. I can create a bank account for you and make sure the funds are always deposited."

"That would be fantastic, sir. Since I'm new to the area and not sure where to even open an account, I'd appreciate your assistance."

"That's right. I think you're going to really like it here. Let's move on to term number three. Drugs and alcohol. You are to stay sober and clean while performing here at the Sea House."

Rob held up his hands. "You do not have to worry about that one, sir. I'm completely capable of that."

Mr. Lawrence nodded. "That's good. I don't mind if you drink and have a good time, obviously. We did that last night! But when you're on my stage you need to be able to give it your all. You can't do that if you're not sure what planet you're on."

"Completely agree."

"Fantastic. Now, number four. Distractions and relations. I don't care who you sleep with, Clark. We're men. We have needs. I get it. But the second they start to interfere with your work, that's when things get messy. Like I said, I want you to be the biggest star in the country. Don't let someone take that from you."

Rob immediately thought of Emma Grace. "Yes, of course. I understand, and that shouldn't be an issue."

"All right. And lastly, number five. How much do you want this, Clark? The fame that would come with being America's best jazz singer?"

"Oh, I really want it, sir. I knew the minute I finished my service in the military! That's why I'm here. I came straight home and set out on the path to--"

"I get it. I can tell you want it. That's good. Like I said, if you stick with me, you will be the most famous name in America. There's just one small thing I need from you to make this work, Clark."

"Oh, okay. What is that?"

Clearing his throat, Mr. Lawrence locked eyes with Rob. "I need you to be forever committed to the Sea House. I need you one hundred percent all in."

Rob glanced at the contract and then back to Mr. Lawrence. "Of course. That's easy. I'm one hundred percent all in, Mr. Lawrence."

"How old are you again, Clark?"

"I'm 23, sir."

"23. What a great age. So young and full of energy. The perfect age to remain forever, right?"

Rob chuckled nervously. "Yeah, I guess so."

"Well, if you really want this, Clark, and you're ready to be a star, let's get this contract signed. And then we can start working on the show rehearsals."

"Where's the pen? I–"

"Oh, and one last thing. Let me flip to the end."

Mr. Lawrence turned to the last page of the contract. "As the headliner, you'll have full reign over the creativity of the show. You want it, we can make it happen. But I get the final word. I approve everything. If the show is shit, we don't do it. We change it up. Understand?"

"Yes, of course. I promise I won't let you or the Sea House down, Mr. Lawrence. I'm ready to make this happen."

Mr. Lawrence grinned as he handed Rob a pen. "Well, ladies and gentlemen, I'd like to introduce you to Clark James."

Rob looked down at the contract where the signature lines were, noting that Mr. Lawrence had already signed his portion of the contract. "James B. Lawrence." He scanned the page, hesitating to sign the dotted line.

"Is something wrong?" Mr. Lawrence asked.

Clark nervously smiled back. "Oh, no, sir. But maybe I should take this with me and look it over first? Just to make sure I understand everything?"

Standing up from the table, Mr. Lawrence began to put on his coat.

"It seems to me that you're not really wanting this as much as you claim, boy. And if that's the case, we can just call this meeting adjourned."

Rob's cheeks flushed as his eyes widened. "No, no, no, sir. I absolutely want to do this. I'm so sorry for hesitating."

Mr. Lawrence stood tall over the table, looking down on Rob. "Well, then, you know what to do. Just sign the line."

Rob looked back at the contract in front of him and grabbed the pen on the table, any hesitation replaced with excitement. Quickly, he scribbled "Robert Matthews" on the line.

As he crossed the Ts in his last name, the sound of a clock echoed through the nightclub.

"BOOOOOONG! BOOOOOONG! BOOOOOONG!"

The sound reverberated, swirling in Rob's ears. The third chime seemed to bounce through his body. The final chime was so strong that Rob could feel it heavy in his chest. Launching his body across the table, Rob hugged his chest, his eyes forced shut. It felt as if his heart no longer was beating.

And then everything went silent. The clock stopped. And very slowly, Rob felt a gentle thud return as his heart beat inside his chest. He opened his eyes to see Mr. Lawrence sitting across the table from him.

"I–I didn't realize the time. And what a powerful clock you guys have here." Rob adjusted his posture.

Mr. Lawrence rested his chin against his arm he'd propped on the table, all while maintaining eye contact with Rob.

"Say, what time is it anyway, Mr. Lawrence?"

Mr. Lawrence smiled. "It's 6:28. That silly old clock of ours must be broken. You know how it is, old buildings and such."

Rob laughed nervously. "Yes, of course. We should probably get that fixed before my first show. Wouldn't want a giant grandfather clock going off at random times, right?"

With a giant belly laugh, Mr. Lawrence shook Rob's hand.

"You're a funny guy, Clark James. No, we definitely wouldn't want that. I'll have Joey fix that issue immediately."

Rob smiled hearing his new name. Clark James. He didn't know exactly what was next, but he did know it was time. Finally, it was Rob's time to shine.

CHAPTER II

Present Day

The afternoon sun basked over the deep blue ocean beyond the giant windows. Neal, along with his grandfather, were completely lost in Nana's story of the infamous Clark James. They'd lost track of time and needed to head to lunch soon.

"Wait! So, he just signs the contract like it's nothing? No questions asked? No negotiations?"

Neal seemed flustered as he began locking up the club.

"He was young. When you're young, you don't think to negotiate a contract. And he felt the pressure from Lawrence," said Nana.

Granddad stood up from his chair. "So, he signed the contract. And then what happened?"

"Gentlemen, let's go to lunch. I'm starving. And my head is starting to ache from all this talk about Clark James."

"Wait, Milly. You had to have been just a little kid in 1945. When did you meet him? And how old was he?"

Neal flipped the lights off inside the club and his grandparents followed him out the main entrance. Adjusting her purse on her shoulder, Nana looked at Daniel and Neal. "I met Clark James in 1962. I was 20…and he was still 23 years old."

Neal and Grandad looked at each other and then back to Nana.

"But that's a story for another time. Let's go get some lunch, boys."

Neal took his grandparents to one of his favorite spots, Tuck's, a local dive hidden in the hills of Monterey overlooking the Pacific Ocean. The small outdoor patio offered the best of both worlds: plenty of shade and breathtaking views.

Over bruschetta and cabernet, Neal wanted to know more about his grandmother's connection to Clark James.

"So, Nana, now that we know you met Clark James, you have to tell us what he was like."

Sipping her wine, Nana glanced over at Neal. "He was something. The ladies loved him. They couldn't keep their eyes off him. And the men desperately wanted to be him. I like to think that maybe I was one of the few people in the world who really got to know him."

Grandad cleared his throat. "Meaning?"

Nana swirled her wine glass, her gaze lost in the red liquid. "Ah, Clark James was…like a mirrorball. So many rough edges that shined for the world to see, but there was more than what the surface showed. He was so complex. He longed for deeper connection and love."

"Do you know where he is now? Is he still alive?"

Nana finally looked up from her glass. "No, I don't. We stopped communicating many years ago. Well, I cut the communication."

"And why did you do that?" asked Grandad.

Nana patted Grandad's hand. "Well, because I chose to build a life with you. And that was all I really needed."

"Ha! Nana, the heartbreaker!" Neal winked at his grandmother and took a sip of cabernet.

"I can't believe you never mentioned him, Milly. You're telling us this story, and I can tell that he meant something to you. Why did you never talk about him? "

THE CLUB BY THE SEA

"My relationship with Clark James was complicated. I was completely enamored with him, but now that I look back on it, I realize it wasn't healthy. It was toxic and dangerous on both our parts. I wasn't the best person then either. I–I'll tell you everything, but it's a difficult story to tell. I was very young."

Neal looked at Nana and then at Grandad. "Here's what I can't understand. Miranda has done some research into Clark James, and there's nothing on him after 1962. It's like he just vanished."

Nana nodded her head. "Yes. There was a fall of the jazz club and there most certainly was a fall of Clark James. But before we get to that, there's a little more you need to know."

CHAPTER 12

BIG SUR, CALIFORNIA, 1945

The day after signing the contract, Clark got to work. The sun had barely peeked through his bedroom window when he heard a loud knock on the cottage door. Startled, Clark jumped from bed.

"Uh, coming!" He stumbled toward the front door, still in his knickers.

Clark's hand was on the doorknob as it suddenly flew open. There stood Mr. Lawrence wearing khaki dress pants, his plump belly spilling over the waistband, along with a simple white button-down shirt. He adjusted the newsboy cap on his head.

"Good morning, Clark James! Are we ready to get started?"

Clark covered his body as best he could. "I...uh, yes! Yes, I'm ready!"

Mr. Lawrence nodded. "Well, good! Don't just stand there then. Go get some clothes on and let's get a-movin'!"

"Right! Yes, sir. Just give me a quick minute, and I will be right out." Clark turned to head back to his room.

Within just a few minutes, he was dressed and ready, meeting Mr. Lawrence on the cottage's front porch. Clark smiled as he closed the door behind him.

"All right! Ready, sir." Clark followed Mr. Lawrence, who had already began the trek up to the Sea House.

Briskly walking to catch up with Mr. Lawrence, Clark placed his cap on his head, noting the strong wind that blew off the sea.

"So, what's on the agenda for today?" Clark asked.

"You'll be meeting the band here in a minute. And then you all will jump straight into rehearsals. We must not waste any time before showtime." Mr. Lawrence kept moving forward, his pace brisk.

"This is all so exciting! Did I tell you yesterday that I also play piano?"

Mr. Lawrence turned to look at Clark as they approached the back entrance of the Sea House. "No, you didn't. But that's very good! Our last act, she was just a singer. It will be good to have someone with multiple talents on stage."

Clark smiled as they made their way through the rear entrance of the club, Mr. Lawrence leading the way through the darkened room.

"This is backstage. It's where your dressing room is as well. Joey will show you everything soon when he gives you the grand tour."

Clark nodded as he followed along.

"Clark, do you write your own songs, by chance?" asked Mr. Lawrence as they approached the dining room.

"I have attempted to, sir. And I'm willing to keep trying."

"Yes, that would be good. We need to be authentic and original if we want to make you famous."

"Authentic and original. Got it."

The two men entered the dining room. A group of people were sitting at the front tables chatting with Joey. Mr. Lawrence cleared his throat. "Hmph." Conversation stopped as all eyes darted to Mr. Lawrence and Clark.

"Good morning, everyone."

"Mornin'."

"Good morning, sir."

"Mornin, Lawrence."

Pulling a cigar from his pocket, Mr. Lawrence continued. "As you all know, we are beginning a new era. I want you all to meet your new headliner, Clark James."

Clark stepped from behind Mr. Lawrence, smiling and waving at the group of people. A few waved back. Some just smiled.

"I want you all to completely forget everything that we did with our last act. We are moving forward, and if Clark wants to make changes, we will," said Mr. Lawrence, taking a puff of his cigar.

Mr. Lawrence turned to his new headliner. "Clark, you already know Joey. Allow me to introduce you to the members of the Sea House Ensemble. Up first, we have Larry on the bass."

A tall, husky man stood up from the booth. Wearing jeans and a snug white t-shirt with rolled-up sleeves, he extended his calloused hand to Clark.

"Hi ya, Clark. I'm Larry. Pleasure to meet you. Welcome to the Sea House." He firmly shook Clark's hand.

"Nice to meet you, Larry. Looking forward to working with you, sir."

Larry returned to the booth, slicking back his dark hair with his hands.

"Then, you have Jane on the backing vocals as well as guitar," said Mr. Lawrence.

Adjusting the belt around her black pencil skirt, Jane smiled and walked toward Clark.

"Mr. James, it's a pleasure to be working with you. Welcome!" She flashed a bright smile.

THE CLUB BY THE SEA

Clark gushed. "Oh, please call me Clark. Looking forward to singing with you, Jane."

"Next we have Teddy on the saxophone," Lawrence said, pointing to a short, rotund man at one of the tables.

Teddy stood up and removed his boater hat, revealing a shiny bald head.

"Mornin', Clark. I'm not just the saxophone guy. I also play clarinet, trumpet, and a little bit of the trombone. Guess you could say I'm your horns guy," he said, a wide smile spreading across his face, revealing a gold bottom tooth.

Clark laughed. "All right, a Renaissance man. Nice to meet you, Teddy."

"And last but not least, we have Beverly on the drums," said Mr. Lawrence.

Chewing gum, Beverly adjusted her curly blonde bangs as she strutted her way toward Clark.

Stopping just a few inches from him, she blew a bright pink bubble. "Hey there, Toots. Beverly. Call me Bev, Babes, Baddie. Whatever ya want."

Clark took her hand right and gave it a quick peck.

"Nice to meet you, Baddie Beverly. Say, I've never met a girl drummer before."

"And she's a real big flirt too!" laughed Larry from the booth.

Beverly's eyes darted toward Larry and she stuck out her tongue. "Bite me, Larry. So, yeah, I'm on the drums. Got a problem with that, Clark James?"

Clark shook his head.

"Bev, easy. He's just a baby. Come on!" Jane pointed to Clark.

"Yeah, simmer down, Beverly. Nobody's shitting on you for playing the drums," Mr. Lawrence said with an arched eyebrow.

"All right, all right. I'm just giving him the ol' welcome wagon special. You're too serious 'round here." Beverly took her seat.

As Mr. Lawrence made his way to the front of the dining room, he continued, "Very well then. As we all know, there is no time quite like showtime. Let's get to work, people. Joey, I'll leave you with this crew. Should they need something, make it happen."

Joey nodded as Mr. Lawrence saluted him while exiting the dining room. The entire room grew silent as everyone shifted their eyes toward Clark. He stood with his hands in his pockets in front of the stage, not sure what move to make next..

"Clark, why don't you tell the gang the vision you have for the shows?" asked Joey.

Clark nodded. "Ah, yes. Good call, Joey."

Everyone continued to stare at Clark.

"First, let me just say that I saw you all performing the other night. And what a phenomenal job you did. I couldn't stop dancing!"

A few forced smiles appeared on the band members' faces.

"So, I know you all have the experience and talent. I think–"

"Listen, Toots! No need to butter us up, 'kay? I know, we know, Joey even knows we're good. The question is, are you good?" Beverly crossed her arms as if she was issuing a challenge.

"Beverly!" gasped Jane.

Shrugging, Beverely continued, "Oh, c'mon, Jane. We're all thinking it."

Larry stood up, crossing his arms. "She's right on this one. With all due respect, Clark, we know you don't have much experience with performing. So, how can we expect you to elevate this new era here at the club?

Clark ran his hands through his hair. "You all are certainly right. I don't have much experience. But I know that feeling, that rush when you've poured your heart and soul into a performance and the crowd just eats it up. When it's so good, they can't help but make their way onto the dance floor."

Larry smiled. Beverly kept her arms crossed across her chest.

"Gee, that is the best feeling, isn't it?" gushed Teddy.

"That's right, Teddy. And I don't know much about you all, but if you're like me, music might just be the only escape you've had in your life. I grew up on a farm in Tennessee. And when the Depression hit, we had nothing."

Jane placed her hands on the table as she locked eyes with Clark, listening intently.

"My mom and dad did what they could during that time to get by, Dad busting his ass on the soybean and tobacco crops, Mom and I going to the farmer's market every weekend to try to make some money. But when people started losing their jobs, they weren't able to frequent the farmer's market as much as they used to."

Clark took a seat at the table with the band.

Beverly slowly uncrossed her arms and folded them in front of her atop the table.

"Spirits were low. It seemed like everyone around us was going through it. My mom played piano in church growing up, and she taught me as I was growing up. One day when we weren't selling much of the crops, my mom came up with an idea. She asked dad if we could haul the old piano with us on our next trip to the farmer's market."

Teddy's face lit up as Clark continued the story.

"Dad thought she was one crazy woman, bringing a piano to the farmer's market. But she thought it would provide a good boost of happiness. So, she and I practiced playing together all week. And by that following Friday, we had a little routine down pat."

"You guys put on a show at the farmer's market?" asked Larry.

Clark nodded. "We sure did. We pulled up to that market, unloaded the piano, and got right to it. At first, we had several gawkers watching us. Who the hell brings a piano to a farmer's market?"

Beverly laughed. "Please tell me you and your mutha gave those people a show."

Smiling, Clark continued. "Oh, did we! Mom started playing the keys and I belted out 'This little light of mine. I'm gonna let it shine.' Then Mom, still playing, started harmonizing with me. Before you knew it, the crowd grew bigger and people were clapping along."

"They loved it, didn't they?" asked Teddy, hanging on Clark's every word.

"Teddy, they loved it. We started performing every weekend. Not only did it bring a smile to their faces, but guess what else?"

"What?" asked Jane, leaning into the conversation.

"People bought soybeans. They threw a little money into the hat we'd placed beside the piano. And Dad loved it," said Clark.

Teddy clapped his hands. "Ooh, good!"

Clark smiled. "I eventually went into the service as I was looking for new experiences. And that's where I truly leaned into music. The music, especially live performances at the nightclubs in Paris, were really what got me through the war. And I just knew that if it did that for me, it could do that for others."

"Paris?! You know what, Clark? I think this might be a good route for us! We give the show a little bit of that French flare? A little bit of *je ne sais quoi*!" Jane shimmied her shoulders.

"Ha! Yes, a little bit of, uh, what do you call it? Ah, *ooh la la!* Have all the audience swooning in love." Larry chuckled as he swayed his hips.

Clark laughed. "I think we're onto something, guys! So, like I said, I don't have that much experience, but I know we can perform a show that is unforgettable, a show that makes people experience every emotion, a show that makes people want to dance their hearts out."

"Clark?" Beverly twirled a strand of her hair between her thumb and forefinger.

"I think we can take you under our wings," she continued as she flashed a smile.

Clark nodded. "I love the sound of that. Jane, since you do backing vocals, do you write your own songs?

Jane sat up straight. "I've written a few tunes."

"Good! I'd like to get together with you and work on some original pieces. Joey, how are we with costumes and set design?"

Joey cleared his throat. "We have a team of seamstresses that can make pretty much anything happen. As far as the set goes, for now what we have is what we've got. We can spruce it up with a little paint for now. But until more money starts coming in, the stage production will stay similar to what you saw the other night."

"Fair enough. But as we get bigger, I'd like to add more razzle-dazzle. Pyro, better stage lighting–"

"PYRO?!" exclaimed Teddy, rising from his seat.

"All the fireworks, Teddy. Sparks, fog, the full cha-bang!"

"All of which can happen one day, Teddy. But for now, let's focus on getting this room packed full of people. A happy crowd brings happy money. Happy money makes Lawrence happy. And that will allow us to create bigger and better shows, which will make us all happy," Joey explained.

Clark nodded. "Right! So let's get to work, friends!"

CHAPTER 13

For nearly a month, Clark and the band rigorously worked to create a show that was going to captivate an audience. The days started early, usually with light choreography rehearsals beginning around 7:30. The band rehearsed from mid-morning, sometimes through lunch, with more rehearsals into the early evening. If they weren't on stage, Clark and Jane were writing new songs together, sometimes late into the night. And when there was nothing going on musically, Clark was in costume fittings and production meetings with Joey and Mr. Lawrence.

Eventually, opening night rolled around and it was time to put all their hard work to test. Thirty minutes to showtime, Clark stood nervously in front of the mirror in his dressing room. The bright bulbs surrounding the mirror highlighted the fact that all the color had drained from his face.

Clark offered himself a pep talk. "Breathe. Relax. You got this. This is what you've always wanted."

Suddenly, the door flung open and Joey stepped inside. "Are you ready, Clark?! It's almost time!"

Clark laughed. "I think so. I'm so nervous. I keep having to remind myself to breathe."

Standing in the doorway, Joey looked at Clark. "You got this, man. You've worked so hard and it's time to show the world what you're made of. Let's get the crew in here."

Clark nodded as he dabbed his sweaty forehead with a handkerchief.

"Guys! Larry, Bev, Jane, Teddy, come in here! Clark's so nervous, he's about to shit himself," laughed Joey.

Beverly strutted into the dressing room with her hair in spiral curls, wearing her black sequined opening-number dress.

"Aww, Toots. Whatsa matter?" she asked, pulling a tube of lipstick from her cleavage.

"Hey, Bev. I'm just a little nervous, that's all."

"Aww. That's adorable." Beverly leaned toward the mirror and swiped the lipstick across her full lips.

"It's okay to be nervous, man. We all get nervous at times," said Larry as he walked into the dressing room wearing a black tux complete with bow tie and cummerbund.

"To be honest with you, Clark, I'm a little nervous too," Jane said as she made her way into the dressing room wearing a dress identical to Beverly's.

"Yes, completely normal! We just gotta get out there and knock their socks off," Teddy exclaimed.

Joey looked at his pocket watch. "Fifteen minutes until we take the stage, folks!"

Clark took another deep breath. "Okay, gang. Let's all huddle up real quick. Joey, you too."

Everyone circled up, shoulder to shoulder in the middle of Clark's dressing room.

"I just want to say that it's been an absolute pleasure working with you all to prepare this show. We've busted our asses to get here tonight.

Jane, we could not do tonight's show if it wasn't for you and your assistance with the songwriting."

Jane smiled.

Clark continued. "Larry, your knowledge and experience is unmatched. You're able to keep everyone on track, and when I get too excited and screw up, you help me get back in line every time."

Larry laughed. "That's right, brother."

"And Teddy. I've never seen someone play the saxophone or trumpet with as much power as you."

"Hey! Don't forget the trombone," Teddy chimed back.

"Of course. And then Bev. You bring the spunk and confidence that really makes us shine. You keep the beat rockin'. This show wouldn't be possible without you."

Beverly twirled her hair. "Well, isn't that the truth?! Put ya hands in guys. Let's knock 'em, sock 'em, rock 'em, and maybe fu--"

"All right, Beverly! We get it," Jane scolded.

"Let's do this, guys! Let's make some magic tonight!" said Clark eagerly.

The band cheered and started to make their way toward the stage. Everyone took their places behind the red velvet curtain that separated them from the audience.

The set was designed on three large risers. Beverly had the top riser to herself with the drums situated in the center. Teddy stood on the middle riser surrounded by his horns. On the bottom riser was Larry and his base, along with Jane and her microphone stand.

The show would start with Clark under a trap door in the middle of the front of the stage. He would be crouched down low where the audience couldn't see him as he sang the opening lines of the song. Then right before the key change, the stage crew would pull a lift that would raise Clark to the stage, front and center.

"Good luck, guys!" Clark whispered as he stepped onto the platform. He took his place, crouching low with his back to the crowd. Holding his microphone against his chest, he closed his eyes and waited for the cue.

The pre-show announcement boomed through the dining room.

"LADIES AND GENTLEMEN, PLEASE TAKE YOUR SEATS AS THE SHOW IS ABOUT TO BEGIN."

"IT IS WITH GREAT PLEASURE THAT WE WELCOME YOU TONIGHT TO THE SEA HOUSE! PLEASE GIVE A WARM WELCOME TO THE SEA HOUSE ENSEMBLE!"

The red velvet curtain opened and Clark could feel the warmth of the stage lights.

"AND NOW...MAKING HIS GRAND DEBUT...LADIES AND GENTLEMEN...CLARK JAMES!"

Thunderous applause rattled through the room. Teddy played the first few notes of the opening number, a saxophone solo.

Still crouching under the stage, Clark brought the microphone to his lips. "Oh, when the California sun goes down..."

Beverly tapped her drumsticks on the symbols, creating a dramatic crescendo.

"And the stars shimmer in the sky," Clark sang.

Larry picked up the bass. The lift on which Clark stood began to rise.

"I know a place where we could escape," sang Clark as he slowly started to stand.

"Yes, I know a place."

The lift was almost completely raised and Clark could now feel the heat from the stage lights on the back of his head.

"Say, pretty lady."

Now fully standing on the stage, Clark's back was to the audience.

"Won't you meet me at the Sea House?" Clark belted the lyrics as the band played along.

Clark spun around and faced the audience. The stage lights pierced his eyes, making it difficult to see the crowd. But he could feel the audience members' eyes on him. They were intensely watching, waiting to see his next move. Clark was making quite a first impression.

By the end of the first number, as he belted out the last few lines of the song, the audience began to roar with excitement. Applause rolled like thunder through the room. A few women in the audience even screamed.

Sitting in the front row at his table, Mr. Lawrence took it all in. The audience was completely in the palm of Clark's hand. And this was just the beginning. When Clark finished the final note, every person in the room stood up, applauding.

Mr. Lawrence jumped out of his seat and joined in the applause. Clark locked eyes with Mr. Lawrence, just as the club owner raised his glass to toast the performance.

With a wink, Clark placed the microphone in its stand and faced the crowd, a huge grin on his face.

"Good evening, ladies and gentlemen. I'm Clark James. Welcome to the Sea House!"

It didn't take very long for Clark James to become a sensation. Within a few days of the headliner's first performance, the streets of Big Sur began to buzz with excitement about the Sea House's new act.

Every Thursday through Sunday, the dining room was packed full of people from all over the Golden State who'd traveled to see Clark James. The attendance numbers continued to rise and so did the profits for the Sea House. Mr. Lawrence was particularly fond of this.

The roar of the crowds, their screaming, dancing, and cheering his name, gave Clark a rush unlike any other. But while the thrill was exhilarating, things weren't always pleasant. Like one particular Friday night when Emma Grace returned to the Sea House to see her former fling perform.

It was mid-song when he noticed her sitting in one of the front-row booths. Her wavy blonde hair was pulled partly back, showcasing her beautiful face. Wearing a one- shoulder black gown and red lipstick, she was simply stunning. Clark couldn't help but notice her as he peered from the stage.

After his first set of six songs, he stepped off stage to join Emma at her table.

"Well, hello there, Miss Emma Grace." Clark grabbed her hand and gave it a gentle kiss.

Laughing, Emma looked up at Clark, her big eyes wide. "Ah, *the* Clark James, the Sea House's finest act. It's so good to see you!"

Clark slid into Emma's booth. "You are looking ravishing tonight. Hollywood must be treating you well."

"Ah, not as well as it must be for you. Seems like everywhere I go, people are talking about you. I even heard them mention you on the radio the other day."

Clark gushed. "The radio?! No way. Which station?"

"I believe it was 41. Raving about how the Sea House has the best jazz singer in the state of California."

"Gah, I haven't listened to much of the radio. There's not much time in between rehearsals, wardrobe fittings, shows, and just sleeping. But that's just crazy!"

Emma laughed and placed her hand on Clark's arm. "You really did it! You became the jazz singer you always wanted to--"

"CLARK! My boy, it's almost time to get back up there for your next set."

Clark and Emma looked up into a cloud of cigar smoke to find Mr. Lawrence standing at their table.

"Ah, I remember you. Welcome back to the Sea House. It's nice to see you, Miss..."

"Grace. Emma Grace."

"Right! Well, it's nice to see you again. What do you think of our boy, Clark James?" Mr. Lawrence gave Clark a friendly punch to the arm.

"I can't believe it! It's just amazing to see him up there on the stage." Emma smiled as she pulled Clark's arm close to hers..

Clark gave her arm a gentle squeeze. "Yes! All thanks to this man right here! Mr. Lawrence changed my life!"

Clark slid out of the booth and gave Mr. Lawrence a pat on the back. Placing his cigar in the nearest ashtray, Mr. Lawrence let out a loud laugh. "Nonsense, my boy. You changed everyone's life here at this club. We're all reaping the benefits of your show. So you must get back out there! Give the people what they want!"

"Yes, yes! It's showtime! Emma, let's catch up on my next break!"

The band began to play as Clark raced up the steps to the stage. "All right, everybody! Are we having a good time tonight?!"

The crowd roared. "That's what I love to hear! Well, this next song, I'd like to dedicate it to someone special right here in the front row. Miss Emma Grace, the most beautiful woman in the room!"

All eyes shifted from the stage to Emma Grace's booth where she laughed, her cheeks blushing. A few women in the crowd stood up to get a better look at Emma. If Clark James was giving her a shoutout from the stage then she had to be someone important.

At Mr. Lawrence's table, one of the women sitting with him smirked. "Now Lawrence, who is *she*?"

Mr. Lawrence laughed as he sipped his cocktail. "Oh, her? Don't worry about her. She's just a soon-to-be former short-lived romance. Nothing special."

"Well, she must be something special. He's claiming she's the most beautiful woman in the room. I didn't come here to hear Clark James rave over some other woman."

Mr. Lawrence placed his glass on the table. "Listen, she's nothing. Clark James isn't dating anyone. He's not allowed to."

The woman took a sip of her champagne. "Like I said, Lawrence, look around. Every woman in this room is here because they want to be seen by Clark James. They want to feel like they're the only girl in the room, that he's singing only to them.

"You are absolutely right. And Clark does a fantastic job making the entire room swoon, don't you think?" asked Lawrence as he lit a cigar.

"Well, all I'm saying is that it dampens the mood when he's over here giving some C-list actress a shoutout."

Mr. Lawrence flicked ash from his cigar. "I can assure you that she'll no longer be an issue after tonight."

CHAPTER 14

The next morning the rain woke both Clark and Emma Grace. Although rain in Big Sur was common, Clark was getting used to waking up to the sound of raindrops. Since he didn't have to be in his dressing room until later in the evening, it was a perfect morning to enjoy some downtime.

Clark rolled over and looked at Emma Grace. "It's been such a long time since I've done this."

Emma smiled, "Done what?"

"This. Just laid in bed and relaxed. With a beautiful woman wrapped in my arms," he said as he pulled Emma closer.

Emma giggled. "Well, relaxing looks good on you. You should do it more often."

"I've been on the go since returning to the States, and it feels like I'm just now getting to where I can do that, actually."

"Can I ask you something?" she said as she ran her hands through his hair.

"Of course."

"Why the name change? What was wrong with Rob?"

Clark cleared his throat. "Oh, Mr. Lawrence said it needed to be something legendary. Something that people would never forget. So, we settled on Clark James."

"Ah, I see. I don't know, though. Rob could've been legendary."

Clark laughed. "Oh yeah? How many guys out there do you know with the name Rob?"

Emma Grace chuckled. "A lot, actually."

"See? Exactly!"

Clark rolled out of bed. "I'm going to make a cup of coffee. Would you like one?"

"Yes, I would love that."

Clark was brewing the coffee when he heard the kitchen door open.

"Mornin', Clark! Hell of a show last night!"

Clark turned to see Mr. Lawrence standing in the doorway.

"Oh, good morning! Thank you, sir."

"Hey, listen. You got a minute to step outside and chat real quick?"

Clark looked back toward the hallway leading to his bedroom and then back at Mr. Lawrence.

"Ah…I…have company right now. Emma Grace stayed the night. Could we possibly talk later this afternoon?"

Mr. Lawrence adjusted the cap on his head. "Clark, it will only take a few minutes. Let's step outside," he said as he opened the kitchen door.

Clark put down the coffee pot and followed Mr. Lawrence out to the front porch.

"What's this about? Everything okay?"

Mr. Lawrence took a cigar from his blazer pocket.

"Oh, everything's great, Clark. You're doing an amazing job. But we have just a small concern."

Clark crossed his arms to cover his bare chest from the breeze.

"Oh, okay. What's that, sir?"

Mr. Lawrence struck a match to light his cigar. "Well, it's the girl. Miss..."

Clark shook his head, confused. "Grace. Emma Grace."

"Ah, right!" Mr. Lawrence said, snapping his fingers. "Miss Grace. I'm worried about her."

"Why are you worried about her?"

"Well, I'm worried that she doesn't have the best intentions in mind when it comes to you. Have you all discussed her acting career?"

Clark leaned against the porch railing. "We haven't talked about her work in a while. We've just been catching up."

"Clark, she hasn't had any acting gigs in months. They're saying she's extremely difficult to work with."

"Well, I find that hard to believe, sir. I mean you've seen her! She's sweet and sincere all the time."

"I know. And that's what I think she wants you to believe. She wants you to fall in love with her, Clark."

Clark shook his head.

"She needs money, Clark. You're her way in. She's hoping that she can use you to become famous."

Clark stood up. "I just don't know about that. With all due respect, sir, I can't see her doing that."

"Have I ever done you wrong? Have I led you astray so far?" asked Mr. Lawrence as he stepped closer to Clark.

Clark stood up straight. "No, sir, you haven't. And I appreciate everything, truly. But I just don't understand why this is an issue."

"She's going to take you for everything you have. And if you want to throw it all away for some girl, then fine. But don't say I didn't warn you, Clark."

Clark turned and looked out at the foggy sea. "So, what am I supposed to do then? Tell her she's not welcome here anymore?"

"You just tell her that you are focusing on your career. You have a way with words. You'ill know how to say it."

Clark turned back around to face Mr. Lawrence. "Yeah, it's not that easy."

Mr. Lawrence stepped off the porch and began walking toward the pathway that led to the Sea House. "Well, you'll figure it out. In fact, you have to figure it out. She's not good for you, and in the end you'll see that. Have her out of here before the show tonight, Clark."

Clark couldn't believe it. Any of it. How could Mr. Lawrence just walk into his house and tell him to get rid of a woman he had feelings for? Was Emma Grace really that bad of a person?

When he walked back into the kitchen, he found Emma Grace sitting at the table.

"Hi," she said softly as she held up a cup of coffee.

"Hi. Sorry, I got distracted. I see you found the caffeine."

"I did. What was that about? Looked like a serious conversation."

Clark pulled up a chair and took a seat at the kitchen table. "Oh, that was just Mr. Lawrence wanting to go over some housekeeping items for tonight's show."

"Ah. Such as?"

Clark looked down at the table. "Emma, I really had a great time with you last night. And you're such a beautiful woman—"

"But what? I'm a freeloader? I'm taking advantage of you?"

Clark could feel the blood rushing to his cheeks as he looked up and met eyes with Emma Grace.

"No, no that's not it all. I just have to really focus on my career right now and–"

"Clark, I heard everything he was saying to you. I'm not trying to take advantage of you or use you for some stupid fame."

Clark grabbed Emma Grace's hand. "Hey, listen. I know! I didn't believe him for a second, truly. But...he's right in a way. I have to really focus on my career. And the shows are needing my undivided attention."

Emma Grace stood up and walked toward the bedroom. "There's no need to explain yourself when I heard every damn word of your conversation. I get it completely."

Clark followed her. "Em, I'm sorry. I know that this sounds like I'm–"

Emma Grace quickly put on her dress from the night before. "A sellout? A coward? Because that's exactly what you are!"

"Okay, well, you don't have to be so harsh about it. I'm trying to do what's best for me right now, which is something you would understand if you actually gave a shit about your career, Emma Grace."

"OH! You really are something. No need to worry about breaking my heart because I am out of here, *Rob*."

Clearly upset, the young woman dashed past Clark and started making her way toward the front door.

"Hey, hey hey. Emma, I don't want to upset you."

Emma turned and faced Clark. "It's too late for that. You had an opportunity to defend me when that scumbag was feeding you lies. And you just stood there!"

Clark took Emma's hand. "I told you that I don't believe him. But what am I supposed to do? Everything I have is because of him. This cottage that we're standing in right now is because of him."

Emma dropped Clark's hand. "Yeah, well, like I said, sellout. Have a nice show tonight, Rob. And have a nice life."

With that, she was gone. Clark stood alone in the kitchen as the rain began to pick up, pelting the windows of the cottage. He had done exactly what Mr. Lawrence wanted him to do, but it didn't feel right. But this was the life he'd always wanted, and he was willing to make some sacrifices.

CHAPTER 15

BIG SUR, CALIFORNIA, 1950

As the years passed, his fame rising, Clark eventually adjusted to his new life. The Sea House was becoming known throughout the country as the home of Clark James. His headlining shows continued to bring crowds to the Sea House. Because the demand was so high, Mr. Lawrence decided to do something for the first time in the club's history: he added more shows to the weekly lineup.

Clark had a fully packed schedule. Mondays were for press and radio interviews. Tuesdays were rehearsals and wardrobe fittings. Wednesdays through Saturdays were show days. And Sundays were off days.

The rigorous schedule meant Clark operated on autopilot. But no matter how tiresome the schedule got, nothing could beat the rush of stepping on stage each night. Clark had the entire crowd in the palm of his hand and that was all that mattered to him.

There was one particular Wednesday night when things began to shift for Clark. As he was getting ready in his dressing room, Clark and Joey discussed the night's crowd.

"Clark, this crowd is insane tonight. They're all super-excited to see you perform," said Joey.

Clark checked his reflection in the mirror and adjusted his gold bow tie. "Oh yeah? That's like music to my ears, Joey. How about the women out there?"

Joey chuckled. "Dressed to the nines and looking like dimes. A lot have bought passes to the after-party on the terrace."

"Hmm…the after-party on the terrace. How could I forget?"

Joey opened a bottle of bourbon and poured some on ice. "Yeah, it does seem a bit much, don't you think?"

"You know how Lawrence is. If he sees a money-making opportunity, he's going to take it."

Joey handed the glass to Clark. "That's right. But hey, cheers to being the hottest singer in the country right now."

Clark laughed and took a sip of bourbon. "I'll definitely toast to that anytime!"

"Oh, hey, by the way, there is an older couple in booth four asking to see you. I know how fans can get at times, so I wasn't sure if you knew them or not. But I wanted to let you know before you went out there."

"An older couple?"

Joey poured more bourbon into Clark's glass. "Yeah, they seem pretty insistent on talking to you. In fact, they called you by your old name."

Clark brought the glass to his lips, lost in thought. "Can you do me a favor, Joey? Can you bring them back here?"

"Right now? You go on in 30 minutes. Are you sure?"

Clark put down his glass. "Yes, I'm sure. Send them back discreetly, please."

Joey nodded and left the room. While he was waiting, Clark slicked his hair back and did one last check in the mirror. Bow tie? Check.

Blazer on with only the bottom button fastened? Check. Shoes tied? Check.

"OH MY GOD! IT REALLY IS YOU!"

Adjusting his cufflinks, Clark looked up to see the older couple in the doorway of his dressing room. Time stood still. Clark could barely believe his eyes.

"Hi, Pops. Hi, Mom."

The woman ran to Clark and threw her arms around him. "I thought you were dead! I cannot believe this is really you!"

"Yeah, I, uh–it's a complicated story, and I really can explain."

Clark looked at his parents with disbelief. They had certainly aged since he left home more than a decade ago. A wave of guilt enveloped Clark.

"We saw your photo in the paper, ya know?" said Clark's dad.

"Oh? I didn't realize the papers were getting all the way out to Nashville now. I do these press interviews and–"

"A simple letter would've done the job, Robert. Just a simple letter saying you are alive."

Clark's eyes remained focused on the floor. "I know, Dad. But it's a bit complicated."

"No, complicated is having to tell your friends and family that your son must have died in the war or that he was being held prisoner in another country."

Tears began to stream down his mother's face. "Honey, we really did think you were dead. I'm so glad to see you now, but it would have been nice of you to stop in Tennessee before heading out here to California."

Clark gently placed his arms on his mother's shoulders. "I know. I am so sorry, Mom. I just didn't think you guys would understand. I felt like if I returned home, I would be stuck there. None of this would have ever happened."

Suddenly, there was a knock on the door and Joey appeared in the dressing room. "Sorry to interrupt, Clark, but it's showtime."

Clark gave his mom a gentle squeeze. "Right, showtime! Joey, these are my parents. Can you make sure that they are taken care of very well tonight?"

Joey nodded. "Well, of course. It's a pleasure to meet you both. Everything is on the house tonight. Please follow me right this way."

Clark's mom smiled and gave her son a quick hug. "Good luck tonight, Sweetie. We will be watching from the front row!"

"Thanks, Mom. And Dad, I know you're upset with me. After my show, I would love to invite you all back to my place so that we can catch up. You guys can stay in town for as long as you'd like."

And with that, the singer and his parents parted ways. Clark rushed backstage while Joey escorted the couple to their seats.

Once Joey had Clark's parents settled, he set out to find Mr. Lawrence. After searching the dining room, he found Mr. Lawrence off to the side of the stage watching the opening number of Clark's set.

"Lawrence, I think we might have a problem."

Not taking his eyes off the stage, Lawrence cleared his throat. "Ah, yeah? What's that?"

"Rob–I mean Clark's parents are here. And they seem concerned."

"His parents? Where? And what do you mean concerned?"

Joey pointed toward booth four where Clark's parents were sitting. "Yes, that's them right there."

"Hmm..."

"I gathered Clark didn't tell them where he's been the past several years. They thought he was dead."

"Well, look at them, Joey. Do you blame the guy? His father looks like the biggest stick-in-the-mud. Hasn't even clapped once since Clark took the stage."

"Yeah, I think it's just a complicated situation. And it might get more complicated because Clark is wanting to catch up with them."

"Complicated, yes. But there's nothing wrong with him catching up with his parents. I'm not a monster, Joey."

Mr. Lawrence let out a laugh while giving Joey a playful shove.

"I understand, sir. But what do we do when his parents want him to leave and he realizes that he can't do that?"

The sly smile on Mr. Lawrence's face quickly faded. "Oh, that won't be necessary. I'll make sure they are gone before that discussion even happens. Let's give the boy his reunion, but keep a close eye on them at all times. I don't want them messing with his emotions."

Joey looked toward the stage. Clark was performing his heart out. "Yes, agreed, sir."

"We can't have Clark James sad. When he's sad, he doesn't have his heart fully in the show. And I can't stand to see a grown man up there on stage looking so..."

"Heartbroken?" said Joey.

"No. Embarrassing and pitiful."

Clark finished his set for the night and went to find his parents. When he returned to the dining room, they were no longer at booth four. Clark tapped Joey on the shoulder as he was finishing up an order at one of the tables.

"Hey, Joey. Have you seen my parents?"

"Ah, Clark! Great show! Yes, they are actually on the terrace with Mr. Lawrence."

"Oh yeah. I forgot all about the after-party. Thanks, man!"

Clark dashed in between groups of people and gave a few quick hugs while making his way to the terrace. When he arrived at the VIP party, he noticed his parents chatting with Mr. Lawrence near the terrace railing. Clark didn't know his parents to drink alcohol, but at this particular moment both had a cocktail in hand.

Clark approached the three of them and placed a hand on his mom's shoulder.

"CLARK! What a fantastic show! Mr. Lawrence was just filling us in on all the amazing work you've been doing," said Clark's mom, proudly.

"Yes, Clark. I've been telling them all about your sold-out shows and how impressive you are. They're lucky to have a son like you."

Clark's dad let out a sarcastic laugh before taking a sip of his drink.

"Lucky. We're so lucky. Lucky to know he's been alive all this time."

Clark nervously cleared his throat. "Dad, I didn't know you were a drinker. When did you start that?"

"Picked it up a few years ago. You know, when I thought my son was dead."

Mr. Lawrence exhaled smoke from his cigar. "Gentlemen, we're having a grand time. Let's not let something from the past get in the way of tonight's fun."

"Yes! I agree! Let's enjoy this night, Honey. We're back with our son and that's all that matters," said Clark's mom as she drained the last drop from her glass.

"She's absolutely correct. And it looks like we need more drinks. Joey! Oh, Joey!" shouted Mr. Lawrence. He signaled to Joey for another round of drinks.

Clark adjusted his bow tie. "I don't know. It looks like you guys have had enough to drink for tonight. Maybe we could just take it easy and–"

"Oh, you think you're so grown up now that you can tell your old man what to do?" Clark's dad swapped his empty glass for the new one from Joey's tray.

"Honey–"

"No, stop. I'm tired of this pretend bullshit. We've been acting like everything is hunky-dory all goddamn night. And it's not."

Clark grabbed his dad's arm, pulling him in close. "Dad, cool it. Let's sit down and talk this out like adults."

Clark's dad pushed his son away. "*Adults?* You don't know the first thing about being an adult. Get your fucking hands off of me."

Clark could feel the blood rushing to his head. How dare his dad come into this establishment and do this? Clark adjusted his dinner jacket and took a step toward his father.

"Jesus, Dad. You got a lot of nerve coming into *my* house and making a scene like this."

"Oh, do I? Are you listening to yourself right now, son? You don't even realize what hell you've put your mother and me through."

"ENOUGH! I told you I'm fucking sorry, Dad. I don't know how many times I have to tell you that. I'm sorry that you're upset, but this is not the place–"

"What are you going to do about it?! Mr. Hollywood thinks he's bigger than his own father. Tell me, Rob. What the fuck are you going to do about it?"

Clark's dad threw back the last of his drink and wiped the sweat dripping off his forehead. Leaning in close to Clark's face, he whispered. "Tell me. What the fuck are you going to do about it?"

"Dad, get out of my face."

Clark's mom began to cry. "Stop this! Stop it right now! Let's all just go back to having a good time."

"Oh, we're having a BLAST! Our son has been lying to us for years. But guess what, honey?! He's alive and doing quite well, rolling in fame and fortune in the Monterey fucking hills."

Mr. Lawrence cleared his throat and put his cigar in the nearest ashtray. "All right, all right, all right. It's been a real pleasure having you both here tonight, but I think it's time to leave now."

Clark held a hand up to Mr. Lawrence. "No, this isn't necessary. Dad, let's just go back to my place and we can discuss this in private. Stop making a scene!"

"Ha! A scene? I'll show you a fucking scene!" Clark's dad threw his glass to the ground. The shatter caused everyone in the room to turn their heads toward the commotion.

Clark's dad grabbed his son, threw him to the ground, and pinned him down, his hands tight around his Clark's throat.

"You stupid little shit. YOU HAVE NO IDEA–"

Guests on the terrace collectively gasped and ran toward the two men.

"SOMEONE HELP HIM! GET THAT MAN OFF HIM!"

Sobbing hysterically, Clark's mom screamed, "GET OFF OF HIM NOW! YOU'RE GOING TO KILL HIM!"

Pulling off his party jacket, Mr. Lawrence crept around behind Clark's dad. "All right, now I told you to stop and you didn't listen." Leaning back, Mr. Lawrence swiftly kicked Clark's dad in the lower back.

Clark's dad let out a sharp scream. "AHHHHH! Mother–"

Clark and his father lay sprawled on the terrace, gasping for air.

"NOW I SUGGEST YOU GET THE HELL OUT OF HERE BEFORE I KILL YOU, YOU SICK, SORRY PIECE OF SHIT!" screamed Mr. Lawrence.

Joey and a few bystanders approached the scene and grabbed Clark's dad, pulling him from the ground.

"Clark James, ladies and gentlemen, is a fraud. Ya, hear me?" yelled Clark's dad as he was led from the nightclub's terrace. "He's a fucking fraud!"

Clark stood up, feeling slightly woozy from having his windpipe crushed by his own father's hands. He ran his hands through his hair and adjusted his bow tie.

All eyes were on him. "Uhm-uhm." He cleared his throat. "That was quite a spectacle, wasn't it? Everyone, please go back to enjoying the party. I'm so grateful for each and every one of you. Please! Drink up as the night is still young!"

Some of the guests gave sympathetic nods and smiles, while others kept their eyes on Clark. His mom dabbed her eyes with a handkerchief she'd pulled from her clutch.

"Mom, let's get you to bed. You can stay at my place tonight."

Wrapping his arms around his mother, Clark began to lead her out of the nightclub.

"Mr. Lawrence, thank you for what you did tonight, but I think we've had enough fun for one evening. We're going back to my cottage, if that's all right."

Mr. Lawrence patted Clark on the back. "I think that's a fine idea, kid. So sorry about tonight, but it'll all be okay."

CHAPTER 16

The next morning Clark woke up to the warmth of the bright morning sun shining through his bedroom window. He stood up and stretched before walking to the living room. Through the front window, Clark saw that his mother was already awake and sitting on the front porch.

Clark stepped outside to find his mother leaning back in a red metal chair, still in her party dress from the night before.

"Good morning."

Clark's mom looked up from the stunning view of the sea below the cottage and gave a forced smile. "Good morning, Honey."

"Did you sleep okay, Mom?"

She nodded. "Yes, slept like a baby, but perhaps that was because of all the wine. The views here are incredible. I can see why you love it here."

Clark took a seat in the chair beside his mom. "Yeah, it's my favorite. When I have a quiet moment, I like to just sit out here and take it all in."

"It's been a wild ride for you the last few years, hasn't it?"

Clark nodded. "Yes, you could certainly say that."

"I mean, you went off to fight for our country, returned home, and went off to fulfill your dream a million miles away from the only home you'd ever known. And here you are, a sensation...someone I barely know."

"A sensation. I don't feel like that most days, but I do feel like I'm where I'm supposed to be."

"I can see that, Honey." Clark's mom patted his hand.

"Well, clearly Dad cannot."

Clark's mom stood up and leaned against the porch railing, crossing her arms.

"Your father does love you, Clark. He always has and always will. You know he has a tough way of showing that."

Clark rolled his eyes. "Yes, I definitely felt the love when he was strangling me last night."

"I agree that was a bit extreme."

"A bit extreme?! Mother, do you hear yourself right now? It was absurd and embarrassing."

Clark's mom quickly turned to face the ocean. "You're right. It was all of those things. But he has not been the same since you left for the war and didn't come back to Tennessee. And honestly, can you blame him?"

She grabbed a blanket from a nearby basket and wrapped it around herself. "Your father has always had a bit of a melancholy soul. It comes in waves, but the day that we realized–or we thought–you were never going to come home, something in him just cracked."

Clark crossed his arms. "I know. I should've written or called. I realize that now."

"You know, we had a little celebration of life ceremony for you, Rob. We invited the Brooks and the Smiths. And Pastor Danny. You know, all of your childhood crew. We learned to move on. We tried to, at least. We tried our best to come to terms with the idea that our son might never return to us."

"Mom, I am so sorry."

Clark's mom adjusted her blanket and shifted in her chair to face him. "Your father started drinking. On especially bad days, Clark, he turns into the man you saw last night."

"Mom, has he ever laid his hands on you?" Clark rose from his chair.

"Oh, God no, Honey. He has his issues, but he would never do such a thing. Your father is a good man, but there are many nights when he just doesn't come home. He'll stumble through our door in the early hours of the morning."

Clark looked off, saddened by what his mother was revealing.

"But something in him changed one day when we opened the morning paper and there you were. Clark James. In a swanky suit and tie. Singing on the big stage."

"Mom–"

"So, we saved up the money. We found out you were doing regular shows here at the Sea House and decided to come see you. And maybe talk our boy into coming home."

She began folding the blanket into a neat square. "But I know. I see it in your eyes. You're not coming home. This is your life now."

"Mom, I would love to come home for a few days, but I just don't know if I can make that work right now. I have rehearsals, interviews, events, parties. Not to mention, all the people you met last night at the club depend on me. The more people I draw in for shows, the more they make. My performances help them provide for their families."

"I know, Honey. It's okay. I selfishly thought you might come home with us. I hoped the trip out to see you might help save your father from himself.

Clark put his arm around his mom and pulled her in for a hug. "Mom, you can stay here as long as you need. We can help you find a place. I can give you money."

She wiped tears from her cheeks. "No, no, no. That's nonsense. Your father needs me, and I'm going to stick with him no matter what. We'll get through this. I'm just so glad you are alive and well. But when you're ready to return home–when the fame has settled or it's all become too much–you know that you can always come back to us."

Clark squeezed his mom tightly. "I know, Mom. I know."

CHAPTER 17

Later that afternoon, after a cab had taken Clark's mom back to the hotel where his father slept off his hangover, Clark met with Mr. Lawrence in the club's dining room.

"Well, that was quite a night, wasn't it, boy?" laughed Mr. Lawrence.

"Sure. It was definitely something. I'm sorry that happened in front of everyone and that you had to get involved."

Mr. Lawrence poured himself a glass of water. "Ah, families are complicated, Clark. I get it."

Clark nodded. "Yeah, ain't that the truth. My mom says that my father's not been doing well. And I feel terrible. It's because of me."

"*Because of you?*" Mr. Lawrence rolled his eyes. "Let me tell you something, boy. Your father's actions last night were not because of you. He's just a mean ol' man."

"I know. But he apparently hasn't been doing well since I chose not to return home after the war. And I get it. He thought I was dead."

"And then he discovered that you're not. You're alive and doing damn well. What we saw last night was a result of jealousy, Clark."

Clark shook his head.

"Just listen to me, Clark. Your father is jealous that you are doing very well out here on the West Coast. I mean you heard the absurd things he was shouting at you last night."

"I know. And I agree, Mr. Lawrence. But I think I might need to help my folks out. I don't know. Maybe I need to take some time off and return home. Just for a little while."

"Not happening, Clark."

Clark looked Mr. Lawrence in the eye. "I know, my schedule is slammed, but I was thinking we could move some things around."

Mr. Lawrence lit his cigar. "Like I said, Clark, it's not happening."

Clark felt his blood begin to boil. "So, that's it, huh. It's just not happening? No reason? Just no?"

"Yes, it's a definite no. And you want to know why, Clark?"

Clark folded his arms across his chest and nodded.

"Because I know people like your father. You get out there and you try to save him. And he just sucks the damn life out of you. Then a few weeks turns into a few months. And then a few months turns into a year. And then just like that you're stuck back in Tennessee. I simply cannot allow that to happen to you."

Clark stood up. "Oh, well *thank you*. But I am going to have to disagree with you on this one, Lawrence. I need to do this for my family. I need to make it right with them."

"Clark, you can't."

Standing up, Clark slapped his hands on the table, making the drinking glasses rattle. "For the love of God, I don't care! My mother needs me and I–"

Mr. Lawrence threw his cigar into the ashtray as he jumped out of his seat to meet Clark face-to-face.

"We're your family, kid! Me, Joey, and everyone else who helps make your show go on. We're your family, not your trashy parents from some hick town in Tennessee."

"Oh, so that's what it is. They're *trash*. Well, like I said, I don't care. I will be going home for a few days."

Mr. Lawrence flipped the table over, his face red and angry. The sudden commotion caused water to splash all over Clark's shirt.

"You're not going anywhere! You hear me! You made a deal with me. And that deal stands."

"What the hell are you talking about?" asked Clark while slowly backing away from Mr. Lawrence.

"The contract. Oh, you mean to tell me you didn't read what you signed?"

"I read the contract. But what are you talking about?"

"You must not have read it well enough, then. Article 10, Paragraph 3. 'Subject agrees that he becomes property of the Sea House the day he begins his residency.' You signed the dotted line, Clark"

"Okay, so what?!" Clark said, throwing his hands up in the air.

Mr. Lawrence inched closer to him. "*So what?* So that means, Clark, that you belong to me."

Crossing his arms over his chest, Clark stood tall. "I'm sorry?"

"You are no longer, Robert Matthews. You are Clark James. And Clark James is a product of the Sea House and—most importantly—a product of *mine*. The day you signed that contract Robert Matthews disappeared."

"I don't believe this. This is complete bullshit."

Throwing his navy blazer over his broad shoulder, Mr. Lawrence began walking toward the front entrance of the club. "It may be bullshit, Clark. But you signed the contract. You agreed."

"Yeah. Well, I want out. I'm not going to stay here if it means this!"

Mr. Lawrence stopped in front of the door and slowly turned around. A malicious grin spread across his face as he looked back at Clark.

"There is no out. You are forever that 23-year-old man who signed his life away. You are forever a part of the Sea House."

CHAPTER 18

Present Day

Neal woke up earlier than usual for a morning off work. He rolled over and looked at the alarm clock on his nightstand. 7:00. Perhaps it was the two bottles of wine they went through the night before or the details of Nana's story. Either way, Neal was eager to hear more about Clark James.

Before he got out of bed, he reached over his puffy, white duvet and grabbed his iPhone from the nightstand. The black-and-white framed photo on the corner of the nightstand caught Neal's eye. It was a picture of him and Josie from their first road trip together. Neal brought Josie with him to Tennessee for a long weekend to celebrate Grandad's retirement from the railroad.

He had not planned on bringing her along as he traveled back to Knoxville to celebrate the end of an era for Grandad. But after sharing many childhood stories of moments with his grandparents, Josie said she would love to meet them. Neal seized the opportunity. It was a big deal for both of them. Neal had never brought anyone back to meet his entire family. And Josie was able to meet people that Neal held really close to his heart.

The photo showed Neal and Josie smiling big with their arms wrapped around each other on the dock of Nana and Grandad's lakehouse. It was taken after a long, hot day on the water. Both of them were still in their bathing suits with cheeks red from a bit too much summer sun. Neal wore navy swimming trunks, his blonde hair slicked back. Josie's black bikini straps showed from underneath the old concert tee she was wearing as a cover-up, her brown hair wet and stringy.

Seeing the photo of the two of them made Neal wonder what Josie was up to in LA. He also questioned why he'd not yet replaced the photo in the frame. He opened the Instagram app on his phone, typing in Josie's name.

They still followed each other on social media. Neal was not quite ready to disconnect. And honestly, he enjoyed seeing the updated stories she shared of her life. Sometimes he intentionally posted scenery of the house or the cliffside views to his Instagram, hoping Josie would see it. It was a modern way of signaling he was still in love with her.

He scrolled through the collection of moments from Josie's life. The photo of her smiling big when she started a new job as head graphic designer at the marketing agency, California & Co. The photo of Neal and her on Catalina Island for Josie's sister's wedding, Josie in her gold silk bridesmaid dress, her brown hair pulled up in a ponytail, Neal in a black suit with matching bow tie. The caption read, "The best weekend with the best wedding date."

Neal smiled, zooming in on the photo. They looked great together. And he remembered that weekend so well. It was just a month after Josie met Neal's family in Tennessee. On the flight back to California, Josie asked him if he would like to attend her sister's weekend wedding festivities. He happily accepted the invitation.

He was nervous to meet her family. And her dad and little brother did give him a bit of the cold shoulder at first. But by the end of the weekend, after a few too many games of beer pong with Josie's dad and brother, Neal was part of the family.

So where did they go wrong, Neal asked himself. When did Josie begin to get annoyed with him? When did he start to read her text messages and not immediately reply? What did her family think?

Neal could feel the sadness creeping in, but now was not the time to throw a pity party. Not when his grandparents were visiting. He could smell the morning coffee and heard the occasional laugh from one of his grandparents as they puttered around the kitchen.

He got out of bed and went downstairs to get the day started. When he entered the kitchen, he could hear the coffee dripping into the stainless steel pot. But his grandparents were not at the kitchen table. Neal grabbed a mug from the cabinet above the coffee pot and poured himself a steaming cup of joe, sipping the coffee in silence until he heard Nana's voice.

"Daniel, would ya not smoke the cigar near me? It's making my eyes water! It's too early for all of that."

Ah, they were in the sunroom adjacent to the kitchen. Neal walked to the door near the kitchen table and slid it open.

"Good morning!" Neal said, seeing his grandparents in the sunroom. Nana was still in her pajamas, sitting on the white couch. Grandad was lounging in his robe and faded brown suede houseshoes.

"Morning, Neal! About time you got up," said Grandad.

"Good morning. I think the wine kept me up last night. What about you guys?"

Nana took a sip of her coffee. "Oh, well, we certainly drank enough wine last night for that to happen. But it had the opposite effect on me. I slept like a baby."

Grandad nodded and held up his coffee mug. "Same here."

Neal took a seat beside his grandparents. Grandad puffed on his cigar. "So, I can't stop thinking about the story of Clark James," said Neal.

Grandad tapped ashes from the end of his cigar into the metal ashtray on the side table. "Yeah, you and me both. Milly's been holding onto this one for years."

Nana laughed. "Well, it's not the easiest story to tell. It's a wild one."

Neal adjusted his chair to get the sun out of his face. "So, Clark realizes that he is in deep shit with the contract."

Grandad laughed. "Deep shit. That's one way to put it."

"And then what? He just continues to do shows?"

Nana put her coffee mug down. "Well, yes and no. He continued to do the shows. But it wasn't always as glamorous as it seemed. He struggled with feelings of insecurity and not feeling like a human being at times."

"I mean...I can't believe it. He's frozen in time? Like, stuck at the age of 23?"

Grandad tightened the belt of his robe. "Hell, I'd love to forever be 23."

"I'm sure you would," Nana replied sarcastically. "But for Clark, it was almost like a prison sentence. He felt trapped, oftentimes putting himself in terrible situations in hopes of escaping the loneliness he felt."

CHAPTER 19
Big Sur, California, 1950

After arguing with Mr. Lawrence that day, Clark felt like a part of him was forever changed. When he realized just how serious the repercussions of signing the contract were, he felt stupid, like he'd been blindsided.

It felt as if he was grieving his own life. Time was moving on for everyone but him. This paradise that he'd dreamed of for so long suddenly felt like a rose with a thousand thorns. At first, he did not press much about the contract, mainly because he was afraid of what would happen if he did. If Mr. Lawrence manipulated him into the contract, what else was he capable of? And who else knew about this shady deal? He remained conflicted about what to do until one night after a show.

Clark and the band had just wrapped their set when he noticed a familiar face in the audience toward the back of the dining room. The woman had her back turned to him, and she was talking with Mr. Lawrence. But Clark instantly recognized the heavy wooden cane the woman was holding. It was Miss Vivian who had come to the Sea House.

Clark dashed through the crowd, making his way up through the darkened dining room to Miss Vivian. Her strapless silk gown featured a giant purple bow on the back that flowed down the entire length of the dress. Her curly black hair appeared longer than he remembered.

"Miss Vivian!" Clark said, placing a hand on the woman's shoulder.

Quickly turning around, she flashed a bright white smile at Clark. But when Clark saw her face, he was astonished at how young she appeared. Her wrinkles from years earlier were almost completely gone. And that smile? Clark always remembered her missing a few teeth, but now she had a perfect smile.

"Why, Robbie, baby! Look at you!" Miss Vivian exclaimed.

"Ah, look at you! You look..." Clark struggled to find the right words.

"Ravishing?" Miss Vivian asked, framing her face with her hands.

"I was going to say youthful. It's quite incredible. How did you do it?" Clark asked.

"Robbie, baby. We never ask a woman her secrets to staying young," Miss Vivian gushed.

Clark studied Miss Vivian's face, his eyes scanning from her wrinkle-free forehead to her nose to her smile.

"You were incredible up there tonight. I told you that you were going to be a star! You remember that?" Miss Vivian laughed as she patted Clark's shoulder.

"Yeah, I do. Guess you could say I wouldn't be here without you, Miss Viv."

"Aww, the pleasure is all mine. Love seeing you shine here at the Sea House!"

She gave Clark a wink and began to walk toward the terrace for the after-party. Clark followed.

THE CLUB BY THE SEA

"I don't think I remember. Remind me, how are you and Mr. Lawrence friends?" Clark asked as they made their way outside to the terrace.

"We go way back, Robbie. I can barely remember now."

Clark forced a smile. "Right, of course."

The two parted, Miss Vivian off to find the bar and Clark to talk with Beverly, who was standing at the terrace railing.

"Hey, Handsome," Beverly said as she sipped her dirty martini.

"Hey, Bev. Great job tonight," Clark replied, leaning against the railing.

"Gee, thanks. Can't say you're wrong."

In the distance, Clark saw Miss Vivian at the bar with Mr. Lawrence, laughing over drinks, clearly deep in conversation.

"Hey, Clark. Who's got your eye?" Beverly asked.

Clark looked back at Beverly. "Oh, uh, an old friend is here. And I'm just trying to figure something out."

"Oh yeah? What's that?"

"You see that older—well, I mean, young lady over there? The one talking with Lawrence?" Clark pointed toward the bar.

"You mean Miss Vivian?" Beverly asked.

"Wait, you know her too?" Clark asked, crossing his arms.

"Yeah, she and Lawrence are buddies. She's been around a time or two."

"Interesting. There's something odd going on here, Beverly."

Beverly let out a sarcastic laugh. "You're just now figuring that out? Welcome to the Sea House!"

Clark leaned in toward Beverly. "Bev, what do you know?"

Beverly threw back the rest of her drink and exhaled. "Look, Toots. I've probably said a little too much. Just mind your business. Things stay better that way, okay?"

"Hmm...I don't think so, Bev. I'm tired of minding my business," Clark replied sharply.

Joey walked by Beverly and Clark carrying a tray of filled champagne flutes. Clark sidled up to Joey and grabbed two flutes from the tray. Returning to Beverly's side, Clark wasted no time, swallowing his champagne in one gulp.

"Aww, thanks for the bubbly, Clark!" Beverly said, reaching for the glass.

Quickly pulling back his hand, Clark replied, "Sorry, Bev. This isn't for you. It's for me." In a single motion, he downed the champagne.

"Jesus, Toots. Maybe take it easy?"

Shaking his head, Clark put the flutes down on a nearby cocktail table.

"Why do that? I'm just getting started," Clark said with a sly grin. He buttoned his blazer as he dashed away toward Miss Vivian and Mr. Lawrence.

The pair were deep in conversation, engulfed in smoke, Miss Vivian smoking a cigarette and Mr. Lawrence puffing on a cigar. Mr. Lawrence looked up, noticing Clark.

"Ah, there he is! Our bright and shining star, Clark James!"

Miss Vivian laughed. "Yes! There he is!"

Clark smiled. "Hey, you two. What are you guys talking about over here?"

Mr. Lawrence took a pull of his cigar. "We actually were just catching up. It's been a long time since we've seen each other."

"Oh really? Remind me again, Mr. Lawrence. How do you two know each other?" Clark asked.

Mr. Lawrence puckered his lips and rubbed his thick mustache. "You know, boy. It's been so long, I can't seem to remember."

"That's funny. Miss Vivian said the same thing," Clark replied.

Miss Vivian forced a faint laugh as she rubbed the miniature skull figure on her cane.

"So, Miss Vivan, I just can't shake this new, young look you have. It's almost as if you're aging backward," Clark said.

Mr. Lawrence smiled as the cigar rested between his teeth. "Well, Clark, that's a blessing!"

Nodding in agreement, Clark tapped the lower portion of the cane with his foot. "It's almost like you don't even need this cane anymore, right?"

Miss Vivian's lips tightened. "What's going on?"

"You tell me. What are you doing here? How do you two even know each other?" Clark asked, stepping closer.

The smoke combination from Miss Vivian's cigarette and Mr. Lawrence's cigar surrounded Clark's face, a wave of nausea imminent. His heart raced as the three of them swapped glances. Not wanting to draw attention from the crowd, Clark kept his composure, crossing his arms across his chest.

Timidly tapping his foot, Clark continued, "I'm waiting. Let's hear it. I would love to hear more of this elaborate story right now."

Reaching for the nearest ashtray, Mr. Lawrence aggressively smashed his cigar into a pile of black soot.

"Clark, we've already answered that question. So, why don't you just tell us what's going on?" Mr. Lawrence arched his right eyebrow as if to challenge the young singer.

"I think you two are up to something. Something that I don't like."

Miss Vivian leaned in close to Clark, her signature scent of patchouli mixed with smoke causing his stomach to churn.

"You're a smart boy. But you do not want to dance with fire, Robbie," she whispered.

"Or what? What's going to happen, Miss Viv?" Clark pushed back.

Grabbing the lower part of her wooden cane, she pushed the miniature skull head up to Clark's face, grazing his cheekbone.

"Oh, child. Sweet, sweet, child. The answer is simple."

Clark slowly batted his eyes, not backing down.

"I'll end you, forever," Miss Vivian scoffed, moving the skull under Clark's chin.

"Now scram!" She forcefully pushed Clark's head back with the cane.

A shiver rolled up Clark's spine, making its way down his arms. The wind from the sea rushed through his hair, causing him to slightly lose balance as he shuffled backwards. He quickly nodded to Mr. Lawrence and Miss Vivian, understanding his presence was no longer welcomed.

"Right. You both have a great evening," he whispered as he hurried back to the opposite end of the terrace.

Returning to Beverly, Clark's head began to spin, causing the color to drain from his face.

"Toots, are you okay? You don't look so good!" Beverly said, adjusting her posture against the iron terrace railing.

"I think...I think I'm going to be sick," said Clark as he clasped his hands over his white button-down shirt.

Beverly grabbed Clark's sweaty hand. "Let's get you out of here, before you hurl all over the guests. Come with me!"

Clark held on as Beverly zig-zagged through the dining room full of people dressed in colorful ball gowns and tailored suits. They rushed out the front entrance of the Sea House, making their way down the curved trail along the cliffside leading to Clark's cottage. The darkened night sky engulfed them as the sound of waves crashed against the cliffs below. Beverly, still leading the way, rushed past the tall sea grass as the wind blew through.

"Beverly!"

Beverly continued to lead Clark quickly down the trail.

"Bev!"

The sight of the cottage appeared as the yellow glow from the kitchen light glowed through the porch door window. The ancient redwood trees surrounding the cottage creaked and swayed as the wind continued to grow stronger.

"Bev, stop! I'm going to–" Clark let go of Beverly's hand and hunched over.

"BLAGH!" Clark winced as he vomited the champagne he'd downed just moments before, his eyes watering. His stomach cramped as he crouched on the pathway.

The wind whipped through Beverly's hair as she rubbed Clark's back.

"Get it all, Toots. I remember my first glass of champagne."

Clark felt the warmth slowly return to his cheeks as he wiped his mouth with the sleeve of his black party jacket.

"It wasn't the champagne, Bev. It was that creepy, old hag, Miss Vivian." Clark steadied himself as he stood up.

"Oh yeah? Ya sure it wasn't the two glasses of champagne you downed in five seconds?" Beverly reached into her silver beaded clutch.

Holding the clutch open towards the full moon, Beverly rummaged through it as she used the bright natural light to help her find what she needed. She dug through the tubes of lipstick and mascara until she felt the thin wax-papered package.

"Here, you need this," Beverly said as she held out a package of Black Jack chewing gum.

Clark took a stick of gum. "That bad, huh?" he laughed.

Beverly nodded. "Just trying to help you regain some dignity after you ralphed everywhere."

Using his fingers to wad the paper into a tiny ball, Clark took a deep breath as he chewed the gum.

"Okay, the champagne probably didn't help. But Miss Vivian scared the shit out of me."

Beverly held the beaded clutch against her chest, doing her best to block the wind. "She's a character. Can we go inside your place now, Clark? This wind's freezin'!"

Clark nodded and grabbed Beverly's hand. This time he led the way as they continued to the cottage.

CHAPTER 20

Present Day

The mid-morning sun beamed through the large paned windows above Neal's kitchen sink. As Nana shared her story, the three had enjoyed breakfast and a few too many cups of coffee. Neal leaned back in his spindle back dining chair and stretched his arms high above his head, noticing the time on the nearby wall clock. 10:30. The intriguing story of Clark James was getting wilder by the minute, and as much as Neal wanted to hear more, it was time for them to start their day. Neal stood up and began to collect the dirty dishes from the table.

"Neal, Honey, let me help you with those," Nana said, taking a sip from her coffee mug.

Neal shook his head as he carried an armful of dishes toward the sink. "It's fine, Nana. I got this. Sit down and relax, please."

Grandad adjusted his fuzzy black robe around his belly. "Milly, I just don't understand where all this is coming from."

Taking off her red-framed glasses, Nana held them up to the sunlight that was beaming through the window.

"My goodness, my glasses are dirty! No wonder I can't see a dang thing." She brought the glasses close to her mouth and breathed a thick layer of fog onto the lens.

"Milly." Grandad crossed his arms as he leaned back in his chair.

"You know, Neal, I was thinking we could go to the beach today. Looks like the perfect day for it. I could even pack us a–"

"Milly!" Grandad repeated, rubbing his tired eyes.

"Daniel, what?!"

"Stop doing that thing where you nervously change the subject to any random thing that runs across your brain. Where is all of this coming from? Why didn't you mention it to me?" asked Grandad.

"Daniel, I don't know. Why would it matter? Tell me what good it would have done for our relationship if I just randomly told you one day that I once dated Clark James?" Nana nervously picked at her nail polish.

"Well, if I'm being honest, it doesn't make me feel very good. Makes me think you've never trusted me," Grandad said.

"That's far from the truth. I trust you, and you know I love you. But it took me years to rationalize what happened that summer with Clark James. I asked myself for years, was it love? Infatuation? Or was it just the trauma that we experienced together?"

Neal leaned back against the kitchen sink, looking over the island at his grandparents as they discussed the sensitive subject. As a child, it was rare that he saw his grandparents argue. And when they did have a disagreement, it seemed they were able to resolve the issue by day's end.

"You said he wrote you letters. Did you continue to write to him after we got together?" Grandad asked as he stood up from the kitchen table.

"Yes, but I stopped after you proposed."

"Oh. So for a good bit, still," Grandad quietly responded.

"I stopped writing to him because I chose to be with you, Daniel. I needed stability, someone who could help me recover from all the mistakes that I'd made."

"But how could I have done that when I didn't even know, Milly?!" Grandad said, throwing his hands up in the air, seemingly defeated.

"Daniel…I'm sorry," Nana said, standing up from the table and making her way to Grandad. She leaned in close to him, putting her hand on his crossed arms.

"No, Milly, I'm sorry. I'm sorry that you went through this and it hurt you so badly that you felt you had to keep it hidden all these years." Grandad placed his hand over Nana's.

Neal watched from the kitchen as his grandparents talked it out. He admired how they didn't raise their voices during heated conversation. He and Josie hadn't done that either. Neal was proud of this. No matter how mad they were, neither would raise their voice to belittle the other.

"Hey, guys," Neal said as he walked toward the kitchen table. "I think we should start getting things together if we plan to go to the beach today. If we want to make our dinner reservation tonight, we need to get moving."

Nana patted Grandad's chest and looked back at Neal.

"Okay, let's do it! Let's all put on our sunblock and suits. I'll make a quick picnic lunch for us," Nana said. "Let's be ready to leave in the next 45 minutes or so. Sound like a plan, guys?"

"Yeah! Meet you back down here in a few!" Neal dashed up the stairs to his bedroom to get dressed.

Nana looked back up at Grandad, placing her hand on his cheek. "Babes, I love you."

Grandad smiled. "I know. Same team, always."

Nana laughed. "That's right. Now go finish your cigar and get ready!"

CHAPTER 21

The hazy California sunlight beamed through the breaks of the towering redwood trees as Neal drove his 1989 charcoal gray Ford Bronco down Highway 1. It was a beautiful day, and Neal had removed the Bronco's doors and hardtop in preparation for their drive. It was the perfect time to enjoy a leisurely day along the coast.

Neal's mid-length blonde hair coiled in the wind, his black Ray-Ban square frames preventing the loose strands from getting in his eyes. Nana took the front seat, looking like a California '60s queen. Her stark white tunic dress, doubling as a bathing suit cover-up, sashayed in the wind. Nana thrived in any type of convertible setting and always came prepared. So, it was only natural for her to wrap her salt-and-pepper hair with a teal headscarf.

As they drove past beautiful cliffside scenery, The Everly Brothers' "All I Have to Do is Dream" played through the radio.

"Oh, how I love this song! Turn it up, Neal, would ya?!" Nana laughed, leaning her head back in the wind. Sunbeams occasionally reflected off the lenses of her sunglasses.

Neal adjusted the radio's black rubber knob, making the '50s hit grow louder as they approached Garrapata State Park.

"Only trouble is, geeeeee whiz..." Nana gleefully sang along.

Neal fixed his eyes on the rearview mirror to see Grandad singing along in the backseat, his black t-shirt blowing in the wind. He swayed his head along to the music as the wind tousled his thinning brown hair.

"...all I have to do is dream..." Grandad mouthed, grabbing ahold of Nana's hands as she reached back from behind her head, the two singing and swaying together like teenagers.

Neal smiled as he took a gravel exit off Highway 1 which led to a beach-access parking lot. Clouds of gray dust blew from the Bronco's tires as the vehicle continued to crunch down the gravel path until Neal pulled into an unmarked parking spot.

The parking lot overlooked a thicket of green vegetation with red flowers blooming here and there and led down a bank to meet the sandy beach, which stretched for miles into the distance. Deep blue waves rushed onto the shore, leaving patterns of seashells and coiled seaweed on the wet sand.

"Oh gosh, just look at it. You never forget the beaches of Big Sur," Nana said with a big smile.

From the middle console, Neal pulled a black trucker hat with a red-and-white patch on the front that read "Big Sur Brewing," one of his favorite local taverns to hit up for a drink or two. He placed the cap backwards and admired his reflection in the rearview mirror.

"We ready?" he asked, turning to look at his grandparents.

"Let's do it!" Grandad said, tapping on the headrest of Nana's seat.

Nana adjusted her tunic. "Yes, let's go!"

They gathered their blankets, cooler, and umbrella from the Bronco's cargo area. Nana carried the blankets, Grandad held the umbrella, and Neal got the honor of dragging the cooler through the thick sand.

They began their descent down a short, sun-bleached wooden boardwalk that connected the parking lot to the beach. Nana led the

THE CLUB BY THE SEA

pack out onto the flat beach until she found the perfect spot, not too close to the water, but not too far away either.

She laid the thin quilt on the sand as Neal screwed the umbrella into the sand. Smoking his cigar, Grandad sat back and observed the two in action. When the group got settled on the blanket, they laid in silence for a few moments and took in the views.

Straight ahead, giant stone archways rose from the ocean's floor. Deep blue waves crashed against the jagged formations, leaving a waterline. The sun reflected off the blue waters onto the beach.

"Want to go for a walk, Neal?" asked Nana as she stood up, dusting the sand off her hands.

"Sure," Neal replied, kicking off his worn leather flip-flops.

Nana linked arms with Neal as they walked along the beach, ocean water lapping at their ankles.

"Oh! I forgot how cold the Pacific can be, even in the summer!" laughed Nana.

"Yeah, it's not like the beaches of Florida, that's for sure."

The two continued their walk, occasionally looking back at Grandad who appeared to have fallen asleep on the quilt.

"Neal, I've been thinking about Josie," said Nana, looking down at her feet and her red-painted toenails.

"Oh, you don't say?" asked Neal, sarcastically.

"Was it really so bad that you can't talk to her anymore?"

Neal adjusted his Ray-Bans with his left hand. "Nana, I don't know. She doesn't want to have anything to do with me anymore."

"And what makes you so sure of that?" replied Nana.

"Well, she told me that when she broke up with me."

"She literally said, 'I don't want to have anything to do with you anymore,' Neal?"

Neal rolled his shoulders back. "No, not exactly. But she made it clear when she said she didn't want to move in with me."

The two continued down the beach, looking ahead at the range of cliffs towering over the sand.

"Okay, did she give you a reason for not wanting to move to Monterey?" asked Nana.

"Uh, yeah. She did."

"Which was?" asked Nana.

"She felt that I no longer made her a priority, that my job was more important than she was."

"You know I'm not taking sides. And I would never dare take someone else's side over my Sweet Pea's, " gushed Nana.

Neal grinned as they turned around to head back toward Grandad.

"But you are a workhorse. You've been that way for quite some time," said Nana.

"Yeah, I would agree with that. But is there really a problem with prioritizing success?"

"There's absolutely nothing wrong with prioritizing success, Neal. But what fun is success when you have nobody to share it with along the way?" Nana replied, adjusting her sunglasses.

Neal slowly nodded his head. "I would also agree with you on that."

"You can love what you do and work hard doing it. But at some point, you need to be willing to adjust your work-life balance, so you can be there for the ones who love you the most."

"Okay, Nana. But she also needs to be more understanding. I can't always turn off my phone. And some nights I am going to have to work late," said Neal.

"And I'm sure that's something you could communicate to her. But you're going to have to talk with her first."

"Communicate. That's odd coming from you right now, Nana," Neal said, crossing his arms.

Nana shrugged her shoulders. "Touché. But this is where you learn from your elders, okay?"

Neal nodded. "All right, I'll think about it. How about that?"

The two were approaching Grandad, who had awakened from his nap.. He stood at the water's edge, his toes wiggling in bubbly surf. A large wave surprised him, its force causing him to jump a few inches back.

"Oh, look at him, jumping like a little ballerina!" laughed Nana.

"What's the matter, Grandad? Is the water too cold?" Neal shouted, cupping his hands around his mouth like a megaphone.

Grandad nodded as the two made their way toward him.

"So, Nana, what did Bev say to Clark that night when she went back to his cottage?" asked Neal.

Nana paused to think for a moment. "Oh, let's wait until we get back to your grandfather. Because he's fully invested in this story as well."

Neal smiled. "Did you ever meet Bev?"

Nana shook her head. "I didn't, unfortunately. She was no longer working at the Sea House when I arrived."

"What happened to her?" asked Neal.

"Well, it wasn't good. I'll tell you all the details. Don't worry, Sweet Pea," said Nana, tapping Neal's arm as they joined Grandad in the surf.

CHAPTER 22

BIG SUR, CALIFORNIA, 1950

Beverly and Clark made it back to Clark's cottage. The dark wood-paneled walls and complementary cabinets made the space feel even smaller at night. The kitchen's only light source was a tiny fixture with a milk glass dome mounted to the ceiling. A transom window above the door from the porch let in the moon's faint light.

Clark leaned against the paneled wall. He was still wearing his black party jacket, but he'd draped his bow tie across the back of a nearby chair. Beverly sat on the white hexagon tile countertop, her silver beaded dress covering her legs.

"So, tell me what's going on, Bev," Clark said.

Beverly rolled her eyes, placing her clutch down on the countertop. "Listen, Toots. Can you at least be a good host and offer me a drink first?"

Clark nodded. "Oh yeah. What would you like? I've got beer, wine, and champagne," he said, opening the slim, rounded ruby red refrigerator.

Clark rattled various glass bottles in the fridge. "Oh, and there's bourbon, of course, in the living room bar."

THE CLUB BY THE SEA

"Hmm...I'm thinking it might be a bourbon kind of night," said Beverly.

"Very well," Clark replied, shutting the fridge door. Spinning around, he quickly moved into the living room, which was adjacent to the kitchen. The clinking of bottles echoed in the small space. Returning minutes later, Clark held up a half-filled glass bottle of Old Fitzgerald.

"There we go, Toots!" Beverly released the golden clip with pink floral emblems and green vines from her hair setting off a cascade of curls down her back.

Clark took the metal ice trays out of the freezer and dropped a couple of the square cubes into a pair of highball glasses. He poured the spiced brown liquid into a glass for each of them, handing one to Beverly.

"Cheers!" She smiled, her red lipstick almost completely faded.

"Cheers!" replied Clark, as they clinked their glasses.

The sip of bourbon instantly warmed Clark's entire throat. After just vomiting the champagne, he began to second guess his choice of bourbon. Setting the cold glass down beside Bev's, he continued the conversation.

"All right, Bev. Tell me everything."

Beverly took another sip of bourbon, closing her eyes as she savored the taste.

"Listen, Clark. I can't really say much. But you're on the right track with Lawrence and Vivian."

Clark crossed his arms over his chest. "Okay, come on, Bev, stop being coy. Would you just give it to me straight, please?"

"All right, all right, all right," Beverly replied, dramatically holding up her hands in surrender..

"Lawrence and Vivian are business partners. He owns the venues; she discovers the talent."

"So the bar in New Orleans? Miss Vivian doesn't own it?" asked Clark.

"Nope, Lawrence does," Beverly replied, shaking her head. "She just manages that one, and when she finds someone that she believes would be a great fit for the Sea House, she sends them off to meet Lawrence."

Clark cupped his cheek with his hand, shaking his head. "And here I thought I was special. I thought she was doing me a favor by helping me out and sending me here."

"Oh, you're special, all right. I don't know their exact plans for you, other than to be a draw for the Sea House. But they are loving you," said Beverly as she took another sip of her drink.

"Okay, Bev. Let me ask you this: Did you have to sign a contract with Mr. Lawrence?"

Beverly let out a sarcastic laugh. "Of course I did, Toots. That's standard protocol."

Clark placed his hands on his hips. "No, that's not what I mean, Bev. I mean does your contract have some crazy terms and stipulations?"

Beverly seemed confused. "What kind of crazy things, Clark?"

Clark stared intensely into Bev's green eyes. "You know what I'm talking about, Beverly."

"No, I'm not followin'. But if you're wondering, we all owe something to Lawrence. Each and every one of us here has struck a deal with him."

"Oh yeah? And what's yours?" Clark challenged.

Beverly adjusted her position on the countertop, sitting up taller. "Jesus, Clark. You're in rare form tonight. What's goin' on? Why the interrogation?"

"Aw, come on Beverly! Cut the cute act and stop being a ninny!" Clark said, leaning in closer to Beverly.

"Fine! You want to know what I know?"

Clark nodded his head, placing each hand on the countertop beside Beverly's hips. He leaned in closely, allowing only a few inches between them. "Mm-hmm."

"Number one. The only one who's a ninny, Clark, is you." Beverly jabbed her slim finger into Clark's chest. "I mean seriously! Who doesn't carefully read their contract? You should've known what you were gettin' yourself into."

Beverly jumped off the countertop, putting her face-to-face with Clark.

Clark leaned back, his eyes wide. "Oh, so you do know more about my contract than you let on."

"Clark! We all know! Every single damn person who works at the Sea House knows!" Beverly shouted.

"What kind of sick hell is this--"

"And would you stop complainin'!? You wanted this, right?"

Clark slowly nodded his head, confused by what he was hearing.

"So you got what you wanted. Ladies and gentlemen, *Clark James*! The biggest jazz singer in the world!" Beverly mockingly said, clapping her hands slowly.

"Beverly, what the hell is wrong with you? Am I missing something?"

"We're all miserable here, Clark! Wake up! We're just livin' for the applause each and every night."

"And how old are you, Bev?! You stuck at the age of 23 too?" Clark snapped.

"No. And that's where we're different, Clark. Everyone here is tied to Lawrence in some sorta way. But you, you're the only one who is forever. And I can't seem to figure that part out."

Clark stood there with his mouth slightly agape, unsure what to say next. Running her fingers through her hair, Beverly exhaled.

"What happened to the last act before me, Bev? Bonnie Frank?"

Beverly rolled her head back, letting her golden locks drop off her shoulders, bringing her hands to her cheeks.

"I don't know. I came to work one day and she was gone. The next thing I knew, we were meetin' you."

"And nobody thought to ask questions?"

"Jesus, Clark. Ya don't see it, do ya? Askin' questions 'round here is a dangerous game. Lawrence doesn't like to be questioned. You do that and you're just cruisin' for a bruisin'." Beverly placed her hair clip inside her clutch.

"So, that's it? We just continue to be beholden to Lawrence, never questioning a damn thing?"

Beverly threw the silver chain of her clutch on her shoulder. "Start gettin' creative, Clark. Use your talents to fight back, I don't know what else to tell ya."

"My talents? What do you mean?" Clark followed Beverly as she made her way to the kitchen door.

"You're a songwriter, Clark. Use your words," said Beverly, opening the door.

"That's actually a great idea."

Beverly turned around as she stepped onto the front porch. The sound of distant waves and buzzing cicadas rushed through the open door.

"There ya go, Toots. Use that creative brain of yours to fight back. Thanks for the drink."

Clark nodded. "Of course. And thank you for sharing this information with me."

Beverly pushed a few loose strands of hair out of her eyes as the wind picked up. "I was divorced with nowhere to go. That's how Lawrence got to me."

"Oh. I'm sorry, Bev. I didn't know."

Beverly shrugged. "Like I said, we all got a story. Mine just happens to be that I finally escaped my deadbeat husband. Came up to Big Sur for a weekend getaway with the little bit of money I had to my name. I met Lawrence, and the rest is history."

Clark leaned against the door frame. "And what did he promise you?"

"Freedom. And that no man would ever lay his hands on me again. And as sick and twisted as he is, Lawrence has held up his end of the deal."

"I see," Clark said, adjusting his hand on the door frame.

"I quit school after ninth grade. And what do ya think happened as I was tryin' to make a life of my own? Nobody wanted to hire the dumb, divorced broad, that's what." Beverly made her way across the front porch.

Clark stepped out onto the porch, the kitchen light casting his shadow onto the wooden floorboards.

"And you don't quit playing at the Sea House because you have no other place to go?" asked Clark.

"Bingo, Toots! You're finally seein' the big picture. Who knew playin' the drums was going to be my ticket to a new life?" Beverly said, stepping off the porch.

Clark watched as she started to make her way up the path to the Sea House, the wind blowing her hair in the darkness.

She turned around one last time, crossing her arms across her chest. "Oh, and by the way, my ex *hated* me playing the drums. Said it wasn't sexy. So, guess what?"

"What?" Clark asked, leaning up against the front railing of the porch.

"Nothin' makes me feel more alive than playing those damn drums every night on that stage. A big 'bite me' to him!" Bev said with a wink.

"You're a knockout, Bev. Never change!" Clark shouted as she turned to continue her walk.

"Night, Clark! You got this!

He watched as Bev's silhouette became smaller and smaller until she was no longer in sight. Clark stepped back into the cottage and closed the door, shutting out the sounds of Big Sur. Picking up his watered-down glass of whiskey, he grabbed a pen and pad, took a seat at the kitchen table, and got to work.

CHAPTER 23

The following week, during a sold-out show, Clark decided it was time to mix things up during the final number of his act. Wearing an all-white suit, Clark stood centerstage, microphone in hand. The spotlight beamed on him, causing small beads of sweat to drip down his forehead.

The applause had come to an end, everyone's eyes fixated on Clark. He dabbed his forehead with the white handkerchief from his blazer pocket.

"Ladies and gentlemen, you have been an absolutely amazing crowd tonight. And we have time for one more song. Would that be all right with you?" A charming smile spread across Clark's face. The crowd roared with approval.

"Well, alrighty. I'm going to do something a little different tonight, folks," Clark said, unbuttoning his white blazer.

He looked back at the band. Larry, holding his bass, had a distant expression on his face. Teddy's eyes bounced back and forth from Clark to the other band members, his confusion obvious. Jane nervously smiled at the audience, placing her hands on her hips. Drumsticks in hand, Beverly crossed her arms and awaited Clark's next move.

"Say, can we get a microphone moved over to the piano for this next one?" Clark asked.

Jane eagerly nodded her head, a forced smile glued to her face. Strutting her way across the stage to the black grand piano, her silk dress swaying back and forth with each step, she placed the microphone stand by the piano, adjusting it to the correct height.

Making his way to the piano, Clark gently put his hand on Jane's back, leaning into her ear.

"Trust me on this one, Jane," he whispered.

Facing her fellow band members, Jane looked at them and then to Clark. "Hey! We didn't rehearse this."

"I know. Just go with it," he said, gently squeezing her left arm before taking a seat on the piano bench.

Clark placed his fingers on the ivory keys, lightly tapping them. A soft "da da" rose from the instrument.

"All right, ladies and gentlemen, real quick...give it up for Jane! And while we're at it, how about the Sea House Ensemble? Aren't they such a talented crew?"

The crowd responded with loud clapping and screams. Jane faked a surprised face, waving her hand in the air like a beauty queen. The other members of the band forced a smile while they nervously nodded their heads.

"This final song is one that I've never performed live. It's something that I wrote not that long ago. Would you like to hear it tonight?"

Members of the audience moved slightly forward in their seats, clapping their hands. The room faded into silence, audience members keeping their eyes trained on Clark James. Mr. Lawrence sat in his usual booth, surrounded by his friends. The gentleman on the end of the booth, in a brown party jacket with matching vest, looked back at Mr. Lawrence.

"Psst, Lawrence. Did you know about this?" he asked, nodding his head toward the stage.

Mr. Lawrence nervously forced a smile. "What can I say? It's a night of wonderful surprises!" He fixed his eyes on Clark at the grand piano, holding an unsmoked cigar in his right hand.

"This song's a little story about a boy," Clark said, looking down at the piano keys.

He slowly played the intro to the song while continuing to talk to the audience. "A boy who had one simple wish in life. And everyday he prayed for this wish to come true. And guess what?"

Clark turned his face toward the audience, flashing a cheeky smile. "He finally got what he wanted. But with just one little catch."

Mr. Lawrence looked over at the side of the dining room, noticing Joey standing there with his round tray tucked under his arm. They locked eyes and Mr. Lawrence slowly shook his head. Joey nervously grinned back.

"Yes, he got what he wished for, but he woke up every day stuck at the age of 23," Clark said as he looked out into the audience.

The room was completely silent as Clark replayed the song's intro, louder this time. Clark sang the words.

"He thinks, lucky me, finally living this everlonging dream.

Telling the world all of his stories.

Feeling seen, but it's all a big scheme.

Cause really how lucky is he to forever be 23?"

As he continued to sing the song, Teddy picked up the saxophone, placing it to his lips. Riffing, he soulfully played along. Beverly picked up on the rhythm, gently tapping the snare drum every beat or so. And by the end of the song, Jane and Larry had found a way to join in on the surprise.

On the outro of the song, Clark looked back at the audience, narrowing his eyes directly at Mr. Lawrence.

"Yes, this is the story," he sang with a smirk.

"Yes, this is the story," he continued, feverishly playing the piano keys.

"Of the boy who was forever 23."

When Clark finished the final note, the audience completely lost it. Ladies jumped out of their seats, applauding. Men waved their hats in the air, stomping their feet. All of Mr. Lawrence's table was standing up now, cheering with the audience. The applause was so loud that the dinner glasses on the tables began to rattle.

Everyone cheered, giving Clark and the band a standing ovation. Everyone, except Mr. Lawrence. His beady brown eyes stayed glued to Clark the entire time, as the singer graciously stood up, bowing to the audience with giant, hopeful eyes.

"Lawrence, that Clark James is something else!" said the man at the end of the table, feverishly clapping his hands.

"Ha! He sure is!"

The crowd continued to applaud even as the curtain slowly began to lower. Clark stood in the center of the stage, beaming with pride. He continued to wave at the crowd, taking several bows, until the curtain completely closed.

Grabbing a towel from behind the piano, Clark dragged it over his wet head, dabbing his face.

"And that's how you end a show, folks!" Clark laughed, while walking past the rest of the band members to backstage.

Larry quickly followed Clark. "Hey, Clark, that wasn't cool, man!"

Clark continued to walk backstage, making his way down the hallway to the dressing rooms. "Larry, you wouldn't have approved in the first place. But you gotta admit, they loved it."

Larry grabbed Clark's arm. "It ain't about the audience loving it. It's about leaving us, your team, hanging, making us look like fools up there by changing the set like that at the last minute."

Clark scoffed. "Wait, you can't be serious right now, Larry. You're mad?"

Sounds of pinging rang down the hallway, as Jane quickly sprinted in her black stilettos to Clark's dressing room.

"Clark James! I'm going to kill you!" Jane said, pointing her finger.

"Oh, you think I'm mad. Wait until you see ol' Jane. Here she comes!" said Larry.

"Gentlemen, get inside that dressing room right now. Before the audience hears me!" Jane demanded, her face turning bright red.

Clark went into the dressing room, taking a seat at the chair in front of his vanity mirror.

"Look, I don't understand why everyone is so mad."

"Clark! You should've told us about the new song! We looked like a bunch of cabbage heads out there because of your little stunt," Jane said, feverishly throwing her hands in the air.

"All right, Toots. That was good, but maybe a little heads up would've been nice!" Beverly said as she rushed into the dressing room.

"Yeah, if I had known about it ahead of time, Clark, I would have played an even cooler saxophone solo," said Teddy as he followed into the dressing room.

Clark stood up, adjusting his party jacket. "All right, I get it! You guys are upset. And I'm sorry. But I thought you all wouldn't let me go on with the song if you knew about it ahead of time."

Jane took a seat on the couch. "Well, you're probably right. Not with lyrics like that. You're just asking for trouble from Lawrence."

Beverly put a piece of chewing gum into her mouth. "Oh, c'mon Jane. It wasn't that bad of a song. Nobody out there even knows what it means."

"Oh, really, Bev? So what's your plan when Lawrence jumps on our asses over this?" Jane snapped back, crossing her arms.

Beverly blew a giant pink bubble. "Maybe he liked it. Maybe the crowd got to him."

"Ha! He ain't going to like it," said Larry.

"Listen, everyone calm down. I told Clark to write a tune, use his talents. Now maybe the execution coulda been bettah, but--"

"I'm sorry, Bev. But *you* told Clark to write the song?" asked Jane.

Beverly crossed her arms and leaned back against the wall of the dressing room.

"Yeah, I did, Jane. And what's it to ya?"

"God, Beverly. You're so stupid! You are already skating on thin ice from last time. And now this. You just can't keep your nose out of trouble, can you?" Jane snapped back.

"Oh, stuff it! Ya think ya bettah than me, Jane? I think ya jealous Clark wrote a song without ya."

Jane let out a sarcastic laugh. "Oh, please. No offense, Clark, but it wasn't even that good. The writing was all over the place. And Beverly, you–"

BANG!

Everyone turned their heads to the doorway of the dressing room where Mr. Lawrence stood. His large hand was still on the door from the aggressive smack.

"Evening, Mr. Lawrence," Teddy nervously stuttered from the corner of the dressing room.

Mr. Lawrence slowly scuffed his heels against the checkered tile floor. His eyes darted across the room as he closed the door behind him.

Leaning back on the closed door, he sighed. "So, that was really something tonight, wasn't it?"

Nobody spoke a word. Mr. Lawrence continued. "Real groundbreaking. Practically had the audience pissing on themselves!"

Lawrence walked past Larry, giving his shoulder a squeeze. He continued his way across the room, walking by the back of the couch, grazing his fingers along the top of the cushions. Beverly and Jane's eyes followed him as made his way to the stocked bar by Clark's vanity.

He grabbed a bottle of Old Fitzgerald off the bar, throwing the cork across the room. Beverly and Jane feverishly ducked to dodge it.

"Why, yes, they loved it so much they didn't even bother to read into the words of this original, Clark," Mr. Lawrence said, pouring a glass of bourbon.

Everyone kept their eyes on Lawrence.

"So which one of you baboons gave him the idea?" Mr. Lawrence said, sipping on his bourbon.

"No offense, Clark, but you're not that smart. You couldn't have come up with that idea on your own," Mr. Lawrence sneered.

The room remained silent.

"So, who was it? Someone say something, dammit!" shouted Lawrence.

"Listen, Lawrence. I wrote it on my own, okay? I know it wasn't the best idea and I'm–"

Mr. Lawrence threw his glass of bourbon across the room, the brown liquid splattering. The glass shattered against the wall.

"Clark, shut the hell up! You hear me? You've already pissed me off enough tonight!" Mr. Lawrence spat, launching towards Clark.

He pushed Clark up against the wall, aggressively pushing his palm against Clark's throat. Clark's eyes grew wide from the crushing of his windpipe.

"What's-a matter? Can't sing about how terrible life is now, can you, boy?"

Clark's face flashed red.

"All right, Lawrence. Lay off him. You're gonna really hurt him," Larry yelled.

"Fuck off, Larry!" Mr. Lawrence snapped back.

The vein in Clark's forehead grew bigger and bigger, turning a darker shade of blue. He feverishly tried to get out of Mr. Lawrence's grip, but the strength was unmatched.

"Jesus, Lawrence. Stop already! Ya gonna kill him! It was me!" Beverly screamed, jumping off the couch.

Letting go of Clark's neck, Mr. Lawrence quickly turned around to face Beverly.

"Beverly. Not you, sweet little Bev." Mr. Lawrence mockingly made a crying face.

Beverly stood tall, looking directly across the room at Mr. Lawrence.

"You got a problem with me, Beverly?" Lawrence asked.

Beverly continued to lock eyes with Mr. Lawrence. "No, I don't, sir."

"Because all I've ever done is help you. That's it, Beverly."

"I know, sir. And I appreciate it so much," Beverly quickly replied.

"Do you? Because it seems like you keep going behind my back trying to ruin me!" Lawrence spat.

"I'm sorry. It was stupid. I just thought Clark could use some help and I–"

"Save it, Beverly! Just like how you thought Bonnie Frank needed to be saved too?" Mr. Lawrence asked.

He walked to the door of the dressing room. "Now listen to me. I want all of you to get your asses out there. Put on your happy faces and mix and mingle with the guests on the terrace. And Clark?"

Clark slowly moved his eyes up from the floor to Mr. Lawrence.

"You go out there and have the time of your life. Drink cocktails, kiss the hands of women. And if they ask you anything about that damn song of yours, you better get creative. Say it was all just folklore or something."

Clark nodded.

"And someone clean up this mess!" Mr. Lawrence pointed to the shards of broken glass.

He pulled open the door and exited the room quickly. Everyone remained standing until Teddy finally inched toward the doorway.

"All right guys, I'll see you out there," he said quietly, waving back to the bandmates.

Jane sat up and smoothed the wrinkles in her dress.

"Yes, I guess it's about that time. Hey, Bev?" She grabbed Beverly's hand. "I'm sorry for what I said earlier, okay? You know I didn't mean it."

Beverly smiled. "I know, Janey."

Larry cleared his throat. "Yes, I guess we better see our way out to the terrace. Jane, I'll go with you."

Jane and Larry looped arms, heading out the dressing room.

"Ya guys go ahead. I'll stay here and clean this mess up. And Clark, ya gonna need some makeup to cover that nasty bruise on your neck."

Clark looked in the mirror, letting out a faint gasp at his reflection. The color in his face had returned, but the bruise on his neck was already setting in. A full handprint appeared in black and blue across Clark's throat, making his Adam's apple the size of a golf ball.

Beverly scurried over to the mirror. "Take a seat, Clark."

Clark fell into the makeup chair as Beverly picked up the round case of beauty powder off the vanity. She tapped the thick brown makeup brush into the powder, forcing little clouds of dust into the air.

"Now, let's see if this color matches your skin tone," Beverly said, gently dabbing the brush against the bruise. "Ah, there we go. It's covering up quite nicely."

Clark caught his reflection in the mirror over Beverly's shoulder. He tightly gripped the arms of the chair. Tight feelings of panic danced in his chest. His throat throbbed with pain, causing the makeup brush to feel like needles.

Tears formed in Clark's eyes, making Beverly's appearance blurry. He tried to control it, but like a broken dam, tears began to pour from his eyes. Clark's body shook.

"Oh, Toots. It's okay. We're gonna have it completely covered. Nobody will know, okay?"

"Bev, I'm so sorry," Clark cried.

"No, no no, Clark. It's okay. Lawrence just lost his temper. He'll cool off."

"I shouldn't have done it that way. Now you're in trouble, and everyone is freaking out. I should've–" Clark couldn't get the rest of the words out as his body began to convulse with each sob.

Beverly pulled Clark in for a hug. "It's okay, Clark. We're gonna be okay, Toots. Let's get ya all covered up. Believe you me, I am a pro at covering bruises."

Clark exhaled.

"Okay, Bev. Thank you. Let's get out there and put on a show."

CHAPTER 24

The next morning Clark awoke to a sharp pain in his neck. Sitting up in bed, he winced from the pain as he gently grabbed his neck. He walked over to the wooden dresser with a matching mirror against the far wall of his room.

Taking a long look at the aftermath of last night's damage, Clark froze looking at his reflection in the dusty mirror. His usual slicked-back black hair was now curled and knotted from last night's sleep. But the worst part was his neck, which was swollen with hints of purple and blue. It looked as though a tire had been driven directly across his throat.

"Just great," he croaked, staring at himself in the mirror.

Craning his neck slowly to the left, he examined the damage. The images of Mr. Lawrence's rage vividly replayed on loop in Clark's mind. He was thankful today was an off day and that nobody would have to see him like this except for the band during afternoon rehearsal.

He walked through the cottage to the kitchen to get a glass of water. As he filled the glass with tap water, he wondered how he could do damage control from the night prior. How could he get Beverly off the hook? How could he convince Mr. Lawrence that he would never write a song like that one again?

He went out to the front porch to gather his thoughts. Taking a seat in the red metal lounge chair, he placed his glass of water at his bare feet. Clark leaned his head back and closed his eyes. "Just breathe, Clark," he whispered under his breath. "Take some deep breaths." He inhaled as the waves crashed against the cliffside below him, exhaled as the wind lightly grazed his hair.

Opening his eyes, Clark noticed Larry coming down the trail toward the cottage. Larry walked briskly toward Clark. He wore light jeans, a simple white t-shirt, and a black leather jacket, his hair whipping in the wind.

Clark stood up. "Hey, Larry. You're here early. Rehearsal isn't for a few more hours." His voice croaked with each word. It was difficult to talk.

Larry stood at the bottom of the wooden porch steps, his hands in his pockets. "Mornin', Clark. How are you feelin'?"

Clark leaned against the railing of the porch. "I could be better. Feel like I've been run over by a truck a few times."

"Yeah, you don't sound too good, man. Can I come up?" asked Larry.

Clark nodded, motioning with his hand for Larry to take a seat in the chair next to his.

Larry sat, the chair creaking as he leaned back. He pulled out a crushed paper pack of Camel cigarettes.

"Cigarette?" he asked, offering the pack to Clark. "It might actually help with your throat."

Clark shook his head, "Nah, thanks, Larry. What's going on, man?"

Larry flicked his silver lighter, holding the flame up to the cigarette as he balanced it between his lips. The flame turned the tobacco into little embers until smoke filled the air.

"Clark, we got a problem," he said, exhaling cigarette smoke.

"Okay?" Clark leaned against the railing.

"Last night really didn't end well," Larry said.

Clark took a seat beside Larry and rested his arms on his knees. "What happened, Larry? You're making me nervous."

"Bev's gone, Clark."

"What do you mean she's gone, Larry?"

Larry looked at Clark, hesitating. "I mean...she's not at the Sea House anymore."

"Why? Because of what happened with the song?" Clark said, his voice raspy.

"I'm sure that's got something to do with it. All I know is that last night after you left, Lawrence and her seemed to be in a heated conversation." Larry took a puff of the cigarette. "He was chewing her out, calling her names. 'Stupid whore.' 'Ungrateful little bitch.' And she wasn't holding back either. She was crying and giving it right back to him. She called him a fat bastard."

Clark sat up straight in the chair. "What else?"

"I couldn't stick around much longer. They were going at it in the dining room after most everyone left. Jane and I just happened to catch some of the conversation," Larry said, pulling his leather jacket against his chest as the wind strengthened.

"So, how do you know she's gone?" asked Clark.

"Because we heard it. Lawrence told her she was done. He said he was done helping her and that she was finished."

"No, I don't believe it. She'll be at rehearsal later today, right? Right, Larry?" Clark stood and began to pace.

"I wish I could tell you, yes, Clark. But I can't. She stepped out of line a few too many times."

"Jesus, Larry. I can't believe this. What are we going to do? Can we fix this?"

Larry shook his head, standing up. "Clark, you still have a lot to learn about this place. When Lawrence makes his mind up about something, that's it. She had plenty of warnings."

Clark covered his face with his hands, breathing deeply. "This is all my fault. I should've never performed that song."

"You definitely poked the bear, but now you know what the repercussions are. Moving forward, don't do it again and everything will be okay," Larry said, patting Clark on the back.

Larry stepped off the porch and began to walk back toward the Sea House.

"Clark?" he said, turning around.

Clark uncovered his face and looked down at Larry.

"Don't worry about rehearsal today. There's no way you can sing with that crushed windpipe. We can rehearse tomorrow. You need some time to rest up."

"You sure, Larry? What if Lawrence gets upset about that?" asked Clark.

Larry shoved his hands in his jacket pockets. "Nah, he won't be here today. He never comes on Sunday mornings. Jane and I decided last night this was the best idea. We've let Teddy know too."

Clark nodded his head. "Okay."

"Clark, take it easy today. Be good, okay?" Larry asked.

"Yeah. Yeah, sure. Thanks for telling me all this, Larry." Clark forced a smile

Larry nodded and turned to begin his trek toward the Sea House. Clark leaned back against the railing of the porch, feeling the tight return of panic in his chest. His legs slowly slid forward, making him slump to the porch floor. He pulled his knees up to his chest as tears poured from his eyes.

"Why!? Why, why, why?!" he cried, rocking back and forth. What did he sign up for? Why did he ever sign that contract?

CHAPTER 25

Later that evening, Joey arrived at the Sea House to prepare a few items for the following workday. Mr. Lawrence had made him aware of Beverly's dismissal. He knew that it would be hard not only for Clark but the entire band to digest.

Before stocking up the carts with glassware and dishes for the next day's table settings, he wanted to check in on Clark. It was a rough night for the singer, no doubt, thought Joey. His neck probably was not looking too good after bearing the brunt of Mr. Lawrence's wrath.

Arriving at Clark's cottage, Joey adjusted his boater hat as he knocked on the side entrance. Three swift raps at the door. No answer. Not even the slight rumble of someone moving through the house. Joey knocked again, this time a little louder.

"Clark! It's Joey!" he yelled as he knocked.

Nothing.

Joey slightly twisted the brass door knob. The wooden door creaked open. Joey took a step inside and looked around for any sign of Clark.

"Claaaaark!"

He stepped inside the kitchen. The house was dark and eerily quiet.

"Clark, it's Joey. Just wanting to check in on you!" he said, as he slowly walked through the hallway of the cottage.

The door to Clark's bedroom was open. Joey took a quick peek into the room. Where is he, he wondered. It was obvious that Clark was not in the house.

Joey exited through the kitchen door that led to the porch. He looked to the left of the porch, to the trail that continued down the cliffside. Could he be down by the beach? Usually this hour was not a good time to be down there, as the tide was starting to pick up.

He quickly continued down the trail, weaving through the tall seagrass. To the left of the trail stood tall evergreens and redwoods, providing great shade. The right side of the trail, the cliffside, dramatically dropped off into the deep blue Pacific Ocean. Joey continued, arriving at the wooden overlook with stairs that descended down to the beach.

The old, tattered wooden boards were held up by stilts that were driven deep into the cliffside. Clark loved coming to this spot, especially escaping to the beach below. But it was not Joey's favorite. The creaking of the boards and the way the deck occasionally swayed in the wind was enough to scare Joey away. Not to mention the worn steps that descended along the cliffside, often slippery from the sea mist and moss.

Joey leaned over the railing, hoping to get a view of the beach. He couldn't see much, just the curling of the foamy waves as they rushed onto the rocky shore. Carefully grabbing onto the wooden railing, Joey carefully placed his feet on the steps. Looking only at his feet and the next step below, he took deep breaths.

"You got this, Joey. Just one foot in front of the other," he whispered to himself.

The steps came to a break in the staircase where a smaller overlook bridged the gap. Now closer to the beach below, Joey was able to get a better view. He slowly moved his head, scanning the beach. No Clark

James until he noticed a person laying on the thick powdered sand that was further away from the shore.

"Clark!" Joey yelled as he carefully descended the remainder of the steps.

"I can't believe you're getting me down here! You know how I feel about that ol' deck. Not to mention my fear of heights!" Joey yelled through deep breaths as he made his way onto the beach.

Relieved, he stepped onto the sand. Clark didn't look like how Joey expected him to. Wearing wet khaki pants and no shirt, Clark lay passed out, his face directly on the sand, mouth agape. His wet hair was mashed into the sand, and empty liquor bottles surrounded him.

"Oh no, Clark!" Joey yelled, running through the thick sand. "What have you done?!"

Joey dropped to his knees, tapping Clark on the cheek.

"Clark, wake up! Clark!"

Clark's body slightly twitched as he let out a faint groan.

"Huuuuh."

"Clark, you gotta get up, man. How much did you drink?" Joey held Clark's head up from the sand.

Clark's sandy, soaked body was limp as Joey continued to talk to him, trying to wake him.

"Clark! I need you to wake up! We gotta get you out of here!"

Clark's eyes slowly fluttered, the sand in his eyelashes moving up and down.

"Joe...Joey..." he groaned.

Joey pushed Clark's torso up, trying to get him to sit up.

"Clark, can you sit up, buddy? Let's get you out of the sand."

Sitting in the sand directly beside Clark, Joey wrapped one arm around him for stabilization while Clark leaned against Joey's shoulder for support, his slick hair leaving a sandy water residue stain on Joey's shirt.

Clark's eyes slowly opened as his head tilted toward the sand. His vision was hazy as tears dripped from his eyes. Slowly, he lifted his head, looking at Joey.

"I don't know what happened, Joey," he said with a whimper.

"How long have you been down here, Clark? Do you remember?" Joey asked, feeling Clark's full body weight against him.

"I, uh, I was listening to records in the living room," Clark said, dazed.

"Okay...and then what?"

"I had a few drinks. And must've gotten the idea to come down to the beach."

"You don't remember coming down here at all?" Joey asked, pulling Clark's head up so he could look him in the eyes.

"Vaguely. I remember running into the ocean. And laughing. I was swimming in my clothes and just laughing my ass off."

Joey looked toward the water as it rushed onto the shore, the waves gaining strength.

"Clark, you're lucky you're not dead. You know how dangerous the steps down here are. And then you somehow fell asleep, which is also just asking for death."

Clark closed his eyes, leaning his head back against Joey's arm. "Yeah, well maybe that would've been best after all."

Joey rolled his eyes, pulling Clark's hair back tightly, forcing Clark to look at him.

"Are you kidding me, Clark?! I never want to hear you say something crazy like that again!"

Clark's eyes widened. "Ow, Joey!" He grabbed the back of his head.

"Oh, that hurt? Well, just imagine if you had busted that dumb head of yours on the stairs!"

Clark leaned up, sitting straight on his own. He ran his clammy hands through his hair, taking a deep breath.

"I don't know, Joey. It just feels like this is all getting to be too much."

"I understand, Clark. The last few days have been."

"Joey, you don't know. You don't get it," Clark said.

"Oh, I don't get it? The guy who has been working for Lawrence the longest around here? Is that so?" Joey replied sarcastically.

"Yeah, and why do you do it? Why do you stay here?"

Joey looked out toward the ocean, the sky filling with heavy, dark rain clouds. The wind began to pick up as the smell of lingering rain filled the air. The waves were curling faster and slamming onto the shore.

"We better get going, Clark. A storm is rolling in and this is the last place I want to be when that happens."

"Answer my question, Joey," Clark demanded.

Joey pulled his legs up against his chest, grabbing onto his shins. "Ah, Clark. Fine. I don't leave because where else is there for a man like me to go?"

Clark focused his eyes on Joey, not knowing what to say.

"Exactly. Opportunities don't come easily for me like they do for people of your kind, Clark. My ancestors moved here during the gold rush, hoping to make a big break in the free state. They left everything they had in Mexico."

Clark nodded. "But Joey, you sound…"

"Like a white man? Like I don't speak a lick of Spanish?"

Clark nodded, his cheeks red.

"I was born and raised in California. My parents worked their asses off to provide a life for my siblings and me. One thing they wanted was for us to have opportunities. So, we grew up learning English and attended school in America."

Joey stretched his legs out on the sand. "But guess what happened after high school?"

"What?" asked Clark.

"Nobody wanted to hire a Mexican. It didn't matter that I spoke English better than any of the White boys in school. Or that I'm bilingual. People like me are only destined for jobs in factories, on farms, or doing hard labor."

"So, how did you end up here at the Sea House?"

"I got a job working as a waiter at a nearby restaurant. But I was more of the trash man than anything, and the pay was terrible. I passed by the Sea House every day on my commute. The flashy, grand entrance caught my eye every time. I thought if I'm going to be in the restaurant industry, that's the one I want to be in."

Clark covered his bare chest from the wind with his arms, looking up at the dark sky.

Joey continued. "I stopped by every day for two weeks asking for a job. Front ladies denied me every time. But then one day, Lawrence happened to be in the lobby and overheard the conversation. He followed me out of the restaurant as I was leaving and asked what kind of job I was looking for."

"And that's how you got here, huh?" asked Clark.

"Oh, it wasn't that easy. I told Lawrence that I could outwork any person in the establishment. And he said, 'All right, prove it.' He gave me a month's trial."

"And you crushed it?" asked Clark with a smile across his face.

"Oh, absolutely. I did everything. I washed dishes, I scrubbed the stage, I watered the plants, I reset the tables, I hand-washed the linens. Learned every bit of the restaurant operations. And at the end of the month, he told me I could stay."

"Now look at you. You're Mr. Lawrence's right-hand man," Clark said, playfully punching Joey in the shoulder.

Joey let a smile slide from the corner of his lips. "I don't know about right-hand man. But I have worked my way up to being in charge of many things around here. But when you say that I don't understand you, believe me, I do."

Thunder clapped above them, the sound ricocheting off the cliff-side walls.

"Geez! We better get out here, huh?" asked Clark.

Joey nodded, standing up and dusting the sand off his pants. He grabbed Clark's hands, pulling him up from the ground. Clark held his hands out to his side to help with his balance, but he stumbled.

"Woah, sorry. I think I'm still a little drunk," Clark laughed.

"A little? Clark you're radiating bourbon. Let's try to make it back before we get struck by lightning!" Joey responded, pulling Clark's arm around his shoulder for support.

The two slowly made their way to the wooden staircase, Joey out of breath from having to support Clark through the sand.

"Okay, Clark. You go up first, and I'll follow directly behind you. Hold on to both railings and I'll be there to support you if you need it," Joey said, pointing at the staircase.

Clark nodded, placing his hands on the railing. He slowly began the trek back up the cliffside. The wind was now fiercely blowing off the waves. Thunder continued to boom above their heads.

"But anyway, Clark, I've seen people come and go for years around here. I've had my fair share of arguments with Lawrence, much like yours the other night."

Clark swayed to the right, slightly losing his balance as they approached the middle landing of the staircase. Joey forcefully held his hand up to Clark's back, pushing him forward with all his strength.

"I don't get it, Joey. How do you do it? How have you stayed by his side all these years?" Clark shouted.

They reached the middle landing, both out of breath. Clark threw his body against the wooden railing, leaning his head over.

Joey took a deep breath. "Ah, I just do it. Because like I said, there's nowhere else for me to go. Nobody is going to pay me like Lawrence does. "

"Everyone here is trapped. Just like me."

Joey nodded his head, pointing to the final steps. "Yes, you're correct. Now let's get moving!"

The two continued their trek up the staircase. As they made it back to the top observation deck, both dropped to the ground. Clark laid flat on his back, his hands covering his face as his chest rose up and down. Joey's white shirt was now soaked with sweat and sticking to him.

"Clark, don't make me ever have to go back down there again," Joey said, breathing heavily.

Clark rolled over onto his stomach to face Joey. "I think I'm going to be sick."

"Really? Couldn't see that one coming."

Clark quickly stood up, running to the railing of the overlook. Dropping his head, he vomited the day's bourbon. Each time, his body painfully convulsed. The thick gray clouds above them opened up as heavy rain began to pour. Joey quickly jumped up from the ground.

"Clark! You almost done getting it all out, man?!"

Clark turned and looked at Joey with tired, weak eyes. Wiping his mouth on his arm, he nodded as the two dashed back to the cottage.

Both stood under the porch, watching the storm beat on the rough sea below. Both men were completely drenched.

"I don't know, man. I don't know if I have the drive in me anymore to continue with this," Clark said, flopping into the metal lounge chair.

Joey squatted in front of Clark. "Listen to me, Clark. You do have it in you. You know how I know?"

Clark leaned his head against the cottage's wood facade.

"How?"

"Because of that first day when you met the band. When you shared the story of growing up in Tennessee. You're doing it, man. You're doing the damn thing that you always wanted!"

Clark looked at Joey, his eyes full of sorrow.

"Do you want to go back to Tennessee? Be back on the farm with your parents? Live a life not knowing if you're going to have enough money to put food on the table?" asked Joey.

Tears rolled down Clark's flushed cheeks. "No...but I need to help them. My parents. I need to do something for them."

Joey looked up at Clark. "Okay, what's that?"

"I want to send them money. Specifically, Mom. I need to help her, Joey. I can stay through this if I know I'm helping my folks."

Joey stood up and ran his hands through his wet hair. He quickly nodded his head. "Okay. I can help you with that, Clark. I can get that set up. How much and how often?"

"Can we send a thousand dollars a month?" Clark asked.

"I–I don't know about that. That's a lot of money. I can see Lawrence questioning that," Joey replied, crossing his arms.

"Jesus, why do we have to tell him? Why can't we just do it? It's my money."

"You're not wrong, Clark. But he controls the funds. Your money is more than likely locked up in the safe in his office. Let me see what I can do, okay?"

Clark nodded. "Okay."

"I got you, Clark. Now, I best be getting home and out of these wet clothes. Can you do me a favor?"

Clark stood up. "What's that?"

"Can you not do this again, please? This crazy shit?"

Clark sheepishly smiled. "Yeah, it was pretty stupid, wasn't it?"

"Just a little bit."

"Thanks for helping me out, Joey."

"Of course. Now go inside and get to bed. Sleep off that hangover that's setting in. I can tell you're dying," Joey commanded, pointing toward the door.

Clark quietly laughed and nodded his head.

"That sounds like a good idea. Take care, Joey."

"See ya later, Clark!" Joey replied, as he turned and made his way back toward the Sea House.

CHAPTER 26

PRESENT DAY

A slight breeze rolled off the water onto the deck of Jack's Marina where Neal and his grandparents had stopped for a snack. This was just one of the many marinas in Monterey. Nested between a mix of rundown fishing boats, catamarans, and yachts sat the marina's dive bar that locals simply coined "the restaurant."

The small wooden shack with faded navy shaker siding featured a small indoor dining area where the worn hardwood floor planks creaked under every step. The walls boasted numerous permanent marker messages from people from all over the world, and the seating consisted of mostly small round tables and stools.

Behind the shack was a small outdoor seating area where a few black iron tables and chairs stood with a faded black umbrella perched over each table. The smell of sea air and deep-fried fish filled the air. It was far from fancy dining, but Neal loved the relaxed atmosphere. And after a few beers, he swore the hot dogs were the best in all of California.

Nana leaned back in her iron chair, pushing her now wavy salt-and-pepper hair off her shoulders. "What's good here, Neal?"

Neal slid the simple, one-page menu that had been creased a few too many times across the table toward Nana and Grandad. "Well, your options are limited. To drink you got a small selection of bottled beers and the cheapest glasses of wine possible. To eat, well, there's peanuts, chips, and pizza, and if you're brave enough, raw oysters."

Grandad's brown eyes peered up from behind his glasses as he looked at the menu, "Oysters? Something tells me at a place like this we don't want the oysters."

Neal laughed. "Right. But you could go for the hot dog. I'm not exactly sure what it's made of, but after a few beers, it's really not that bad."

"Tell you what Neal, why don't you just order for us. You're the local," Nana said, right as the young server arrived at their table.

Neal smiled. "Hey, Sarah. How's it going today?"

Sarah's platinum blonde hair was loosely pulled back in a ponytail as she sported the restaurant's simple employee attire: black t-shirt, khaki shorts with a black apron tied around the waist, and black Converse sneakers.

Pulling out a worn yellow notepad from her apron, Sarah replied, "Good. Almost quitting time for me! Who do we have joining you this afternoon, Neal?"

Neal pushed his black Ray-Bans up on top of his head. "These are my grandparents, Amelia and Daniel, otherwise known as Nana and Grandad. This is Sarah, the best server at the restaurant."

Sarah flashed a bright white smile. "Neal's learning from the old fishermen who come here. He's a big schmoozer. Nice to meet you both. What will you be having?"

"Let's see. For Nana, let's do a glass of pinot grigio. And for Grandad and me, let's do two Millers. And we'll take three hot dogs, cause why not?!"

Sarah quickly jotted down the order, her colorful threaded bracelets moving against the yellow notepad.

"You guys got it," Sarah said, grabbing the paper menus from Neal. "I'll be back shortly with those drinks and dogs."

"Take your time. We're enjoying the views," said Neal as Sarah turned to make her way back to the shack.

Grandad leaned back in the chair, his arms resting on top of his belly. "She's cute, Neal."

Neal laughed. "She's a college student, Grandad. She's living the college life, waiting tables at the marina, and occasionally offering surf lessons."

"Oh, really?" said Nana with surprise.

"Yep. She's offered to teach me, but I haven't made the time."

"Well, you should try it, Neal. That sounds fun!" laughed Nana.

Sarah returned to the table with their order.

"All right, the glass of wine for you, Nana. And the beers for the gentlemen. And last but not least, the hot dogs. Be careful, they're extremely hot. I just grabbed them off the hot dog roaster," Sarah said, tossing a handful of crinkled condiment packets onto the table.

"Thanks, Sarah. This looks perfect," said Neal.

"Enjoy!" Sarah said. She turned to the help the patrons who had just been seated.

Grandad picked up the toasted hot dog bun out of the red-and-white checkered paper container. "Oh! Shew...that's hot!" he exclaimed, dropping the hot dog back into the container.

"Well, yeah, Daniel, she just told us that. What did you expect?" asked Nana, bringing the glass of pinot grigio up to her lips.

"Yeah, they don't mess around with their hot dogs here," Neal said.

"Apparently not," replied Grandad, quickly shaking his hand.

"So, Nana, how do you know all of this stuff about Clark James if you didn't meet him until later on?" asked Neal.

Nana sipped her glass of wine and carefully placed the glass on the table. "Well, he told me. Once he opened up to me, he shared with me so many stories and details of his life."

"Did Mr. Lawrence agree to send the money to Clark's parents?" asked Grandad.

"Yes. And no," said Nana. She took a small bite of the hot dog, steam wafting as she placed it back in the container.

Holding a thin paper napkin to her mouth, she continued. "He did agree to send the money to Clark's mom, but it was not the amount Clark wanted."

"What was the amount?" asked Grandad.

"I believe it ended up being five hundred dollars a month insead of the original idea of a thousand."

Neal shook his head. "Unbelievable. It was *his money*. He should've been able to do whatever he wished with it."

Nana nodded her head in agreement. "Of course, that's what everyone would say, right? But life at the Sea House was far from ordinary."

"Did Clark continue to shake things up? Or did he decide to stay quiet?" asked Neal.

A smile flashed across Nana's face. "Oh, he continued to shake things up. And unfortunately, there were more moments like that day at the beach."

"Oh, so he kept drinking?" asked Grandad.

"Yep. He was completely spiraling. That is until I came along," said Nana.

CHAPTER 27
Big Sur, California, 1960

The years slipped by, and Clark James remained fairly the same. The shows continued and the crowds kept coming. Clark would watch people pack into the dining room of the Sea House every night he was scheduled to perform. The fashion trends changed, the people changed, and staff came in and went from the Sea House, but Clark remained the same.

To keep people from speculating about abnormalities, Mr. Lawrence made sure that as the years went by, Clark appeared to grow older. They could only blame good looks for so long. The makeup team would subtly make Clark appear older and more mature. The costume team would always keep Clark's clothes up to date with the latest trends.

Clark moved with the recurring routine of life: the rehearsals, meet-and-greets, shows, parties, repeat. When he didn't have to be in the spotlight, he would retreat to his cottage. There he often would allow the lonesome blues to take over and the liquor to flow.

As the years went on, Clark knew that he was drinking more, but what did it matter? Did he really have anything to lose? One night, it was an hour until showtime and he still had not made his way to the dressing room backstage at the Sea House.

Joey, the only one who Clark had not completely shut out, could feel something was off. Where was Clark? He should be in his dressing room by now.

Joey quickly walked to the cottage and knocked on the side door.
BANG! BANG! BANG!

Nobody came to the door. But Joey could hear loud music blaring through the cottage's walls.

"Clark! It's about an hour to show time! We need you to come to the club, buddy," he yelled loudly over the music.

Nothing. Turning the knob, Joey realized that the door was unlocked. He stepped inside. The music blared. Joey screamed Clark's name as he searched for him.

"CLARK! IT'S JOEY! WE GOTTA GO!"

Joey turned and took a step into the living room. There stood Clark. He was pouring a glass of bourbon with his left hand and holding a cigarette in his right hand. His hair was disheveled, and he wasn't wearing pants. His white dress shirt covered his knickers, and black dress socks were pulled up to cover his shins.

"Oh, hey, Joey," laughed Clark, realizing he was no longer the only person in the room.

"Clark, we gotta go, man. The show starts in an hour. You need to be backstage."

Clark took a big gulp of his bourbon. "Right, right, right. It's *showtime*!"

Joey looked around the room and noticed the many empty glass bottles.

"Jesus, Clark. How much have you had to drink tonight?"

"Hey! It's just a part of the show. A little something-something to get me ready for tonight, ya know?" laughed Clark.

"Where are your pants?"

Clark stumbled backward and let out a childish laugh. "My fucking pants. That's what I need. I knew I was missin' somethin'."

"Oh God, Clark. You're trashed. Let's get you together. Come on," said Joey. He grabbed Clark's arms and forced him into the bathroom.

Turning on the sink's cold water, Joey knew he was in charge. "Take your shirt off and stick your face in the water. Now."

Clark leaned against the bathroom wall for support. "Joey, my man. Joey. Whats-a-matter?"

Grabbing ahold of the back of his friend's head, Joey quickly removed Clark's shirt, pushing him up to the sink. "Hey, man, we gotta get you to the show. We can drink all the bourbon and cocktails later, okay?"

"Joe. Joey…"

Joey grabbed Clark's head and forcefully plunged him into the cold water.

"Aghhhhh!"

"I know, I know," said Joey as he pulled Clark's head out of the water. He dunked him a few more times.

"JOSEPH, ya gotta stop. I'm good!" Clark gasped.

Joey grabbed a towel and threw it over Clark's head.

"All right, Clark. Where are your pants? Let's get those on."

Leading Clark into the bedroom, Joey searched the room for a pair of clean dress pants. It was a bit of a challenge as there were empty liquor bottles covering the floor.

The bottles clinked together as Joey kicked them out of the way. He came across a pair of black dress pants that were partially peeking out from under Clark's bed.

"Put these on. Now. Then your shoes, and let's go!"

Clark stumbled into the pants, letting out a drunken laugh. "Think I'm gonna *break a leg* tonight?"

Joey didn't bother to answer Clark, as he pulled him down the hallway into the kitchen.

"I don't know, Clark. But what I do know is that you need some water."

"Water is in bourbon," chuckled Clark.

"You're right. But here," Joey said as forcefully brought the glass of water up to Clark's lips. "Now, let's go. And let's get you some food as soon as we get you backstage."

What typically was a brisk five-minute walk to the Sea House took about 10 minutes because of Clark's inability to walk without stumbling. When they finally made it to the dressing room, the backstage crew was waiting.

"All right, people, move it! Clark James coming through!" barked Joey while pushing Clark into the dressing room.

"I need hair and makeup in here, stat. Tell Wardrobe we need a well-pressed shirt that doesn't have stains all over it, and someone please get this man some food!"

Clark threw his body onto the couch in his dressing room. "You heard the man! Food and a shirt and a bourbon."

"Anybody who hands this man a glass of bourbon or a sip of alcohol is fired! Let's move, people!" shouted Joey.

The backstage crew flew into action. People zoomed in and out of Clark's dressing room. Clark moved to the makeup chair and a stylist began fixing his hair while someone else shoved bread into Clark's mouth.

"Someone tell me how much time we have until showtime!" shouted Joey as he grabbed the freshly pressed shirt from a stagehand.

"Twenty minutes!"

"Jesus, 20 minutes. This man can barely keep his head up, and he's supposed to take the stage? Where's Lawrence?"

"At the front table!"

"Okay, whatever we do, people, let's keep that man from coming backstage. Tell the waitstaff to keep the drinks and food going out to his table."

"On it!!"

Clark giggled. "Yeah, feed the pig what he needs Bring him the Cuban cigars and whores!"

Joey rolled his eyes. "Jesus, Clark, you are in rare form tonight. What the hell is going on with you, man?"

Clark took a bite of a chicken breast. "None of this matters, Joey. It's the same thing. I go on stage and I sing. The crowd screams. And then I do it all over again tomorrow. So…if I drink a little too much, guess what? Same ol' shit's going to happen tomorrow."

Joey sat across from Clark. "Hey, listen to me. You're better than this. You know that! All these people here love you. They care so much about you."

"Good one, Joey. I got NO ONE."

Joey patted Clark on the back. "That's not true, buddy. You've got me."

"Yeah, well, that's a fucking lie."

Joey grabbed Clark's chin. "HEY! That's it, man! Cut this shit out. What the hell's the matter with you?"

"It's all just a lie, Joey. Stop fucking lying. You know it. Everyone backstage knows it. I'm just frozen here at this damn club."

The remaining stage crew nervously looked around the room, returning their gazes to Joey.

THE CLUB BY THE SEA

"Look, Clark. I hear you. And I know that this has been hard on you, but right now we need to put on the best show possible. Can we pull it together just for the night?" Joey held up the black blazer for Clark to put on.

Stumbling out of the chair, Clark ran his hands through his hair as he took one last look in the mirror. "God, you're just like the rest of them."

"No, Clark. I'm your friend. And I just want you to be able to get through this without Lawrence finding out."

"SCREW LAWRENCE! YOU THINK I–"

"Shh! Shh!" Joey grabbed Clark's shoulders. "Clark, I get it! You're sad. I can see it. It's written all over you. I promise to help you, but you have to get out there and put on this show."

Clark rolled his eyes and scoffed.

"I will. I will do whatever I can to make this easier for you. I can talk to Lawrence, get things through his head. I am your ally, Clark."

"Okay," Clark said, looking Joey in the eyes. "Let's go put on a damn show."

CHAPTER 28

The show started right on time. For everyone's sake, the crew decided that it would be best for Clark to sit on a stool for the opening number. Even though he was still intoxicated, he managed to sing his way through the first three songs on the set list with no issues.

Joey stood against the right wall of the dining hall, keeping one eye on the stage and the other on Mr. Lawrence's table. This might just actually work, thought Joey, until Lawrence signaled for him to come over to the table.

"Yes, Mr. Lawrence? How are we doing tonight?"

The ladies around Mr. Lawrence giggled, clinking their wine glasses together.

"What's going on with Clark tonight?" asked Lawrence, looking up at Joey with a confused expression across his face.

"Something seem wrong with him, sir?"

"Why is he sitting on a stool? That's not typically how a show opens."

"Oh, I believe I overheard him say something about doing something different tonight. It's this new idea he had to make the performance seem intimate, I think."

Mr. Lawrence took a sip of his cocktail. "Intimate? How so?"

Joey nervously clicked his pen in his hand. "I'm not sure, sir. I'm not an expert, but I believe it has something to do with making the crowd feel as if they are just hanging out in the same room with him. Like, it's as if we are all in his living room."

Lawrence chuckled. "Living room?! That's hilarious. I love it."

Joey nodded. "Me too."

"Tell him to get his ass up on the next set, though. There's something off about him tonight. I can feel it."

"Oh, okay. Got it, sir. Anything else I can get you all?"

Mr. Lawrence held his gaze on Joey while lighting his cigar. "What do you know, Joey?"

Joey nervously adjusted the collar of his shirt.

"I know lots of things about cocktails and the menu, sir."

"ENOUGH."

"What do you mean, sir?"

"Joey, you're not a good liar. You've never been a good liar. That's why I keep you around. Now what the hell is going on with the boy?"

Joey cleared his throat. "He just had a little too much to drink tonight. That's all. Nothing major. I recommended that he start the show sitting down."

"Because he's too drunk?"

Joey nodded.

"To stand? Too drunk to stand up?"

Joey nodded.

"Ah, I see. Well, we can't have that now, can we?" asked Mr. Lawrence, standing up from the table as he began to make his way toward the backstage door. Joey followed right behind.

"Look, sir. I know it's stupid of him, but I think he just needs a break."

Continuing backstage, Mr. Lawrence laughed. "A break?! Not on my watch, Joey!"

"Sir, I think he's just—"

Mr. Lawrence spun and pushed Joey up against the backstage wall.

"He's just WHAT?! The guy who pays your salary?!"

Beads of sweat dripped from Joey's hairline.

"Joey, if he screws this up," said Mr. Lawrence, gesturing widely, "all of this could be over in an instant."

"I–I know, sir. But I think he is having a hard time."

Mr. Lawrence punched Joey's chest, knocking the air out of him.

"A hard time? Oh, because having *everything* given to you is so bad."

Gasping air, Joey replied, "I know. But I have some ideas, sir."

"Go ahead then. Let's hear it."

Joey adjusted his shirt, his breathing regulated. "He's lonely, and it's becoming very obvious. I think that's the reason he's drinking more."

Mr. Lawrence rolled his eyes.

"And I think that maybe if he had a companion, things would be easier for him. Maybe he could find the will to continue. Right now, it seems he no longer cares about anything. Nothing matters to him."

"A companion? Joey, he gets way too distracted when someone comes into his life. He stops caring about his work when he's in *love*."

Joey crossed his arms on his chest. "I agree. But wouldn't we rather have him happy and putting on a hell of a show versus him drinking his sorrows away and then doing...*this*?" Joey pointed toward the stage.

Mr. Lawrence walked away and back toward the dining hall.

"All right, so we're done here, sir?"

Quickly turning around, Mr. Lawrence replied. "Fine. He can have a *companion*. But when that happens, I want to meet her and approve."

"Yes, sir."

"In the meantime, Joey. Get back to work and do a better job of keeping Clark in line."

CHAPTER 29

BIG SUR, CALIFORNIA, 1961

After that night, Clark James didn't have as many outbursts of drunken behavior prior to shows. Joey let him know that he was allowed to start dating, which seemed to help Clark's spirit.

Although, he was not really dating anyone. Because of his situation, Clark felt that a relationship would never work. Nobody would ever truly understand his contract with Mr. Lawrence, and trying to explain it could cost him everything. So, he became more of a ladies' man, taking different women back to his cottage after each and every show. For the most part, the thrill of sharing the night with someone did fill the void in his heart.

As for the shows, they continued as scheduled. While Clark still loved performing, it was starting to lose its spark. In the earlier days, he would wake up eager and ready to start rehearsal. These days, he slept in as long as he could and rolled into rehearsal just as it began.

Oftentimes, Clark felt like the world was moving on while he was stuck in a repeated scene of unfulfilling nights in a dimly lit ballroom. When the shows were over and he could slip away from the late terrace parties, he would return to his cottage and sit on the front porch. While sitting back in the old, rusted metal chairs, Clark would stare out into the dark sea, dreaming of days outside of the nightclub. Sometimes when he was feeling really lonesome, he would go into the living room and put on the record of old soulful songs, reminding him of his childhood back in Tennessee. Sitting in the dark on the hardwood floors, with his back against the wood-paneled living room walls, Clark would sing along to the songs of his childhood.

"This little light of mine…I'm gonna let it shine," Clark whispered along, in the dark room, the glow from the moon shining through the small living room window. The memories rushed back to times spent singing at the piano with his mom.

"Don't worry Mom and Dad. I'm making it up to you, guys," Clark said as tears rolled down his checks. "I'll spend forever making it up to you."

This was the only motivation remaining for Clark to continue with the shows. On days where he really thought about throwing in the towel and telling Mr. Lawrence he was done, Clark thought of his parents. Without the Sea House, he would not be able to continue to send them money each month.

But one night that all changed. Feeling more energy from the crowd than usual, Clark gave the audience his all. So much so that during the final song of the evening, beads of sweat dripped from his face, leaving his dark hair curled and slick. During the standing ovation, he noticed through the blinding spotlight Joey talking with Mr. Lawrence at his table.

Joey quickly glanced back and forth from the stage to Mr. Lawrence. Mr. Lawrence shook his head and held his pocket watch out for Joey, as if it was not the time for Joey's shenanigans.

"Ladies and gentlemen, we have absolutely loved performing for you all tonight. Can you please give one more round of applause for my incredible band?!"

As requested, the crowd roared with screams and applause. "I'm Clark James, and once again, thank you! Thank you very much!" Clark waved to the audience as he walked toward the back of the stage, the band continuing to play.

Waiting in the dimly lit space at the back of the stage, Joey leaned against the wall, holding a small towel. Clark walked up to him, glistening with sweat.

"Great show tonight, as always, Clark!" Joey said, tossing the towel to Clark.

"Thanks, man! Felt the energy from the crowd tonight. It felt like life was coming back to me!" Clark said, dabbing the towel on his face.

Joey nodded, following alongside Clark as the two continued down the hallway to Clark's dressing room. Inside the dressing room, Clark quickly pulled off his suit jacket and tossed it onto the velvet couch. His damp white shirt stuck to his chest.

"How much time do we have until the VIP party on the terrace?" Clark asked, making his way to the pitcher of water on the vanity by the makeup mirror.

"Clark, I think–"

Clark slammed his empty glass onto the vanity. "Ahh. Where's my next pressed shirt? I don't see it on the rack."

"Clark, it's not there because–"

Tuning Joey out, Clark rushed over to the makeup mirror surrounded by giant glass light bulbs. "Man, I am really sweaty. I should probably freshen up before going out there. Can we get hair and makeup in here?"

Joey looked at Clark's reflection in the mirror, a soft smile on his face.

"Joey? Why are you just standing there?" Clark asked, turning to face Joey.

"Clark, something has happened. And I don't think you should go to the terrace party tonight."

Running his hands through his dark hair, a confused look flashed across Clark's face.

"What do you mean?"

"It's your parents, Clark," Joey said, inching a little closer to Clark.

"My parents? What do you mean? What's going on?" Clark asked, crossing his arms.

"Clark, they were in a terrible accident. And I'm afraid that..."

"Afraid that what, Joey?" Clark straightened in his chair.

"They didn't make it, Clark. I'm so sorry."

Clark stumbled backward, leaning against the wall of the dressing room for support.

"No, Joey, no. You don't know what you're talking about!"

"I–I know. I'm so sorry, Clark." Joey's voice broke.

Clark's legs gave out, causing him to drop to the floor. He leaned against the wall, pulling his legs up against his chest. The cinder block walls of the room felt like they were collapsing as Clark buried his head in his hands.

Joey dropped to the floor beside Clark. "Clark, this is a lot to take in. You take all the time you need to recover from this. Maybe go home tonight and get some rest. Skip the VIP party."

Clark lifted his head, his face flushed and wet from tears. "What the hell happened?!"

Swallowing the lump in his throat, Joey forced the words. "Your dad was driving. He'd had a few too many. Your mom was in the passenger seat."

"Oh, God. This can't be happening!" Clark cried.

Joey placed his hand on Clark's shoulder, giving it a tight squeeze. "Clark, I'm so sorry."

"When did it happen, Joey?" Clark asked.

Joey looked to the floor and then back to Clark. "Uh...I'm not sure those details matter."

"No, tell me. When did this happen?" Clark's voice rose in anger and sadness.

"Clark, I don't think it's going to make anything better."

"Joey, when did this fucking happen?!" Clark yelled, his face now crimson.

"We found out this morning, I'm afraid," Joey replied softly.

Clark's lips curled. "This morning?"

"Clark, I know."

"No, Joey, you don't. You know nothing!! My parents died this morning and you are just now telling me?! It's fucking ten at night, Joey!"

"I'm so sorry. But you know that no matter what, Lawrence would've made you perform tonight. I couldn't do that to you before you took the stage."

Clark's body shook as he inhaled deeply. "This doesn't even feel real right now. What am I doing here!?"

Larry and Jane entered the dressing room, wearing the second outfits for the night. Jane's hair was cut in a short bob that rested right at her shoulders. She walked to Clark and cupped his face with her hands.

"Clark, we are so sorry," she said, hugging him.

Larry stepped close to Clark and Jane.

"Yeah, Clark. We're all so sorry. Is there anything we can do?" Larry asked, placing his hand on Clark's shoulder.

Clark's face was red and blotchy. "You guys all knew too?" He whimpered into Jane's shoulder.

Jane gently rubbed Clark's back. "Yes, I'm afraid so."

THE CLUB BY THE SEA

"But, hey, man, you did put on one hell of a show tonight. You were on fire out there, Clark!" said Larry.

Clark slowly lifted his head up from Jane's shoulder, pulling himself out of her arms.

"What?" Clark whispered back.

Larry nervously pulled on the collar of his white turtleneck. "You were amazing out there tonight, Clark."

"Larry, my parents are dead. And all you can seem to say is that *I was on fire tonight*?!"

"I'm sorry man. I just don't know what else to say." Larry nervously twirled the button on his blazer.

"Well, that's the thing, right? Nobody knows what to say. But you all definitely knew about it and kept it a secret from me all day, so that you could still make your damn money!"

Jane let out a sigh. "Clark, it's not like that at all! We're devastated for you."

Clark crossed his arms, making a sarcastic face. "Oh, are you, Jane? Are you really?"

Larry straightened, crossing his arms over his chest. "All right, Clark. We know you're hurting right now, but you don't get to be an asshole to us and talk down to Jane like that."

"Ha! Save it, Larry. You don't get to tell me about being sad or being an asshole. None of you do, you hear me?!" Clark spat his words while pointing his finger at the three of them.

"Clark–"

"NO! Screw you guys! And screw the Sea House! I should've never come here. If I would've just returned home that day, none of this would've happened," Clark wailed.

"Oh, Clark, Honey. I'm so, so sorry," Jane said as Clark burst into tears.

"I think we call it for the night and get some rest, Clark. Let's get you back to the cottage, get you some shuteye," Joey said, grabbing Clark's arms.

"What are we going to do about the funeral, Joey?" Clark asked, as Joey pulled him out of the dressing room.

"We will do whatever it takes, man. We can talk more about this later. Let's just get you back to the cottage, okay?"

"Joey, what am I going to do?" Clark cried.

Joey stopped and turned to Clark. "If there's anything I know, Clark, it's that you will do what you always do. You will press on. And you will be strong. There are a lot of questions and details to work out. And we will."

"I have no one," said Clark.

"Wrong, Clark. You have us. And we are going to take care of you," Joey said, giving Clark's arm a squeeze.

CHAPTER 30
Big Sur, 1962

Things began to change in the summer of '62. While the shows were still greatly attended, California was changing. Jazz was having to compete with rock and roll and major blockbuster tours across the country. Clark James was slowly becoming old news in the music industry. That was until Amelia May showed up to the Sea House.

Amelia May was a young reporter for a rising music publication that was becoming well known across the country. She was the magazine's youngest employee, and while her job was to sell ads, she had bigger aspirations. Amelia dreamed of the day when she could write stories about the country's biggest musicians. After many months of begging, her boss finally gave her an opportunity to showcase her writing skills. She was assigned to write a piece on Clark James.

Sure, he was not the latest sensation, but Clark James was still catching people's attention. And although Amelia didn't know much about jazz, this would be the summer she would learn everything she needed to know.

Amelia arrived at the Sea House on a Monday morning around 11. She was to spend the week with Clark to write a potential cover story.

It was a rare glimpse into the private life of one of the most prolific jazz singers in the country. And if she did it right, this piece would help skyrocket Amelia's career.

When she walked into the club, all of the lights were on and staff members were beginning their daily routine of getting the space prepped for the evening's guests. The bars were being restocked, the floors were being cleaned, fresh linens were being added to the tables, and the tables were being set with dishes and glassware.

Joey noticed Amelia as she peeked into the dining room. "Ah, you must be the reporter."

Amelia switched her black composition notebook from her right hand to her left and extended her petite hand toward Joey.

"Yes, Amelia May. Pleased to meet you."

"I'm Joey, manager of the Sea House, head of the staff, and most importantly for you, your go-to guy for Clark James."

Amelia nodded. "Go-to guy?"

Joey briskly walked past Amelia to adjust the tablecloth behind her. "Yeah, I'm the guy who makes it all happen. I'm the one who suggested we do this interview."

"Ah, I see. Well, thank you very kindly. I'm looking forward to spending the next few days with you all and Mr. James."

Joey laughed. "Mr. James?! He's going to get a kick out of you."

Opening her notebook to a clean page, Amelia asked, "Hmm. So, where is he anyway? I was thinking I could introduce myself and get started."

"If I had to guess, Clark is probably in his cottage right now. If he's not on stage or working, that's where he can be found."

"And where might this cottage be? How far away from the club is it?"

Leading Amelia over to one of the tall windows in the dining room, Joey pointed. "Oh, he's not that far at all. You see that little house right over there?"

Amelia leaned in to see where Joey was pointing. Faintly spotting the cottage through her squinted eyes, she continued. "His cottage is on the property?"

Joey nodded.

"Interesting."

"Oh, and look, his guest of the evening is just leaving."

Writing feverishly in her notebook, Amelia looked back at the cottage. And there he was... except he wasn't alone. Clark James was shirtless on the front porch of his cottage wearing only blue jeans. He was kissing a woman wearing an evening dress.

"His guest of the evening?" asked Amelia.

Walking past her, Joey let out a laugh. "Yes. You'll quickly discover that Clark is a ladies' man. Now come on. I'll take you down there to meet him."

While walking down the gravel trail, Joey and Amelia passed the woman they had just seen kissing Clark.

Joey nodded at her. "Goodbye, Miss. You have a fantastic day now."

She smiled and blushed as she continued past them. Amelia let out a sarcastic laugh.

"You really must be his go-to guy. You even wish his lovers a fantastic day."

Moving forward and leading the way, Joey replied, "Well, we are in the hospitality business after all. And we want Clark's fans to return to the Sea House for another show."

"You can't be serious, right?" Amelia gawked while pushing her straight black hair behind her ears.

"You gotta love groupies," Joey chimed.

Arriving at the cottage's side door, Joey turned to face Amelia. "If you don't mind, please wait here. I'll let Clark know you're here."

Amelia nodded and stood on the porch while Joey escaped into the cottage. She took a look at the cottage and the views. Quaint and cozy. Surreal views. Not something she would picture someone with Clark James' status to be living in, though. It appeared to be small and awfully close to where he worked.

Amelia noticed wet clothes hanging over the painted white railing. Water dripped from the white t-shirt, blue knickers, and two white tube socks.

Joey reappeared, surprising her. "Amelia?"

Amelia quickly turned around to face Joey. "Oh, yes! Sorry, I was just noticing the beautiful views."

"Sure. He's ready for you. You can go on inside. I have duties back at the club, so please excuse me. If you need anything, Clark will give me a ring."

Amelia thanked Joey and then proceeded into Clark's cottage. She was surprised to immediately see him standing in the kitchen.

Clark had put on a button-down shirt and blue jeans. Soft jazz echoed from the room next to the kitchen where Clark was pouring coffee into two mugs.

Amelia cleared her throat. "Mm-hmm. Good morning, Mr. James. I'm Amelia. Amelia May."

Clark looked up at Amelia as he finished pouring the coffee.

"Ah, Amelia May. Please, call me Clark. Mr. James is so formal." He extended his right hand to Amelia. When she reciprocated, he took her hand and brought it to his lips, softly kissing it.

"The pleasure is all mine, Amelia. Thank you for taking time out of your busy schedule to write this article."

THE CLUB BY THE SEA

Amelia subtly wiped the back of her hand on her skirt as she cringed. "Yes. Well, thank you for agreeing to do the interview. I know they're not necessarily your thing, considering you stopped doing them a while ago."

Clark placed the coffee mugs on the kitchen table, taking a seat. "Yes, being famous really isn't my thing."

He held his hand out toward the empty seat across from him. "Coffee? Please have a seat, Amelia."

Amelia nodded, taking her place directly across from Clark. "I see. So, you don't like that you were crowned the *King of Jazz*?"

Clark chuckled as he sipped his coffee. "I mean, it's flattering. But no, I don't necessarily care about being crowned anything."

"But there must be some amusement or enjoyment you get from fame."

Clark took another sip of his coffee, placing the mug back on the table.

"Well, it seemed like you were enjoying the comfort of a fan's arms earlier this morning," Amelia said cheekily as she opened her notebook.

Clark scoffed. "Amelia May! The reporter has jokes!"

Amelia smiled. "Well, am I wrong, though?"

Clark sat up a little straighter in his chair. "No, you are not wrong. The fans are...they are great, let's just say that."

Amelia wrote the day's date at the top corner of the page and then looked up. "Well, let's get started, shall we?"

Clark nodded.

"You're from Louisiana. New Orleans, right?"

Clark shook his head. "No, the Nashville area, actually. Tennessee."

"Oh, I thought you got your start in New Orleans. I assumed that was where you were from. I apologize."

"I did get my start in New Orleans, but I'm originally from Tennessee. After I served in the war, I went to New Orleans."

Amelia wrote in her notebook. "The war? I didn't realize you were in the service."

Clark took another sip of his coffee.

"And what war were you in, exactly?"

Clark gently placed his coffee mug on the table. "World War II. I was stationed in Paris."

Amelia looked up from her notebook. "Oh. And how old are you?"

Clark forced a slight smile. "I'm 39, turning 40 this fall."

Amelia held her gaze on Clark. "You...you're aging very nicely, Mr. James."

"Please. Clark."

"I mean, Clark. You don't look a day over 25, honestly."

"Well, thanks. But I hope this article isn't just going to be about my dashing good looks. Let's continue."

Clearing her throat, Amelia spoke. "Yes, so you returned from the war and moved to New Orleans. Why jazz?"

"While in Paris, I frequented many nightclubs in the city. Fell in love with the atmosphere of the jazz bars. There's something about jazz. It can be so many different things. Soothing, intriguing, sexy, exciting."

"Would you say it's a challenge to bring in people to a jazz club when disco and rock and roll are so heavily influencing the market today?"

Clark laughed. "I would say it's a challenge for the Sea House. It's not a challenge for me."

"You've been with the Sea House now for nearly two decades?"

Clark nodded.

THE CLUB BY THE SEA

"Why not branch out and try to tour the country? Sign with a record label?"

Standing up from the table, Clark began to walk toward the front door. "Because I told you, Amelia. I have no interest in being famous."

"But you are, in a way, very famous."

Clark turned to Amelia. "Oh yeah? And what does that even mean?"

Amelia stopped writing in her notebook, looking up at Clark with confusion in her eyes.

"I–I don't know. I guess I just mean you are well-known around–"

"It doesn't mean a damn thing, Amelia. Being famous...it's nothing."

Amelia slowly nodded her head.

"And if there is anything that I want you to understand or get out of this interview, it's that."

Amelia nervously tugged on her blouse. "That you hate being famous?"

Clark scoffed. "You don't get it. Just like everyone else. No, it's that I am more than just a jazz singer."

Amelia resumed taking notes. "Very well then. And if you could tell the world there's more to you than your job, what would you say?"

Clark opened the front door of the cottage and stepped out to the porch, letting the sea air blow into the kitchen.

"Alrighty, then." Amelia whispered under her breath, before following him onto the porch.

"Beautiful views, Mr. James."

Keeping his back to Amelia, Clark replied.

"Certainly. It's where I spend most of my time."

"So, you're a homebody. If you're not doing a show, you love to spend your time at home?"

Clark scoffed while turning to face Amelia. "Yeah, sure. I'm a homebody."

Amelia continued to take notes.

"But I think that's enough questions for now."

Amelia paused, looking up at Clark. "Oh?"

"I need to start preparing for tonight's show. Why don't you join me in my dressing room this evening at around six? We can continue our discussion then."

Amelia closed her notebook and nodded. "Yes, of course. That sounds great."

Clark gently squeezed Amelia's arm as he walked by her and back into the house. Pausing in the doorway, he glanced back at Amelia and gently smiled. He stepped inside and closed the door, leaving Amelia alone on the porch.

CHAPTER 31

Amelia had never been to an upscale club like the Sea House before. Nor had she ever really spent time with anyone famous. She hoped that her black polka-dotted dress would be appropriate for tonight's show. To make it seem more upscale, she made sure to wear a bold red lipstick and her matching pearl earrings and necklace.

Arriving at Clark's dressing room at exactly six o'clock, she gently knocked on the door. Joey quickly opened it.

"Hey, Amelia. Come on," he said as he held the door open for her.

"Hi, Joey. It's nice to see you again."

Amelia stepped inside to find Clark James sitting in a chair at his vanity mirror surrounded by light bulbs. He was wearing white dress pants and a white button-down shirt.

"Amelia! You're right on time!" said Clark as he looked at her reflection in the mirror.

"Yes! I'm excited to be here and to see the show tonight. It's my first time at the Sea House."

Clark turned to face Amelia. "Your first time? Well, that means the pressure is on!"

Joey put a white blazer on one of the dressing room sofas. "Clark, here is your jacket for tonight. I'll let you all continue the interview, and I'll be back in about 25 minutes to get you."

Amelia took a seat on the sofa closest to Clark, pulling her notebook out of her purse.

"Okay, so how does Clark James get into the zone before a show?"

Clark stood up and walked to the other side of the room, pouring each of them a glass of water. "Well, it depends on the day. But after we do a midday soundcheck, I like to take a walk around the property."

Amelia began to write in her notebook. "And that helps me gather my thoughts. Rests my mind and helps me get into a good head space for the show."

Clark walked toward Amelia, pausing to set the glasses of water on the coffee table by the sofa. Taking a seat, he continued. "Then, I'll start getting ready. I'll cook a meal and then walk over here until showtime."

"You cook a meal?" asked Amelia.

"Yes," replied Clark.

"Why not just eat at the Sea House before the show?"

Clark looked at Amelia as she continued to write in her notebook. "Because I don't want to. I want to eat a meal in my home that I've cooked for myself."

"Gotcha. Back to being a homebody."

Clark laughed. "Yes, we're going back to that."

"So, do you like to have anyone join you for dinner before the show? Or do you prefer to dine alone?"

"It's almost always alone. My time outside of the Sea House is alone."

Amelia looked up from her notebook. "Except at night after the show, right?"

Clark looked at her with a puzzled expression on his face. "What do you mean?"

"That's when the lucky girl of the night gets to come home with you."

Clark laughed. "And we're back to this again. Now, tell me, Amelia May, are you only going to bring up the same topics of discussion during our interview?"

Amelia cleared her throat. "Are you only going to give me very vague answers throughout our interview?"

Clark stood up, grabbing his blazer. "I don't know. I feel like I'm answering everything very truthfully."

"Okay. So, do you miss home? Do you miss Nashville and your family?"

Clark slowly nodded his head. "Every day."

"Do you ever visit? Or does your family visit you?" asked Amelia.

"I haven't been back to Tennessee in many, many years. But my family has visited, yes."

"They must be very proud of you. I'm sure it's so surreal to see their son up on stage."

Clark pulled on his jacket and adjusted the buttons. "Yeah, well, unfortunately they are no longer with us."

Amelia adjusted her necklace. "Oh, I am so sorry. I didn't realize…"

"No, it's okay. You didn't know. They were in an accident last year."

"Oh, goodness. I am so sorry, Clark. That must have been very hard."

Now standing in front of the mirror, Clark adjusted his bow tie. "Yes, it was. My father was an alcoholic. He had way too many drinks before getting behind the wheel one night. His addiction led to the deaths of him and my mother."

"How did you find out?"

"I had just finished a show and was returning to my dressing room when Joey told me."

No longer writing in her notebook, Amelia leaned in. "You must have been devastated."

"I was. And want to know the worst part?"

Amelia looked up at Clark. "They had been dead for nearly an entire day before I was made aware."

"Oh, I'm sure it just took some time for the news to get to you," said Amelia.

"No, it didn't. Everyone here knew. They just wanted me to get through the show before telling me."

There was a knock at the door.

"Because no matter what goes on in life, Amelia, the show must go on. And guess what? It's showtime."

Amelia stood up, adjusting her dress as Joey opened the door to the dressing room.

"All ready to head to the stage?" Joey's eyes darted from Amelia to Clark.

Taking a sip of water, Clark replied, "Yep, all ready!"

"Great. Amelia, come with me. I'll show you to your seat. You'll be sitting at booth four tonight with the owner of the Sea House, Mr. Lawrence."

CHAPTER 32

Amelia was placed at the end of the booth by Mr. Lawrence and his group of friends. Amelia couldn't help but notice that for someone who insisted on hating fame, Clark James really did know how to work a room.

Seeing him on stage and in person felt like seeing a different version of the man that she had been interviewing throughout the day. Clark lit up on stage, and the energy he gave off filled the entire room. As he worked the stage, Amelia knew that he had the band and the audience completely in the palm of his hand.

Oftentimes, Amelia found herself clapping along with the audience. "Wow, he really does know how to make the room swoon."

Mr. Lawrence gently elbowed her. "You're darn right about that!"

Amelia turned to face Mr. Lawrence. "I'm sure you are incredibly proud of Clark."

"That I am. He's been the best investment of my career!"

Amelia flipped open her notebook. "Investment. So, do you have a history of showcasing successful musicians?"

"We've had some great performers in the past, but no one like Clark James. Clark James is a phenomenon. I mean, just look around the room. It's packed with people from all over the country who came to see him on our stage."

"Has he ever thought about leaving to pursue bigger things?" asked Amelia.

Lawrence scoffed. "Bigger things?"

Amelia looked up from her notebook. "Yes, like signing with a record label? Going on tour?"

Mr. Lawrence took a sip of his cocktail and laughed. "My dear, why send Clark James around the country, when people can pay to come see him here at the Sea House?"

"That's definitely an interesting perspective, but has Clark ever expressed any desire to leave the Sea House?"

"No! He has it completely made here. The finest team and staff, wardrobe, fans, and even his living arrangements are taken care of. He's living the dream here!" said Mr. Lawrence.

"So, would you say that he loves being famous?" Amelia asked.

Mr. Lawrence took a puff of his cigar. "You interviewing me or Clark James, little lady? Of course the man loves being famous. Look at him up there, he's eating this up!"

Amelia turned her eyes up to the stage, watching Clark and Jane sing a lively duet at the piano, the beat of the music enticing everyone to sway along in their seats. Clark had made it abundantly clear that he was not into being famous, yet Mr. Lawrence said otherwise. She decided to get Clark's take on Mr. Lawrence's comments after the show.

Until then, she would sit back, enjoy the show, observe the room, and drink a cocktail or two.

CHAPTER 33

After the show, Amelia began to prepare her questions for Clark James. She hoped that they could go somewhere a little more low-key, a place where she could get him to share details of his life. But Mr. Lawrence had other plans.

"You must join us now out on the terrace. This is a VIP experience, and you are just that this week!" said Mr. Lawrence as Amelia stood up from the table.

"Oh, I'm not sure, Mr. Lawrence. I really need to continue my interview with Clark, and I think a quiet place might be best."

"The terrace is exactly that! It's relaxing and subdued. Plus, Clark has to join us for at least an hour. It's part of his responsibilities."

Amelia nodded. "Oh, I see. Well, then yes, let's go to the terrace."

Mr. Lawrence laughed while looping his arm through Amelia's. "Come with me! I'll bring you right to Clark himself."

When they made it out on the terrace, Clark was standing at the bar talking with a group of women, each one gushing over him, throwing out compliments left and right.. Mr. Lawrence pushed through the mass of people circling Clark.

"Excuse me. Coming through. Watch it. Move."

Clark took a sip of champagne, noticing Mr. Lawrence and Amelia weaving through the crowd.

"Ah, Amelia May. So nice of you to join us out on the terrace tonight."

Amelia bashfully nodded, noticing eyes on her after Clark spoke her name.

"Quite a show tonight, Clark."

"Thank you. Would you like a drink? It's on the house."

Glancing at the champagne flute in Clark's hands, Amelia replied, "I'll take one of those, please."

Clark ordered Amelia a glass of champagne from the bar and handed it to her. "Why don't we go over there, where it's less crowded?" He motioned toward the far end of the terrace.

"Yes, that sounds great. You lead, and I'll follow."

Amelia walked closely behind Clark as they weaved in and out of the crowd. Amelia continued to notice the gawkers, each person looking at Clark like he was a golden prize.

"Great show tonight, Clark!"

"You've done it again, Mr. James!"

"CLARK! I LOVE YOU!"

Clark smiled and nodded. Shook hands. Hugged. And somehow they eventually made their way to the opposite side of the terrace.

"Don't worry. We only have to be out here for just a little bit. As soon as my hour is up, I like to get the hell out of here," said Clark.

Amelia took a sip of her champagne. "You really were great in there. Felt like I was seeing a different person."

Clark laughed. "A different person? Oh really?"

"Yes, you were radiating on that stage. I could feel the energy pouring out of you."

Clark leaned against the terrace railing. "It can be therapeutic at times. It's almost like a recharge."

"I can see that. You're very talented. And you do seem to enjoy it."

"I enjoy the art of performing and the work. But like I said earlier..."

"I know. I know. You don't enjoy being *famous*," said Amelia.

"Yes, exactly," Clark laughed.

"So, that must be why you don't want to ever go on tour."

Turning to look out at the ocean, Clark hesitated to reply. "Hmm...yeah, something like that."

"Okay, tell me this, Clark James. If you could wave a magic wand and be anywhere in the world, doing whatever it is that you wanted to do, what would that be?"

Clark quickly turned around to face Amelia.

"Well, Amelia May, I would probably be back in Tennessee. Maybe on a nice farm with a family. Or maybe living in a house deep in the woods. Anywhere I could write songs and send them off for others to sing."

"But then you wouldn't be *the* Clark James," said Amelia.

"No, I probably wouldn't. And that's okay with me."

"So, what's stopping you from doing just that?" asked Amelia.

Leaning back against the railing, Clark studied her. "It's...it's not that easy."

"Seems to me like it could be. You've been in the business since you were 23. Why not move on to new things? You clearly want to experience something new."

Clark looked back to the crowd on the terrace and then back to Amelia. "Because. This is all I know now. I don't really remember what life was like before the Sea House. And I don't think I will ever know that feeling again."

"I don't think I understand," said Amelia.

Clark shrugged. "And I don't expect you to, Amelia."

Closing her notebook, Amelia tucked it back into her purse. "I think we are done for tonight, Mr. James."

Clark straightened up. "What? Why?"

"You're giving me nothing to work with, that's why."

Clark scoffed. "I'm sorry?"

Amelia began to walk away. "I'm wanting to write a piece that is groundbreaking. That really tells the world who Clark James is. And right now I feel like you're giving me vague responses. Confusing ones, I might add. This is a waste of time for both of us."

Clark followed Amelia as she made her way across the terrace. "That's because everything about my life is confusing."

"Mm-hmm." Amelia pulled her purse closer to her body.

"Amelia, wait!" Clark grabbed her hand.

She turned around to face Clark.

"This is all a facade. Clark James. The Sea House. It's…it's not really me."

Amelia impatiently nodded while tapping her foot.

"Can you meet me tomorrow morning at my place around 8?"

Adjusting the purse strap on her shoulder, she quickly replied, "Maybe."

"I'll have coffee ready, and I'll tell you everything you need to know."

"Fine. But there'd better not be an overnight guest leaving your house as I arrive. It's not cute."

Clark laughed. "Deal."

CHAPTER 34

The next morning Amelia arrived at the Sea House at 7:45. And by the time she walked down the gravel trail to Clark's cottage it was exactly 8. This time, Clark was waiting for her on the porch wearing jeans and a white t-shirt but no shoes.

"Morning, Amelia."

Forcing a smile, Amelia replied, "Good morning, Clark."

Clark reached for her hand to help her up the porch stairs. "Coffee?"

"Yes, please. That would be great."

Amelia accepted the coffee mug from Clark and took a seat in one of the chairs. Clark stood in front of her and leaned up against the railing.

"Are you going to take a seat?"

"Who, me?" Clark asked, looking around the porch.

Amelia laughed. "Yes, you. You're making me nervous. And you're blocking the view."

"Making you nervous? Now, we can't *both* be nervous, Amelia," Clark said, taking a seat in the chair beside her.

She placed her coffee mug down beside the chair. "Clark James gets nervous?"

Leaning back in his chair, Clark responded. "Of course I get nervous. I don't really do interviews anymore. Especially one that is this intimate."

Amelia opened her notebook, flipping to the page where she left off. "I'm actually surprised that you don't do more interviews. Why? Do you care to elaborate?"

"In the past, I did not get a say in my schedule or interviews. And that partially remains true today."

"Oh?"

"Mr. Lawrence or Joey schedule press-related appointments. And when I first started performing here, I wasn't allowed to say no or miss a single one. But now that I'm more established, I'm allowed to have more of a say in the interviews I do.

"And what made you say yes to this one?" asked Amelia.

"I didn't. Joey did. I actually found out about you yesterday morning when you showed up at my house."

Amelia's mouth dropped. "You're kidding?!"

"No, I promise! I was just about to crawl back in bed when Joey showed up and told me what was happening."

A shy smile spread across Amelia's face. "Which would explain the lover leaving your house so nonchalantly."

Clark's face turned pink. "Mm-hmm."

"So, you said that partially remains true. What do you mean by that?" asked Amelia.

"Oh, I have a pretty tight schedule. I used to work seven days a week, but after some time I was allowed to have more of a say. And now I'm allowed two days off a week."

Looking up from her notebook, Amelia continued to ask Clark questions. "So, is today an off day?"

Clark nodded. "It sure is. And I thought I could show you some of my favorite parts of the property."

"I'm ready when you are."

Standing, Clark grabbed Amelia's hand. "All right, well then, let's go. I want to show you the beach."

Amelia stood, and Clark led the way down a path Amelia had yet to explore. Going past the cottage, the path weaved through the tall trees until it came to a wooden observation deck with a wooden staircase descending the cliff.

Leaning over the railing, Amelia looked down in disbelief. "Holy–how many steps are there?"

Clark shrugged. "I don't know. Maybe a hundred? Two hundred?"

Amelia looked back at Clark. "And where does it lead to?"

"The beach."

"But we're not going down there are we?"

Clark nodded. "Of course we are, Amelia. Come on, follow me."

Grabbing her hand, Clark started the trek down the stairs. "Hold on to the railing as we go down. The stairs are steep, and they can be slick from the sea mist."

Amelia grasped onto the stair railing, slowly taking each step. At some points, she wanted to close her eyes but knew that would end in catastrophe. As they reached the bottom of the stairs, they were greeted with golden sand and gentle blue ocean waves.

"Look up, back behind you," Clark said, pointing behind Amelia.

Amelia turned around to notice giant walls of rock that formed the cliffs they had just descended down. The beach was a secluded cove.

"Wow, this is unreal," said Amelia.

"Yeah, it's pretty great. Right now the tide is low, so we can really see the beach. But when the tide is high, it's nearly impossible to swim down here."

"How often do you come down here?" asked Amelia.

Clark grabbed Amelia's hand to help her down the last few steps onto the beach.

"Almost every morning, if I get up early enough."

Amelia and Clark walked toward the part of the beach near the rock wall. Taking a seat on a large piece of driftwood, Clark pointed next to him. "Want to sit down?"

Amelia kicked off her shoes and took a seat beside Clark. "Why do I have a feeling that you love it down here because nobody knows it exists?"

Clark took off his shoes and dug his feet deeply into the sand. "Because that's exactly why I love it."

"And I'm sure you bring all the ladies down here too," laughed Amelia.

Shaking his head, Clark laughed. "Nope, just a pushy reporter."

"Very funny. But I find that simply hard to believe."

Kicking some sand in the air, Clark replied. "It's true! This is one of my hiding spots. Everyone else at the Sea House who knows about it is afraid to come down here."

"Why are they scared?" asked Amelia.

"Because of the tide. You just never know when the beach is going to wash away. But don't worry. We have a few hours until that happens."

Amelia nodded. "So, it's just you and me down here. And I don't have my notebook out yet, so we're off the record."

Clark laughed. "Uh-oh. Off the record. This is getting pretty serious now, isn't it?"

Digging her toes into the sand, Amelia continued. "What's something that you wish people knew about you?"

Clark rested his chin on his hand. "Hmm...I don't know."

"Oh, come on!" said Amelia.

Clark threw his hands up in the air in defeat. "What?! That's such a deep question."

"That's the point, Clark!"

Clark looked out to the waves. "Fine. My name really isn't Clark James."

Amelia laughed. "Okay?"

"I'm serious. It's actually Robert. My friends back home and in the military used to call me Rob for short."

"So why change your name to Clark James?" asked Amelia.

"It's silly now, but before my first show at the club, Lawrence wanted me to change it. Rob wasn't that memorable or unique. Clark James was a way of reinventing myself."

"I see. I don't get the best vibes from Mr. Lawrence," said Amelia.

Clark scoffed. "Yeah, he can be a handful."

"I think you mean controlling."

"Yes, he can be that too. But I have to be somewhat grateful for the man. This life that I have is because of him."

"The life that you desperately want out of?" asked Amelia.

Clark's eyes darted back to the ocean. "Like I've said before…it's very complicated."

"So I hear. When was the last time you left the state of California?" asked Amelia.

"I haven't left California since I arrived."

"And when was that?" asked Amelia, crossing her arms.

"1945."

Amelia's eyes grew wide. "Clark–I mean Rob, uh–I don't know what to call you right now, but that's beside the point."

Clark let out a laugh. "It's okay. You can call me either."

"Have you been in Big Sur this whole time?"

Clark nodded.

"As in, you've been here at the Sea House? Working and living here since 1945?"

"Yes," Clark said.

"Well, no wonder you are so over it. You're incredibly burned out. You've been singing to people while they're eating dinner and getting drunk for more than 15 years now."

"I know, it's crazy right?" said Clark as he stood up from the log and made his way toward the ocean.

"Where are you possibly going right now?"

"For a swim! You should join me!" Clark said, running toward the waves while pulling off his shirt.

"I can't swim right now, Clark! I didn't bring a bathing suit," said Amelia, springing up from the log.

Clark ran into the water, plunging into the deep blue waves, popping up just moments later as he flashed a big childlike grin at Amelia. "Of course you can. Just get in."

"In my dress?" asked Amelia, holding out the hem of her emerald green dress that perfectly complemented her figure.

Jumping with the wave, Clark shouted, "Dress or no dress, just get in!"

Amelia shook her head. "Fine. I can't believe I'm doing this. But here I come!"

As she sprinted into the water, jumping right into the waves, Amelia let out a high-pitched scream before going underwater. When she re-emerged, the green dress flowed all around her like a blooming flower. She laughed as she swam up to Clark.

"Feels great, doesn't it?"

"It sure does!" Amelia said, smacking the water and causing it to splash in Clark's face.

"Oh, I see how it is, Amelia May," Clark said, wiping his face. "You shouldn't have done that."

Amelia smirked. "Oh, really? And why's that?"

Clark grinned. "Because... it's WAR now!" With that he swooped Amelia up in his arms, dunking them both under the water.

When they both re-emerged, Clark and Amelia were completely wrapped in each others' arms, laughing. "Is this the best interview you've ever done?" asked Clark, now just inches away from Amelia's face.

Amelia looked up at him. "Shouldn't I be asking you the questions, Clark?"

Clark smiled, giving Amelia's arms a squeeze. "I think it might be time for us to go back up top. The tide will be coming in soon, and we'll lose our shoes and my shirt."

A sudden realization washed over Amelia. She was still in Clark's arms. She could feel the warmth spreading across her face. "Oh, uh, yeah. I think that's a great idea."

CHAPTER 35

Amelia and Clark made the trek back up the stairs in their drenched clothing, arriving at Clark's cottage just 15 minutes later. Amelia was not sure if she should stick around or walk back to her car at the Sea House to drive back to her hotel.

Clark ran his hands through his wet hair. "You hungry? I was thinking I could make us some lunch and we could continue the interview."

Realizing she was still standing in front of Clark James in her completely soaked dress, Amelia began to feel embarrassed. She crossed her arms over her chest.

"I don't know. Maybe I should go back to my hotel and change clothes. I didn't necessarily plan to jump into the Pacific today."

"With the help of the California sun, your clothes will be dry by late afternoon. We can hang them on the porch. I'll give you some of my clothes to wear."

Amelia thought about it for a minute. She did need to continue the interview, and she was, in fact, hungry. Plus, she didn't really want to go back to her hotel. The idea of spending the afternoon with Clark James intrigued her.

"Okay. But don't give me something silly to wear," said Amelia as she followed Clark into the cottage.

Clark walked her into his bedroom, which was at the back of the house. Amelia stood in the doorway as he opened the drawers to his dresser. His bedroom was simple. A mahogany bed and headboard with two nightstands on either side. A white quilt covered the bed. A dresser on the other side of the room. Some black-and-white photos of a person who appeared to be Clark in his younger years standing with various people. Navy curtains hung on the room's single window.

"All right, here's one of my shirts," Clark said, handing Amelia a white t-shirt. "And here's a pair of shorts."

Amelia nodded. Clark stood in his wet jeans with his hands on his hips, staring at Amelia.

"Clark?" Amelia asked.

"Yes?"

"Can you get out so I can change?"

Clark's face flushed. "Oh! Yes, uh, sorry!"

"I'll be out in just a second," she said, closing the bedroom door.

Clark went into his bathroom and changed into a pair of his favorite loungewear pants. He then went into the kitchen to start preparing some lunch, opting for no shirt.

A few moments later, Amelia appeared. "Well, how do I look?" She twirled around the kitchen.

Clark applauded. "All right! Look at you! I would say this is your best look yet, Amelia May."

She laughed and tossed her head, her wet hair tousled. "Thank you for letting me borrow something while my clothes dry."

"Of course," Clark said, moving to the kitchen stove.

"And nice pajamas," laughed Amelia.

"Hey! These are *not* pajamas. They're loungewear pants."

Amelia rolled her eyes. "They're totally pajamas. And if you want to make lunch while wearing your pajamas then that's totally fine."

Clark did his best impression of a bodybuilder flexing. "That's right!"

Amelia laughed. "What's for lunch?"

"Well, I was thinking I could make us something really exquisite. My most famous dish."

Taking a seat at the table, Amelia pretended to be enthralled with Clark's remarks. "Ooh. Do tell."

"My mother's famous Southern mac and cheese," said Clark as he stirred the pot on the stove.

"Wow, ladies and gentlemen. He sings, he swims in the ocean, and he even cooks Southern cuisine!" Amelia joked.

Clark smiled while cooking for them. "You got that right. Make yourself at home. It should be ready in just a few minutes."

Amelia walked into the small living room that was adjacent to the kitchen. She noted the simple furniture. A small blue couch, a record player console against the wall with a stack of records on top, white curtains hanging to cover the large window in the room, and a few other black-and-white photos on the walls. One photo was Clark with a man and woman in the Sea House dining room. Another was Clark in uniform standing beside another man who was also in uniform.

"Lunch is served!" Clark announced from the kitchen. Amelia took a seat at the table and looked at the dish of cheesy goodness. It did, in fact, look delicious.

"So, who are the people in the photos in your living room?" asked Amelia while scooping out some cheesy noodles.

Clark poured two glasses of water. "One is from when my parents came to a show at the Sea House. It was actually the last time I ever saw them. And the other is of my buddy, Kent. We both were stationed in Paris together."

Amelia's eyes grew big as she tasted Clark's homemade recipe. "Wow, this might actually be the best mac and cheese I've ever had."

Clark held his arms out. "See? What did I tell you?!"

While continuing to indulge in the cheesy dish, Amelia laughed. "Do you ever talk to your friend Kent anymore?"

"Sadly, I do not. We went our separate ways when we returned to the States."

"I'm sorry to hear that. I bet you miss him."

Clark nodded. "I miss him like hell. We would spend hours in the French nightclubs. If we weren't working, you could find us throwing some drinks back and out on the dance floor."

"Why does that not surprise me?" Amelia asked as she took a sip of water.

"I haven't talked about my parents or Kent in so long. It's sometimes hard for me to even remember the sound of their voices."

Amelia looked up at Clark as she placed her glass back on the table. "Do you ever hang out with your coworkers here at the Sea House?"

Clark scoffed. "Ha. No, not really. The only person I really trust is Joey. And that's when he isn't being a pain in the ass."

"He seems to care a lot about you, though," Amelia said.

Clark nodded. "I think at the end of the day he does. But also at the end of the day, he's running the Sea House and reports to Lawrence."

"Yes, and then there's him. Mr. Lawrence."

Clark nodded. "Yeah, so what about him?"

"I don't know. I just have an uneasy feeling about him. It's like you're a cash cow to him," Amelia said.

Clark stood up, placing his bowl in the sink. "Yeah, well it definitely does feel that way at times."

"But it's a complicated situation, right?"

Clark smirked. "You're catching on quickly, Amelia."

Returning her empty bowl to the sink, Amelia replied. "I know."

"But the real question is how are your dance moves?"

The heat returned to Amelia's cheeks. "What?"

Grabbing her hand, Clark pulled her into the living room as soft jazz filled the room.

"You're not much of a jazz listener, are you?" Clark asked while pulling Amelia closer to him.

"Guilty. I am not as into the jazz scene as you are."

Swaying in circles around the room, Clark continued. "Jazz can make you feel so many ways, Amelia."

"Oh? How so?" Amelia asked as Clark twirled her around the room.

"Well, for starters it can make you feel powerful," replied Clark, placing his hand gently on her waist and pulling her in.

"And confident," Clark continued, spinning Amelia around to where her back was now pressed against him.

"And even a little sexy at times," he said in a hushed whisper as he spun Amelia back around to face him. He gently dipped her back into his arms.

"Oh!" Amelia laughed.

After pulling her up, Amelia was just a few inches away from Clark's face. They were so close that she could smell the scent of his aftershave, a clean scent mixed with cedar and something slightly sweet. Completely lost in the moment, Amelia threw her arms around Clark's neck, looking into his eyes.

"Maybe jazz isn't so bad after all," she whispered as their lips inched closer.

Before either of them knew it, their lips were touching. Clark brought his arms around Amelia's waist and drew her close to him. Amelia's hands wrapped around the back of his neck as she grazed Clark's hair.

The intensity of the moment quickly washed away from Clark's eyes as he looked back at Amelia. "I...uh...I'm sorry, I don't know if this is the best idea."

Amelia could feel the familiar rush of heat to her cheeks. "It's okay, Clark."

Dropping his hands from Amelia's waist, Clark ran his hands through his hair as he began to pace the living room.

"I don't know what I'm doing," he said, taking a deep breath.

Amelia followed him with her eyes. "Clark, what's wrong? It's okay."

"No, it's not. This isn't supposed to be happening," said Clark, picking up pace.

"I don't understand. Can you just tell me what is going on inside your head?" Amelia asked, grabbing his shoulders.

Clark flinched at her touch. "I think you need to leave, Amelia."

Amelia's mouth opened in protest. "What?"

Standing in the entryway of the living room, with his back toward Amelia, Clark intertwined his fingers and rested his hands on the back of his head. "You heard me! I said you need to leave."

"No, I'm not doing that. I'm sorry, Clark–"

Spinning around, Clark's widened eyes flashed with anger. "DAMN IT, AMELIA! I SAID LEAVE! NOW GET THE HELL OUT!"

She was too stunned for words, standing there in the living room with her mouth wide open and her arms folded against her chest.

"Fine," Amelia said as a lump formed in her throat. She dashed past Clark, bumping into his right shoulder.

"And you know what, Clark?" she said as she turned around at the kitchen door.

Clark's eyes remained fixated on the dark wood-paneled walls as he tried to avoid meeting Amelia's gaze. "I have never met a more pompous ass than you in my ENTIRE life."

He didn't move. He didn't try to convince Amelia otherwise. "The interview is over. I'll be heading back to LA tonight," Amelia said.

Slamming the door behind her, she hurried up the trail to the Sea House. It wasn't until Amelia was almost halfway there that she realized that she was still wearing Clark's t-shirt and shorts.

"Oh shit. My dress," she murmured. Amelia debated on turning around and getting her dress or saying the hell with it and never speaking to Clark James again. Too fired up about the sudden change in mood, she wasn't quite ready to go just yet.

Amelia marched back down the trail to Clark's cottage. Each angry stomp she took caused gravel and dust to kick up into the air. When she arrived, she aggressively banged her fist on the cottage's side door.

BANG! BANG! BANG!

Opening the door with confusion in his eyes, Clark said. "What are—"

"Oh, shut up, Clark," Amelia spit, throwing her hands in the air.

He leaned his body against the doorway.

"You've really got some nerve. First, you sleep with any woman who flutters their pretty little eyes at you. THEN, you finally start to open up to me with real, genuine answers."

"Amelia—"

She took a step closer to Clark. "I'm not finished! THEN, you invite me to this incredible beach and make me feel like I'm the only person who gets to be in your little world."

Clark stood up a little straighter as he stuffed his hands into his pockets.

"AND THEN, you cook and let me wear your clothes. Dance and kiss me. THEN, get all weird and tell me to get the hell out?!"

Clark's eyes darted toward the floor.

"I think you're scared. A scared little boy, Clark James," she said while brushing past him through the kitchen.

"I only came back because I forgot my dress. I'll be damned if I leave here wearing Clark James' t-shirt and shorts."

Closing the door, Clark followed Amelia out onto the porch.

"Amelia."

Amelia grabbed her dress off the porch railing and pulled it over her head, still wet.

"Amelia."

She continued to try to pull the dress down over her borrowed outfit.

"Amelia, stop it. You're right," Clark said as he grabbed Amelia's arm. "Take the wet dress off and come inside."

Feeling defeated, Amelia stopped struggling with the dress. Clark pulled her close to him and brought his lips toward Amelia's. This time neither of them drew back. They began to passionately kiss, dropping Amelia's dress onto the floor.

Grabbing her hand, Clark led the way back into the cottage with Amelia shutting the door behind them. Rushing their way back into the bedroom, Amelia found herself taking off Clark's white t-shirt, their bodies pressed together in Clark's bed.

And for the first time in nearly a decade, Clark felt something inside him light up. A feeling he forgot even existed...love.

CHAPTER 36

Later that evening, Clark and Amelia managed to make their way out of the bedroom. Sitting in the living room, Amelia laid across Clark's lap as they listened to his record collection.

"Amelia?" Clark asked as he ran his hand across her back.

Amelia turned to look back at Clark while admiring one of his live-recorded albums at the Sea House.

"Will you come to my show tomorrow night?"

Amelia replied. "Of course I will. I'm writing a story about you, remember?"

Clark chuckled. "Oh, so it's back on?"

Amelia perked up and sat on her knees beside him, leaning in close to Clark. "It's definitely back on, Clark James."

He kissed Amelia on the forehead. "Good. I can't wait for the world to read Amelia May's groundbreaking story."

"I like it when you call me Amelia. All my friends back home call me Milly," Amelia said as she leaned her head against Clark's shoulder.

"Milly? What a cute nickname."

Amelia scrunched her nose. "It's childish, and I'm not a child anymore."

Clark wrapped his arms around Amelia. "I'll call you Amelia, if you call me Rob."

"Will do, Rob," Amelia said with a chuckle.

"I want to answer some of your questions from earlier too."

"Okay. Go ahead," she said while looking up at Clark.

Clark cleared his throat. "You wanted to know earlier why I never left the Sea House. And the answer is. . .I can't."

Amelia smiled. "Sure, you can. I'm sure it's scary, but you can do it."

"No, that's not it, Amelia. I'm stuck here. When I first came here, I signed a contract that kept me here permanently. As in, forever."

Amelia cocked her head to the side in confusion. "Now what?"

"I know it sounds crazy. I didn't really read the contract Lawrence gave me. I was 23 and young and was just so excited to be offered a job singing."

"Are you saying that you're, like...frozen in time?" asked Amelia.

Clark nodded his head.

"Yes, I guess so. Technically, I'm still 23."

"Clark!" Amelia gasped, straightening her posture. "Be serious. I told you to cut it with the games. Now answer me truthfully!"

Holding his palms out, Clark replied. "And I am, Amelia!"

Amelia's notebook laid open on the floor beside her. She grabbed the black pen beside it and bit down on the end of it. "I don't know if I believe you."

"And I don't blame you! It's crazy. But all I know is that I signed a contract and then a clock struck in the dining room and scared me so badly that I thought I was having a heart attack."

Amelia scrunched her eyebrows as she concentrated on what Clark was saying.

"And then suddenly it stopped. And there I was, 23 forever."

"So, that's your secret? You're forever young?" Amelia jotted down notes in her notebook.

Clark let out a laugh. "Yeah. But it's not as great as it sounds. Everyone just moves on, and I'm just stuck here at this club."

Amelia stood up. "So, let's say you're telling the truth. Surely, there's a way out. You can't continue to sing jazz here for eternity. People will start to speculate something abnormal is going on."

Clark looked up at her.

"I don't really think there is a way out. I've read the contract through and through at this point."

Amelia looked out the window, staring at the dark sea as it glistened in the moonlight. "Does everyone who works here know?"

"Yes, they do. It's this unspoken thing. I gave up years ago trying to fight it."

"And again, if this is real...as you say it is. It's your life, Rob" Amelia said, collapsing beside him.

"I'm sure I can find the contract somewhere around here, if you would like proof, Amelia," Clark replied.

"So...your parents' death. What about the funeral? Did you get a hall pass for that?" asked Amelia.

Looking down at the worn hardwood floors, Clark quietly replied, "No...I did not. Because I can't. "

"What do you mean, you can't? What happens to you if you leave?"

Clark crossed his arms. "It's pretty crazy, Amelia. According to the contract, I'm toast."

"You're toast?!" Amelia was incredulous.

"Not literally. I'm dead. My heart stops beating."

"What in the world, Clark?!"

"I know, I know. I'm the idiot who didn't read the contract when signing it at 23," Clark replied flatly.

"And why didn't you take the time to read it maybe a bit more thoroughly?"

"Well, I was young, and I wanted it so badly. Lawrence also was really pressuring me. He made it seem like it was a sign-now-or-never deal."

"Ah, Mr. Lawrence," Amelia said, shaking her head.

"Yeah, I don't trust him anymore. But after a few temper tantrums and major embarrassing moments on stage, he has finally started to listen to me. He's slowly, over the course of the past few years, given me more freedom."

Amelia rolled her eyes. "Freedom? Such as giving you two days off a week? That's not freedom. He's controlling you. But how long can this continue? The man cannot expect you to sing here forever."

Clark stood up. "I'm not sure that anyone knows the answer to that question. The only thing people see at the Sea House are dollar signs. More shows means more money."

"Which I am sure is extreme pressure for you. But this is so unfair. Your entire craft and now life is dedicated to earning a living for others," Amelia said.

"Does Joey know about this agreement?" she asked, wrapping her arms around Clark.

"He does. And for the most part, he's an ally. Other times, I worry he's a snake in the grass. But he has really helped me throughout the years. Although I couldn't attend my parents' services, Joey, Larry, and Jane pitched in to cover the costs. Larry and Jane are members of my band."

"Well, that was very kind of them. But you still couldn't attend the services," Amelia said, pushing her hair back behind her ears.

"I know. But at this point, the bitterness and heartache are almost numb to me. It's like, how could things really get any worse?"

"I mean, there is something worse. You try to leave and your heart stops beating."

"And then there's that," said Clark.

Amelia shook her head. "I'm still trying to process all of this information. But tomorrow's show is going to be really interesting now."

Clark laughed and gave Amelia a squeeze. "You're right about that."

CHAPTER 37

PRESENT DAY

The afternoon sun was beginning to slip away as Neal and his grandparents pulled into the gravel parking lot of the abandoned club. The new central heating and air had been installed and Neal wanted to check it out. Plus, all this talk of Clark James made him eager to be back inside the historic club.

Neal, Grandad, and Nana made their way out onto the club's terrace. "I'm sure it's so surreal being back in this space, Nana," Neal said.

Nana scoffed. "Hmm. I can say that the day I left this place, I really thought I would never step foot in here again. Yet, here we are."

Grandad took a seat on one of the iron chairs with black paint peeling off of it. "So, what happened, Milly?"

Taking a seat next to Grandad, Neal asked, "Yeah, how long did you stay with Clark James?"

Nana walked over to the railing, taking in the views. "Gosh, it's just so crazy. I look out onto the water and I'm instantly taken back."

She turned her head to the left as the breeze blew her curly hair off her shoulders. "Over there!" Nana said, pointing toward the west side of the property. "That's where Clark's cottage used to be."

Nana turned around to face Neal and Grandad. And boys, did I spend a lot of time in that cottage. After that one day, I was so intrigued by Clark James. So much so that I was supposed to only stay a week, but a week turned into a few more."

"All right, Babes. You can keep those details to yourself!" Grandad said, waving his hands in the air.

"How long did you end up staying after all, Nana?" asked Neal.

"A little over a month. My boss thought I was never coming back!"

"But what happened? Did it all go down in flames?" asked Grandad, flicking the silver lighter he always carried with him.

Nana let out a melancholy laugh. "That's one way to put it. I loved Clark, but I wasn't necessarily the best person for him. I was just like the rest of them here at the Sea House."

Neal looked up at Nana. "What do you mean?"

Taking a seat beside Neal and Grandad, she continued. "Don't worry, Neal. I will explain everything. But just know that things were magical. They really were. Well...until they no longer were."

"What did you think after Clark told you all of those things? Like about the contract and his age?" asked Neal.

Nana let out a sarcastic laugh. "I thought he was pulling my leg at first. Trying to play some weird joke on me. I mean how would you react when you learn something that is so extraordinary?"

Grandad pulled a cigar out of pocket, crinkling the thin plastic wrapper into a ball in his hand.

"You definitely question it, that's for sure."

"Oh, Daniel. When are you going to quit those terrible things? You know they're not good for your heart," said Nana, pointing to the cigar in Grandad's hand.

"Hey, we're not talking 'bout me right now, Milly. This story is completely about you and Mr. Clark James," Grandad said, lighting the cigar.

He held it up to his lips, inhaled, and allowed the end to burn into red embers.

"There has to be a reason why I'm just now hearing this story after all these years. What happened, Milly? Between you and Clark James?"

"Well, you're exactly right, Daniel. Things ended tragically, like you said, in flames."

CHAPTER 38
Big Sur, California, 1962

Amelia's week-long stay at the Sea House turned into multiple weeks. She had ditched her hotel after the first week and began to spend the nights with Clark at his cottage. When he was not working, they were together. Exploring the property, swimming at the beach, staying up late dancing to records. And when Clark was working, Amelia would remain in the cottage, admiring the one photo album of Clark's life before the Sea House.

The album was a small, square leather-bound album containing only a few photos. One of Clark standing beside the piano in a solid white t-shirt with long pants on and no shoes. His short hair slicked to his head, parted in the middle. A wide grin with a missing front tooth as he stood beside a woman sitting at a piano. The woman's frizzy hair was pulled in a tight bun and she wore a solid-colored blouse with short sleeves and matching pencil skirt.

"Is this your mother?" Amelia asked Clark one night while they were laying on the living room floor after a show.

"It is. I must have been around 11 years old there," Clark said, pointing to the photo.

Amelia flipped to the next page in the album. It was a photo of Clark in uniform, appearing much older than the past photos. His hair faded on the sides, with the top longer and slicked back. He was sitting at a small bistro table with a cigarette in his right hand, a soft smile across his face.

"And this was when you were in the war?" Amelia asked.

"Yes, that was a few weeks after we'd arrived. Some parts of Paris were destroyed from bombs, but some parts were in okay condition. There was a café. Oh, what was the name of it?" Clark gazed at the photo, trying to remember details. "Ah! Café Lily!" Clark said, snapping his fingers. "Anyway, Café Lily was owned by a sweet little old man and his daughter. They loved the American soldiers, were always so kind to us. Oftentimes they would provide breakfast for us at no charge. I'm pretty sure Kent took that photo."

Amelia held the photo up closer to her face, examining it and then looking back at Clark. "Gah, you really haven't aged much, have you?"

Clark propped himself up on his right elbow. "See, what did I tell you, Amelia?"

Amelia put the photo down and crawled closer to Clark. "Do you ever show any signs of aging?"

Clark laughed. "No, I don't. And believe me, I spend a lot of time looking at myself in the mirror. Sometimes I am just actively searching for a small glimpse of...*something*. A gray hair, a wrinkle, something."

"Nobody ever says, 'You know what? That Clark James looks awfully young still?'" asked Amelia.

Clark shrugged his shoulders. "Not to my knowledge. But Lawrence is smart about it. He has the makeup team make me appear I'm gradually aging. He's even asked them if we should start dyeing my hair."

"Oh please!" Amelia laughed, running her hands through Clark's curled hair.

"I like your hair without all the product in it. It's curly," she said, laughing.

"Yeah, without all that grease and hairspray. I sometimes daydream about what I would look like older. Like, what would I look like with a beard?" Clark asked, framing his face with his hands

"Well, Clark James, I would say with a beard you might pass for your real age!" Amelia said, pouring wine into the two glasses that sat between them.

"Wouldn't that be the day?" laughed Clark, grabbing a wine glass and bringing it to his lips.

"You have what some people would kill for in this town, Clark. Everlasting youth, you know?"

"Oh, is that the route we're going with for the cover story, Amelia May?" Clark asked, leaning in close to Amelia's face.

"I'm still trying to figure that one out. Might need to see some more shows."

"Oh, I see. Come tomorrow?" Clark asked, his forehead now softly pressed against Amelia's.

"Maybe," Amelia replied with a smile.

"And then the next night?"

"I'll think about it."

"And then the next night after that?" Clark laughed.

"Now, you're really pushing it, Mr. James. But I'll see what I can do."

And Amelia did, in fact, attend every single show that she could. Although she knew about the agreement between Mr. Lawrence and Clark, she never brought it up when they were around the others. In fact, she actually enjoyed being in the audience of Clark's shows.

She was completely engulfed in the world of Clark James. It was truly unlike anything that she had experienced before.

One night during Clark's show, Amelia had a few too many glasses of champagne and decided she was going to speak to Joey about Clark's situation. While Clark was finishing up his second act, she noticed Joey slip backstage and decided to follow him.

Joey made his way through the darkened backstage and into Clark's dressing room. With just a few songs left of the set, Joey needed to make sure Clark had fresh water waiting for him as well as his outfit for the VIP party.

Amelia peeped her head into the doorway. "Psst, Joey."

Joey quickly turned and smiled. "Oh, hey, Amelia! What are you doing?"

Amelia tried her best to walk as normally as possible into the dressing room. "I've got some questions for you, mister."

Joey laughed. "Yeah? And what are those?"

She leaned against Clark's chair for support. "What do you know about the agreement?"

"The agreement?" asked Joey.

Amelia put her hand on her hip. "Oh, come on, Joey. Don't play dumb with me. The agreement between Rob and Lawrence."

Joey took Clark's blazer out of the dry cleaning bag. "Rob? Is that what you're calling him these days?"

"Real funny. Now answer the damn question," Amelia demanded.

Placing the jacket on a coat hanger, Joey answered. "Amelia, I think you've had a little too much to drink tonight. Let's get you some water."

"Joey, just stop. I know about the contract. I know it all."

Joey exhaled and looked at Amelia. "Okay, yes. I know about the agreement. So what?"

"So what?! How about the fact that the man has given plenty of his time to this damn nightclub."

"Listen, I agree. I think it's time for Clark's contract to end. But it's not up to me. It's up to Mr. Lawrence."

"How the hell can you live with yourself? How can any of you? When is it time to give it a rest?" asked Amelia.

"Amelia, I have tried. A couple years ago, I could tell that Clark was no longer happy. I expressed my concerns to Lawrence. But he's ruthless. Doesn't care. Clark is his biggest act to date."

Amelia grabbed the pitcher of water and poured herself a glass. "But there has to be a way out of the contract, right?"

Joey moved past her and began fluffing the pillows on the couch. "I don't know about that, Amelia."

"Oh, bullshit. You know all the secrets of this place. Are you under contract too? Is everyone here immortal assholes?"

"ENOUGH!" Joey screamed as he buttoned his blazer jacket.

"Nobody else has the same contract as Clark. After our previous main act, Mr. Lawrence wanted to scout out the next big thing. So he reached out to his business partner, Miss Vivian from New Orleans. She's the one who sent Clark to Lawrence."

Amelia adjusted the straps of her dress. "Okay. And what does her role have to do with any of this?"

"Well, she's just as involved as Lawrence. She's into some scary things, so I try to stay away from her as much as possible," Joey said, placing Clark's blazer back on the clothes rack.

"Scary things? Like what?" Amelia asked.

"You ever been to New Orleans, Amelia?"

Amelia shook her head. "No, but it's on my list."

"Well, don't go to Miss Vivian's. She's the queen of voodoo."

"Voodoo? Like a witch?"

"Exactly. And I don't know all the things she's done, but I do know that she has done some evil things with her voodoo tricks and spells."

Amelia's eyes grew wide. "Ooh. So she's the one who's behind the curse!"

Nodding his head, Joey continued to prepare the dressing room for Clark. "Bingo, Amelia."

Amelia took a sip of her water. "So, how does one break this curse?"

Heading toward the door of the dressing room, Joey replied, "It's impossible. Well, not impossible. But it's never going to happen."

"What is it?"

He turned around and looked at Amelia. "The club has to be destroyed in a natural disaster."

"What the hell?!" Amelia ran up to Joey.

"A storm, a hurricane, a fire…I don't know. Something has to completely destroy the place. But you think that's going to happen with Lawrence around? People are terrified of that man. Nobody goes behind his back."

Joey started to make his way out the door, but then turned. "The only other way is that Mr. Lawrence willingly agrees to end the contract. But with the amount of money Clark's show brings in, that will never happen."

"And what about the other acts in the past, Joey? What's happened to them?" Amelia asked, blocking Joey from the dressing room door.

Joey rolled his eyes. "Amelia, you're drunk, and I need to work. Move."

"Sorry, can't do that until you answer my question."

Shaking his head, Joey replied. "Ugh, I don't know, okay? I mean, I know it's probably not good. But even Lawrence doesn't tell me that stuff. I'm just the messenger. 'They're out. So-and-so's in. Tell the staff.' That kind of thing."

"But what do you think has happened to them, Joey?"

Joey slipped under Amelia's arm, making his way out of the dressing room and into the hallway. "I don't know, and I don't want to find out. You go around here looking for answers to questions like that, you're asking for trouble."

The alcohol caused Amelia's head to feel a little fuzzy. She leaned against the wall to stabilize herself. "Okay. Well, nice talking to you, Joey!"

"Yeah, yeah! I suggest you get back out there, Amelia, before people start really asking questions," Joey shouted, not looking back as he made his way toward the back of the stage.

CHAPTER 39

Amelia could hear the audience roar with cheers and applause as Joey darted out of the back to the banquet hall to help with the next part of the evening. Amelia couldn't believe it. What was she going to do? How could she help Clark? She wasn't sure, but she knew that she needed to talk to him as soon as possible.

Suddenly, Clark appeared in the doorway. He still had beads of sweat dripping down his face from the show.

"Hey, you," he said, pulling Amelia in for a kiss. "What are you doing back here? We gotta get to the VIP party."

Amelia smiled. "Great show! I wanted to come back here to meet you as soon as you were finished."

Clark quickly unbuttoned his damp shirt, took it off, and threw it on the couch. "Well, I'm so glad you're here. I feel so on fire up there knowing that you're in the audience."

Amelia laughed and offered Clark a glass of water. "Well, you truly did outdo yourself tonight."

"You say that every time, Amelia," Clark said, taking the glass from her.

"And that's because you continue to impress me with each show."

Clark pulled his new blazer over the fresh shirt and held out his arms. "How do I look?"

Amelia smiled. "Very handsome."

"Thanks! Now let's go to the VIP party and then get home," he said as he kissed Amelia on the cheek.

"Okay, but I need to tell you something."

Clark grabbed her hand and started to lead the way out the door. "Okay, can you tell me when we're on the terrace?"

"No, not really. I snuck back here during your final set to corner Joey into telling me more details about the contract."

Clark froze. "What? Amelia, you could get in deep trouble for that. What if Lawrence followed you or found out?!"

"I know! But I know how to end the agreement."

Clark shut the dressing room door and turned toward Amelia. "Okay. I'm listening."

"Well, Joey said something first about a lady named Vivian. And how she's a voodoo queen."

"Vivian? She was who I first worked for when I got a job at a bar in New Orleans."

Amelia opened a bottle of wine and poured herself a glass. "Yes. Well, she's apparently a witch. And she sent you to Mr. Lawrence because he needed the next big thing."

"Come again? A witch?" asked Clark.

"Oh, come on. You say that like it's crazy. Like you're not already stuck at the age of 23!"

Clark grabbed the bottle of wine and took a sip. "Very true. Go ahead."

"Anyway, she put some spell on the contract. And the only way to end it is if Mr. Lawrence agrees to end it."

"Well, that will never happen," said Clark.

"Or if a natural disaster occurs. A fire, earthquake, hurricane. Something just completely destroys the place."

"Again, that will never happen," Clark said while taking another pull of wine straight from the bottle.

"What if we can talk Lawrence into ending it?" Amelia said, inching closer to Clark.

"Amelia, it's sweet of you to try to help. But that is just never going to happen. The man is completely evil."

"I know, but I think we could figure something out. Get Joey to help us. He seemed to be on your side." Amelia grabbed Clark's hand.

"Okay. We can brainstorm later tonight. But we have to get out to the terrace now for the VIP party. I just want to get it over with and then get you back in my bed," Clark said as he went in for a quick kiss.

Amelia laughed. "Okay, but I'm going to need way more wine to get through this party."

CHAPTER 40

The next morning Clark woke up to the golden sunshine peeking through the crack of the drawn curtains in his bedroom. He rolled over and moved his hand across the bedsheets to embrace Amelia only to find that she was no longer in the bed. He sat up, opened his eyes, and instantly felt a throbbing ache above his right eye. Judging by the amount of drinks he and Amelia had the night before, he was not surprised to wake up feeling hungover.

"Amelia?" He croaked, pulling the covers over his head to block out the sunlight. No response. Clark slowly made his way out of the bed and into the kitchen. Still no Amelia. No aroma of coffee brewing. Maybe she was outside on the porch. But when he opened the kitchen door, Amelia was not out there either.

Clark went back inside and pulled on a pair of jeans and a t-shirt, noticing the pile of clothing on the floor from the night before, a mixture of both his and Amelia's. After drinking a few glasses of wine at the VIP party and managing to not mention their recent discoveries, the two stumbled back home to the cottage to continue the party. Once they arrived, they popped open a bottle of champagne on the porch and moved inside to dance, ending their night in Clark's bedroom.

But now Amelia was nowhere to be found. Clark walked to the wooden staircase that led down to the beach. Maybe she was taking a morning swim. That always helped Clark shake off a hangover. But when he peered down over the railing, Amelia was nowhere to be spotted.

"Where is she?" Clark murmured. He began to walk back up toward the Sea House. As Clark entered the back entrance of the club, the cool air from the A/C greeted him. It felt nice. The California sun was already beginning to warm things up this morning. Clark walked into his dressing room and flipped on the light. Still no Amelia. Perhaps she was in the dining hall.

He continued to walk backstage when he began to hear whispers and what sounded like someone crying. Clark slowly made his way closer to the stage, where the thick velvet curtain was closed, separating him from whomever or whatever was on the other side.

"It shouldn't be this way. It doesn't HAVE to be this way!" a voice said. Clark immediately recognized the voice. It was Amelia. But who was she talking to? Clark crept closer to the curtain so he could hear more.

"Oh, shut up," said another person. He'd recognized that voice anywhere. It was Mr. Lawrence.

"You really have some nerve, don't you?" asked Mr. Lawrence.

Amelia sniffled. She was crying. "But how much longer can you really let this go on?! He's done his fair share of time. And you certainly have made your money off of him. You all have!"

Clark was close enough now that he could see slightly into the dining hall through the crack of the stage curtain. Amelia was sitting at the end of a front booth with her head in her hands. Mr. Lawrence was standing in front of the table. He began to eagerly pace in front of the stage.

"Everything was fine. And I mean EVERYTHING. Until you came along. I should have never brought you here."

Amelia dropped her hands into her lap. "You are so full of it. How could you even say that? You don't even know him, much less care about him. He's been desperately craving another life for years now. He has nobody. Not a single person here understands him like I do."

Mr. Lawrence slapped his hand on the table. "ENOUGH!" Clark jumped while leaning in closer to the curtain.

"Now you listen to me, dammit. I did not hire you to come here and wreck all of my plans. I brought you here to befriend the boy. Make him happy. Become his muse. Make him feel like he was in *love*."

Amelia stood up, jabbing her finger into Mr. Lawrence's chest. "AND I DID THAT. I played the part, and I played it well. Until I was no longer acting. I've gotten to know him during these past few weeks, and I just can't continue this."

Clark felt like the floor was being pulled out from underneath him. He couldn't breathe. All of the drinks from last night felt like they were going to come up any moment now. What was Mr. Lawrence talking about? Hiring Amelia? His face began to flush with anger, and his vision became hazy as his eyes filled with tears.

With all the rage in his body, Clark pulled the curtains open, startling the two. Immediately, Mr. Lawrence and Amelia's eyes darted to the stage.

"Oh no," Amelia cried.

"You..." Clark said as he jumped off the stage onto the dining room floor. He walked to Mr. Lawrence and Amelia. "You lied to me, Amelia."

"Rob, I can ex–"

"SAVE IT!" Clark shouted. "I heard everything. And you..." Clark said, turning around to face Mr. Lawrence.

"You've done it. Congratulations, Lawrence. Just when I think you can't stoop any lower, you prove me wrong."

"Clark, this is all a misunderstanding. You've just walked in at the wrong part of the conversation. Take a seat and let me explain." Mr. Lawrence nonchalantly pulled a cigar from his pocket.

"A misunderstanding? Let me get this straight. You KNEW I was miserable. I begged you for years to let me out of here. You saw that I was lonely. So what do you do?"

Tears began to stream down Amelia's face.

"You hire her."

Pointing to Amelia, Clark continued. "A fucking phony. A con artist just like you, Lawrence."

Amelia let out a cry, "Clark–"

"I'm not finished. YOU hire her to pretend to be in love with me. To be–what was it that you said? Oh, my *muse.*"

Mr. Lawrence brought the cigar up to his lips. "All right Clark, that's enough. You've figured it all out. But it was for your own good."

Clark let out a sarcastic laugh. "My own good? What kind of twisted asshole are you?"

Mr. Lawrence exhaled cigar smoke. "You were so pathetic. You were getting drunk and going up on stage looking like a complete idiot. I almost got rid of you, but Joey convinced me not to. Said you were just a *sad, lonely, little crybaby.*"

The heat was returning to Clark's face.

"God, you're so ungrateful, Clark. I have given you everything. And here I was giving you something you desperately wanted...your chance at love," laughed Mr. Lawrence.

Clark turned and headed toward the front entrance of the Sea House. "Yeah, well, you know what? I wish you had gotten rid of me. Because there's nothing worse than being stuck inside this place."

With that, he slammed the door and began the walk back to the cottage. When he arrived, he realized he could no longer hold back last night's drinks. Running into the bathroom, Clark vomited all of the previous night's bad decisions. He wasn't sure which was worse, the stomach cramps, the shattered heart, or the tears that continuously rolled down his cheeks.

But when the rage returned, he got up off the bathroom floor and marched into his bedroom where all of Amelia's belongings were. He picked her green dress off the floor, her pearls from the first night they met, and any other remnants reminding him of her. Stomping through the house, Clark swung open the kitchen door and threw Amelia's belongings out onto the porch.

Clark slammed the door and bolted the lock. He marched back to his bedroom and threw himself onto the bed, tucking himself under the covers. He somehow fell asleep, and through a groggy haze, he could hear a faint knock on the cottage door. But he didn't care. He wasn't getting out of bed anytime soon.

CHAPTER 41

PRESENT DAY

Neal and his grandparents sat on the terrace in complete silence. It was so quiet that they could have heard a pin drop. The sun was setting and within the next half hour, the orange sky would become filled with stars. Crossing her arms in front of her chest, Nana stared off into the distance, reliving every memory that she just shared with Neal and Grandad.

"Were you really working as a reporter?" asked Neal.

Nana cleared her throat and looked at Neal. "Yes, but I was basically an intern for the magazine. I really did want to write the story on Clark James, though. Nobody wanted it, and I took it thinking that it would give me that foot in the door that I needed."

"But how did Mr. Lawrence end up striking that deal with you?" asked Neal.

Nana rubbed her temples with her fingers. "Gosh, I still feel those same terrible feelings today that I did back then. See, I told you that I wasn't the best person during this time period."

"It's okay, Nana," Neal said with a reassuring smile.

"It's really not. But the day after I met Mr. Lawrence at that first concert, he asked to meet with me to go over some ground rules."

Nana continued, twirling the buttons on her blouse "He was a control freak and wanted to make sure I understood that this story had to be very positive and not only put Clark but the Sea House in a good light. And as we were finishing up the conversation he said he had a proposal for me."

"Which was?" asked Grandad.

"If I stuck around a little longer than I had planned and made Clark happy, he would give me ten thousand dollars."

Neal chuckled. "That's it? Ten thousand dollars? Oh, come on, Nana."

"Neal, not everyone is a fancy property developer like you. I was a young woman trying to make it in California as a journalist. That was a lot of money to me. That money was going to help me find a decent place to live, potentially help me get out of the country to see new places. And I thought why not? It would be fun to spend time with a famous musician. So, I went for it."

Grandad stood up. "But you ended up actually falling for him, didn't you?"

Nana nodded. "I did end up developing feelings for him. And I would say that he probably was my first grown-up love. And my first heartbreak as well."

"Did you guys eventually get back together?" asked Neal.

"Well, sort of. Clark didn't see me the same ever again after that. And I don't blame him. I completely broke his heart."

Grandad walked over to the terrace railing. "But you did try to make amends, right, Babes?"

Nana nodded. "Oh yeah. I knew that I had to help him and make things right, even if he no longer wanted to have anything to do with me."

Standing up, Neal turned to walk back toward the club. "I definitely want to continue this story, but it's almost dark. We haven't replaced the lights out here yet. Why don't we go back to the house?"

"That sounds like a great idea," said Nana.

"I agree! Let's get out of here," said Grandad.

CHAPTER 42

Back at Neal's place, they decided to keep things simple for dinner and order pizza. One large pepperoni pizza for the boring pizza lovers and one large Hawaiian pizza for the fun pizza lovers. Neal placed the boxes of cheesy goodness on the kitchen table in front of Nana and Grandad.

Grandad opened a pizza box. "Oh, gross. Not ham and pineapple. You two are psychopaths for liking pineapple on pizza."

Nana looked up from her iPad and peered over her reading glasses. "Hey, you watch it, mister. Pineapple has a home and it's definitely on pizza."

Neal placed plates on the table along with a pitcher of water. "Pineapple has a place on anything."

Grandad rolled his eyes and grabbed a slice of pepperoni pizza. "Whatever you two say."

Neal took a seat in between his grandparents and poured them each a glass of water.

"So, Nana, what happened next at the Sea House?"

Nana dabbed her mouth with her napkin. "Well, it wasn't good. In fact, things began to spiral out of control from then on."

"How so, Babes?" asked Grandad.

"I attempted for days to talk to Clark, but he wouldn't give me the time of day. For the rest of that week, he did not leave his cottage. With his demanding schedule, that was very unusual. But I think Lawrence knew that this was one moment he was just going to have to roll with."

"But what about the shows?" asked Neal.

"Lawrence was not happy about it, but he knew he was walking on eggshells with Clark. So, they told everyone that Clark was feeling ill and would be taking the rest of the week to rest and recover at home. For the first time in almost 30 years, they had a week without shows at the Sea House." Nana grabbed a second slice of pizza.

"Oh, I bet Lawrence hated that, that money-hungry asshole," said Grandad.

"Oh, he did. But as much as he hated it, I gotta hand it to the man. He kept his composure and attitude under control for a few days at least."

"But how did you finally get to Clark?" asked Neal.

"Well, first, I feel like I need to explain myself a little better."

Neal and Grandad both looked up from their plates.

"The day that I was talking with Lawrence in the dining hall, I was trying to convince him to end the contract with Clark. To finally give it up. I woke up that morning feeling so happy and sad at the same time," said Nana.

She took a sip of water and continued. "I was starting to feel guilty for agreeing to the deal with Lawrence. And I was also starting to feel like Clark and I were never going to have any chance if he was to stay at the Sea House."

Nana placed her napkin on her empty plate. "That morning I woke up early. The drinks and the guilty conscience kept me awake most of the night. I went outside to sit on the porch, but I saw Lawrence entering the back entrance of the Sea House and I thought that was my chance to talk to him. But I was silly for thinking that he would ever actually agree with me."

Grandad cleared his throat. "Well, Babes. You shouldn't still beat yourself up over it. That was so many years ago."

Nana gave Grandad's hand a pat. "I know. But talking about all of this for the first time in years has me experiencing those same feelings again. And since Clark was no longer speaking to me, I had to bring in reinforcements. So, I got Joey to help me with a game plan."

CHAPTER 43
BIG SUR, CALIFORNIA, 1962

Amelia continued to show up at Clark's cottage for the remainder of the week, each time waiting on the porch for at least an hour. But he would never come to the door. Eventually, he had to return to the stage. She attended every show the following week, but Clark continued to remain steadfast.

Amelia used to find herself locking eyes with Clark during his sets, but now he kept his eyes forward. He was distant. She was once the first person he would greet after the show ended, but that was no longer the case. Sometimes Clark skipped the terrace parties completely. If he did show, he would shake a few hands and chat with some people while standing at the bar. But after he finished a drink, Clark would sneak out and return to the cottage.

One night, Amelia decided she was going to get Clark to talk to her whether he liked it or not. After keeping him in sight the entire evening, she noticed he slipped away after placing his empty cocktail glass on the bar. She quickly scurried through the crowd and out the front door of the Sea House. Following as quickly as her thin stilettos would allow, she dashed down the windy trail to catch up with Clark.

"Clark!" she yelled.

THE CLUB BY THE SEA

He continued to weave along the trail. "ROB! PLEASE!" Amelia screamed.

He turned around, the wind blowing his slick hair out of place as his untied bow tie fluttered. "WHAT?" he asked sharply.

"Can you please just listen to me. Hear me out, at least?"

Clark threw up his hands. "Oh please, Amelia. What could you possibly have to say that's going to change my mind or make things better?!"

Amelia folded her arms against her body to keep herself warm from the cool breeze. "I know, I'm sorry. I shouldn't have agreed to that deal with Lawrence. But what I ended up feeling with you was real."

Looking off into the distance, Clark shook his head.

"I know you're mad. You have every right to be mad at me, Rob."

"Jesus! Stop calling me that. You don't get to call me by my real name anymore."

Amelia could feel the tears burning her eyes. "Please just let me help you. Let me get you out of here."

Clark walked slightly closer to Amelia. "Yeah, and how are you going to do that, Amelia?! I'm never getting out of here. I'm the idiot who signed my life away for some tiny bit of fame."

"I have a plan!" Amelia said, moving closer to Clark, the wind tousling his hair.

"Oh yeah?! Well, save it. I've watched people come and go over the years. I'm used to it. I can do just fine without you. I don't need you in my life, Amelia."

"Clark, you don't mean that."

Clark wiped his eyes. "Well, I do. Go back to LA. Find someone who will make you happy, Amelia. I'm not that guy."

With that, Clark turned and continued the walk back to his cottage, leaving Amelia in the dark.

When she arrived at the terrace, she was a mess. No longer able to hold it in, Amelia allowed the tears to flow as she sobbed. The air felt like it was completely being sucked out of her chest. She leaned over the railing to support herself.

Joey happened to be passing by with a tray of empty glasses when he noticed Amelia.

"Hey, hey, hey! Amelia, what's going on?"

Peering over her shoulder, Amelia looked at Joey, black mascara running down her face. "He hates me. He wants nothing to do with me ever again."

Joey placed his left hand on her shoulder. "Hey, he's just upset right now. Give him some time and he'll come around."

Amelia gasped for air. "No, no, no. I've messed up so badly. And I just want to help him, but he won't even look at me."

Joey glanced around the terrace and then back at Amelia. "Okay, come with me. Let's get out of here. You don't need anyone looking at you. Or worse, Lawrence coming over here."

Amelia nodded as she grabbed onto Joey's arm as he led the way back inside the Sea House to Clark's dressing room.

When they reached Clark's dressing room, Joey shut the door and turned around to give Amelia his full attention.

"Okay, I want to help, Amelia. Clark is miserable. He's been miserable for years. But then you came along and I could see him transforming. You turned him into someone who I didn't even recognize."

Amelia took a seat on the velvet couch and smiled. "I have a plan, but it's crazy. And I need your help."

Joey nodded. "Okay. How crazy are we talking?"

"Like we're taking this place down."

Joey blinked.

"I know it's crazy. But Clark's never going to be able to leave unless this place is gone. And I know it's your livelihood. And I know--"

Joey held his hand up. "Okay, I'm in. It's time for a change anyway. I've contributed enough to damaging Clark's life. He deserves to be free."

Amelia jumped up from the couch and ran to Joey.

"OH, JOEY! Thank you, thank you, thank you!" She threw her arms around him.

"Okay, okay. I have to get back to the terrace soon. Tell me the plan, please!"

In just a few moments, Amelia unveiled her plan to save Clark James.

CHAPTER 44

The next few days were spent planning *Operation: Save Clark James*. Joey and Amelia divided up the tasks that needed to be completed in order to make the plan go smoothly.

The plan was to take place at the end of summer, but that all changed when one day, Joey overheard Mr. Lawrence talking on the phone with Miss Vivian. Making his way into Lawrence's office to discuss the night's operations, Joey heard him let out a loud belly laugh.

"Well, it's just pathetic, Vivian. I cannot handle it anymore. The boy is moping around here, making everyone feel sad. And I believe it's time."

Joey held his breath as he leaned in closer to the doorway of the office. The thick cloud of cigar smoke rolled from under the door, making Joey's eyes burn.

"Well, what do you mean? I'll do what we've always done," said Lawrence.

Joey arched his right eyebrow, continuing to concentrate on the conversation.

"I mean, it sure has been a long time since I've had to do it, but I'm not afraid to do it again."

THE CLUB BY THE SEA 251

Do what? Joey wondered. What was he talking about?

Mr. Lawrence coughed a deep and loud cough this time. "He's shown his true colors way too many times, Vivian. And the answer is simple: The boy must die."

Joey's eyes widened. Die?!

"It's almost too easy with Clark James though. He drinks a little too much and–*oops*–takes a tragic fall off the cliff and into the sea. And on to the next. I'll just have to figure out what to do about that stupid girl."

Joey slowly exhaled the breath that he'd been holding.

"She'll do anything for money. I could easily offer her another 10k to kill the story and send her on her way. No record of Clark James. And then we find someone with a new talent. Perhaps we will jump on this rock and roll train, finally."

Joey pressed his entire body up against the wall outside of Mr. Lawrence's office. He continued to hold his breath, listening to the conversation.

"Oh, Vivian! It's time! We've made a fantastic profit off of the boy, never mind the fact that we were never actually sending money to his family like he requested. Denying that little request has saved us tons of money, so you're welcome for that."

Joey felt beads of sweat drip down his face. The money to Clark's parents?! It never was being sent. Joey shook his head in disbelief. He should have known. Why would Lawrence ever do something for someone else?

"When, you ask? Well, I would like to have it sooner rather than later. Maybe, let's say, by the end of the month? When can you have a new one out here?"

Joey imagined Mr. Lawrence exhaling cigar smoke in between words.

"Ah, very well then. Let's get to work, Vivian. You find me my next main act, and I'll get rid of Clark James!"

Mr. Lawrence let out a malicious laugh and slammed the telephone into its cradle. Joey made his way back into the dining room. He nervously took his place at the tables, adjusting the crisp, white tablecloths.

"Joey!" Mr. Lawrence shouted as he walked into the dining room.

Joey slightly jumped at the sound of his name being called. "Ah, yes, sir. How can I help you?"

Mr. Lawrence let out a sly smile. "Geez, Joseph. You're extra jumpy today. Everything ready for tonight's show?"

Joey eagerly nodded. "Yes, sir. Same tight ship routine as always."

"Great! Big things are coming soon."

Joey held up a wine glass, breathing a short puff of air onto the rim to give it an extra shine. "Oh yeah? Do tell, sir."

"Well, let's just say some changes are in store!" Mr. Lawrence said, making his way to the Sea House's front entrance.

"Oh, that sounds very exciting. I can't wait to see what all you have up your sleeve, Mr. Lawrence," Joey replied.

"All good things, of course! See you this evening at showtime, Joey!"

"See you at showtime, sir!" Joey said, waving theatrically to Mr. Lawrence.

When he saw Mr. Lawrence's car flash by in the front windows of the Sea House, Joey quickly ran into the office to telephone Amelia. Since she no longer was staying with Clark, Amelia had returned to the hotel where she originally stayed when she arrived in Big Sur. She had given Joey a card at the beginning of her stay with the hotel's phone number and information.

Joey pulled the small rectangular card out of his apron, the edges now crinkled. *The Pink Flamingo Inn* was printed across the card in bold pink cursive font.

Geez, they'll name a hotel anything these days, Joey thought. Quickly, he grabbed Mr. Lawrence's black telephone from the cradle and rotated the phone to dial the numbers.

1, **cling** 5, **cling** 8, **cling**

With each number, Joey's fingers fiercely rotated the dial until the ringing sound echoed in his ear.

"The Pink Flamingo Inn. This is Sue. How can I assist you today?"

"Hi, Sue. I would like to speak with Amelia May, please. She's a guest staying at your hotel."

"Ah, yes. Is Ms. May expecting your call, sir?"

"Uh, sure. We're great friends."

"Very well, then. I will let her know. Please hold one moment while I give her room a ring."

"Thank you, Sue."

Joey held the phone to his ear, listening to the static as he waited for Amelia to answer. He carefully scanned through the black leather notebook on Mr. Lawrence's desk, flipping through pages of scrawny handwriting to find any kind of helpful information.

"Hello?" Amelia's voice suddenly echoed through the phone.

"Amelia, it's me. Joey!"

"Ah, Joey. I was just about to head to the Sea House. How are you?" Amelia asked.

"Not good. We have a problem," Joey replied, continuing to flip through the lined pages of Mr. Lawrence's notebook.

"Oh no. What is it?"

"We need to expedite our plan for Clark. He doesn't have much time left here."

"What do you mean?"

"I overheard Lawrence on the phone with Vivian earlier today. And he's going to have Clark taken care of by the end of the month!"

"Joey, what do you mean *taken care of*? Like, he's ending the contract?"

Joey tapped the page he was looking for with his index finger. "Amelia, no! I mean he's going to have Clark killed."

Amelia gasped. "Killed?!"

"Yes. Murdered. Killed. Kaput. I don't have much time to chit-chat, but we need to make Operation: Clark James happen as soon as possible. There's no telling when Lawrence will act. It could be in days or weeks. We don't have much time."

"Shit, shit, shit! Joey, this is so messed up. Okay, I think we can make it happen soon. We just need Clark on board. And that's going to be hard to do since he'll barely even look at me or speak to me."

"Oh, trust me. He's going to listen to you when we tell him this information. Let's tell him together, okay?"

Amelia let out a sigh. "Okay. I'm completely terrified. But this is the only way."

"You're right, Amelia. It's the only way. I'll see you soon, okay?"

"Okay. Bye, Joey."

Joey hung up the phone and picked the notebook up off the desk. He knew it was in there somewhere. Years ago, Joey had learned how to perfectly snoop through Mr. Lawrence's office without leaving a trace.

He walked over to the massive mahogany built-in bookshelf that occupied the majority of the wall behind Mr. Lawrence's desk. Running his hands along the variety of shaded spines of the different books, he felt the familiar slight break between the hardback book covers. Mr. Lawrence had invested a lot of money into having a custom-made safe that was disguised as stacks of books on his shelf.

Slightly caddy-cornering the disguised safe off the bookshelf, Joey located the small, faded red dial on the side of the books. Such a shame that Mr. Lawrence spent all this money in a cleverly disguised safe only for him to have written the combination of the lock in his notebook years ago.

Joey quickly looked down to read the code from the notebook. He turned the dial with his other hand.

1......9.......8......9.

The safe door opened slightly. Bingo. I'm in, Joey thought. He quickly looked over his shoulder to make sure no one was in the room. Then, he pulled the door open, revealing stacks of banded US dollar bills, the money belonging to Clark that Lawrence had kept all these years. Stolen from him.

Joey picked up the crisp stacks of Andrew Jacksons, placing them in the pockets of his apron. He took as many as he could without it appearing too slim in the safe. Grabbing one last stack from the back of the safe, something caught Joey's eye, the shine of something familiar as the light from the room hit it.

He carefully slid his hand into the safe, feeling for the object. Something cold touched his palm. He pulled out the object and felt his heart stop. It was the gold hair clip adorned with jeweled ivy leaves that Beverly often wore during the shows.

"Oh no. Not Beverly," Joey whispered.

He looked back in the safe and pushed the money aside to see more objects toward the back. One by one, he felt each object, pulling them out of the safe.

The silver broach that the former main act, Bonnie Frank, always wore during shows. The black silk scarf that the former lead guitarist,

William, often wore. Joey continued to graze his fingers along the back of the safe until he felt a small, cold object. So small it was like a pebble. He pulled it out and felt all of the color drain from his face. A faded gold tooth. Teddy's gold tooth.

"Oh, no, no, no, no. Teddy!"

Joey felt the sweat dripping down his back as he looked at the possessions of friends and former colleagues.

"That sick bastard!" Joey realized these were all mementos Mr. Lawrence kept after he arranged the murders of Bonnie Frank, Beverly, William, Teddy, and who knows how many others.

"It's only a matter of time before Clark's next...or even me!" Joey whispered as he frantically placed the items back in the safe. He was careful to put them in the back behind the stacks of money.

He closed the safe's door and placed it back in line with the books on the shelf. He took a deep breath.

All these years of being devoted to Mr. Lawrence, thinking he was somewhat safe from the games and tactics, Joey felt for the first time completely afraid of the man. Not just afraid but utterly terrified. He knew he needed to get Clark and himself away from the Sea House as soon as possible.

CHAPTER 45

They decided to execute the plan the following Monday. And once everything was set in stone, there was just one last thing to do. They had to tell Clark. To prevent any mistakes or nerves from taking over, Amelia and Joey agreed that Clark only needed a 24-hour notice. So, the Sunday before, they knocked on his cottage door.

Clark opened the door, noticing Joey first. "Hey Joey." Amelia appeared from behind Joey, and Clark instantly looked down at the ground. "What are you doing here, Amelia?" he said under his breath.

"Look man, we need to come inside. We have something important to tell you," said Joey.

Eagerly nodding her head, Amelia begged, "Please, Clark."

Clark leaned his arm against the door frame and looked at both of them. "Hmm...okay, fine. Come in."

Once inside, Joey and Amelia took a seat at the kitchen table. Clark remained standing by the door, his arms crossed.

"Sit down, Clark. You're going to want to hear this," said Joey.

Slowly Clark walked to the table. "Okay..."

Pulling out the chair, he took a seat opposite Amelia and Joey. "What the hell is going on?"

Amelia exhaled. "Okay, I know you're mad at me. And I am so, so sorry. I deserve every bit of your hate right now. But what I cannot do is leave here and know that you're stuck."

Clark rolled his eyes and crossed his arms. "Amelia..."

"Clark, listen to what she has to say. This plan is crazy, but we need to get you out of here as soon as possible," said Joey.

"Like it's that easy! A wave of a magical wand and–poof–I'm free!" Clark said, waving his hands sarcastically.

"Clark, Lawrence killed them."

Clark's eyes darted from Amelia to Joey. "Killed who, Joey?"

"Bonnie Frank, Beverly, Teddy...and you're next," Joey said, looking directly into Clark's eyes.

"Have you known this all along?" Clark asked, crossing his arms.

"NO! I've been in the wrong a few too many times, but this is one thing I had no idea about. Lawrence, that sick sick bastard. He kept their stuff, Clark. The items they wore or were known for. Beverly's gold clip. Teddy's tooth."

"Jesus," said Clark.

"It's terrible. I found them in the safe. Along with your money, Clark. We're going to get that for you. But listen to Amelia."

Amelia nervously cleared her throat. "Tomorrow, a taxi cab is going to arrive at exactly 3:30 pm. You will get in it and never look back, Clark. You will never again set foot inside the Sea House."

Clark scoffed. "Okay....again, like it's that easy."

Amelia continued. "There are some things that Joey and I have been working on over the last few days to make this plan work. And so far, it's all ready. But we need you to help play a role."

Clark placed his hand under his chin. "All right."

Amelia continued to unveil the plan to Clark, while Joey interjected with support when Clark questioned anything. When Amelia finished, Clark stood and began to pace the kitchen with his hands cupped around the back of his head.

"Whew. I don't know guys. This is absolutely crazy," said Clark.

Amelia and Joey nodded in unison.

"And this is dangerous. Joey, this could ruin everything for you. And Amelia? You too. Have you guys thought this all the way through?"

"Clark, we have. And it's scary. But you need to get out of here. We both have fucked up badly when it's come to you in the past. So, please let us help you," Joey pleaded.

Taking a deep breath, Clark covered his face with his hands. With tears in his eyes, he looked up at Amelia and Joey and said, "Okay. Let's do this."

Joey and Amelia jumped out of their chairs. Tears glistened in Amelia's eyes. Ever so slowly, Clark finally caved, pulling in both of them for a hug.

"I don't know what to say exactly," Clark croaked.

Joey patted Clark's back. "It's okay, man. You don't have to say anything. We got you."

CHAPTER 46

On Monday morning at 8:30, Clark woke up one last time inside his cottage. He didn't have much time to reminisce because the plan was soon going to kick into action. For a moment, he walked through the house and took it all in. Looking at the few photos he had framed on the walls, remembering all the moments he'd spent both alone and with many different people over the years.

He walked into his room and opened the dresser drawers, pulling out only a few clothing items. Then he took a few different options from his closet: a good rain coat, three button-down shirts, a pair of black slacks, a hat, sunglasses, and a pair of jeans. The toiletry items were going to stay along with the personal photos. If he was going to disappear, Clark needed to make it look like he vanished.

By 10:30, his suitcase, which hadn't been touched since 1945, was packed and placed by the porch door in the kitchen. Back at the Sea House, Joey began preparing for the night like usual, making things seem as normal and ordinary as possible. The only slight difference to his opening routine was placing the three gas containers behind the stage curtain.

At 11:00, the first few members of the opening crew arrived at the Sea House. Joey greeted them outside the front door.

"Hey, guys! Unfortunately, we're having an issue right now and at this time, we're not going to be able to open this evening."

They looked at each other, confused. "What's going on?" one of them asked.

"Oh, we've had a pipe burst and water is everywhere," Joey replied.

"Oh, wow. Can we see?"

"NO!" Joey immediately replied. "I mean it's pretty bad, and I don't think it's safe for us to be walking around in it, you know."

"Ooooh."

"Yes, but we are going to get this fixed, pronto. You guys just take it easy tonight and we'll let you know when it's safe to return to work."

The opening crew got back in their vehicles. Before driving away, one of them yelled out their car window, "Hey Joey, does Lawrence know yet?"

Joey put his hand up to his face. "Oh, gosh. Not yet, but you guys say a prayer for me. I'll be telling him when he arrives later this afternoon."

"Best of luck, dude!" They pulled out of the parking lot. Eagerly waving, Joey nodded his head before returning to the club. In just a few minutes, it would be showtime.

At 11:30, Amelia arrived at the Sea House. She thanked her cab driver and said, "Now remember, you must be here back at 3:30. Please do not be a minute late."

The cab driver, an older gentleman with patchy gray hair, wearing thick square-framed glasses, looked at her and nodded his head. "Yes, ma'am. I'll be here."

Amelia walked to Clark's cottage and knocked on the door. Almost immediately, Clark opened the door. Wearing his usual casual attire–jeans and a simple white t-shirt–he smiled at Amelia.

The wind blew her hair across her face. She used her fingers to pin it back behind her ears.

"Hi," Amelia said.

"Hey, you."

Amelia clutched her purse in front of her and swayed back and forth. "You ready for this?"

"I'm as ready as I'll ever be."

"Nervous?" Amelia asked.

"Oh, I'm nervous as hell right now. But trying to keep it cool. I've got my bag packed, and I'm all ready to go.

Amelia grabbed Clark's hand and gave it a gentle squeeze. "You're going to get out of here, Clark."

He smiled. "Let's see how this all plays out first. Should we go take our places?"

Amelia nodded. "Yes, it's almost that time, isn't it?"

Clark nodded and shut the door to the cottage. He led the way with Amelia following close behind. They walked the usual trails of the property until they got to the deck overlooking the beach. Briefly, Clark stood in front of Amelia and grabbed both her hands.

"Amelia, even if this doesn't work out...thank you."

Amelia smiled, moving her hands to Clark's neck. "It's all going to work out. Just breathe."

Inhaling, Clark closed his eyes and replied, "Okay. Are you sure you're good to do this?"

Amelia nodded. "As sure as I'll ever be, Clark."

He smiled and pulled Amelia in for a hug and kissed her on the check. "I'll see you soon," Clark whispered in her ear.

CHAPTER 47

At 12:15, Mr. Lawrence pulled into the parking lot of the Sea House. He got out of his car and walked in through the main entrance of the club. As soon as he crossed the threshold, he immediately felt something was off. Typically by now the lobby bar would have trays of cleaned glasses sitting on it and someone would be working behind the bar to prepare it for the evening. But there was not a person in sight.

He continued through the dark lobby, making his way into the dining room. Joey was preparing the room like normal, covering the bare tables with fresh linens and pushing the cart of glasses.

"Joey?" Mr. Lawrence made his way down the aisle.

Joey looked up from the table he was setting. "Ah, Mr. Lawrence, how goes it?"

"Well, you tell me, Joey. Is there something going on?"

Joey felt a lump begin to form in his throat. Keep it together. Play it cool.

"Oh, nothing highly unusual right now, sir. Why do you ask?"

"Because there are no clean glasses on the bar yet. Usually by now someone is setting those up and stocking the bar for the show," said Mr. Lawrence with a puzzled look on his face.

"Oh, yes. I forgot about that. Unfortunately, the opening crew all came down with something. A stomach bug, I believe they said."

"A stomach bug?" questioned Mr. Lawrence.

Joey nodded while holding up a spoon and wiping it with a towel. "Yes sir. As soon as I'm done with the tables in here, I'll tend the bar this evening."

Mr. Lawrence folded his arms and studied Joey, who continued setting the table.

"Very well, then. Just make sure we are staying on track. When the other servers arrive, have them get right to it."

Joey nodded, and Mr. Lawrence turned to walk back to the lobby.

"Oh, sir!"

Mr. Lawrence turned around. "Yes?"

"I almost forgot! Amelia is here, and she wants to see you. She's ready to submit her story about Clark, but she has a few questions for you."

Mr. Lawrence arched his right eyebrow. "Interesting. There's no telling what kind of story she's writing now that Clark hates her guts. Where is she?"

"She was walking around. Last I saw her, she was at the overlook."

"Very well. I'll go find her. Thank you, Joey."

Mr. Lawrence began his walk to the overlook. He thought about stopping by Clark's cottage on the way but decided it was probably for the best that he didn't. While Clark's feelings didn't really matter in the grand scheme of things, he wanted Clark to feel rested for the evening's show.

Approaching the overlook, Mr. Lawrence noticed Amelia standing at the end. She had her back to him as she stood close to the steps. Her blue dress and hair fluttered in the wind as she appeared to be taking in the view.

He stepped on the deck and cleared his throat. "Hhmp. You wanted to see me?"

Turning around, Amelia pushed the hair out of her eyes. "Oh, hi. Yes, I wanted to talk to you briefly about the story."

Mr. Lawrence placed hands in his pockets. "Okay. What about it?"

"I've decided to go in a different direction with it," Amelia said.

"Okay? And that is?" Mr. Lawrence shrugged.

Amelia grasped her pearl necklace. "You see, when I first came here, I really set out to tell this story of Clark James, a story that told the world things about him that nobody knew. But then I discovered some things along the way that made me change the narrative."

Mr. Lawrence pulled a cigar out of his pocket and held it up to his mouth.

"Amelia, just get to the point. I don't have all day to shoot the shit."

"Yes, I understand. You're such a busy man, Mr. Lawrence. I've decided that the story is, in fact, going to be about Clark... and also you."

Mr. Lawrence let out a laugh. "Me?"

Amelia nodded.

"Yes. See, you are quite the man, Mr. Lawrence. Opening this fine establishment, seeking out the best talent in the world...and then holding them hostage and manipulating them into fame in exchange for their freedom."

Rolling his eyes, Mr. Lawrence scoffed., "Oh, please, Amelia. As if anybody is going to even give this story the time of day."

"They will if I have multiple sources. Your entire staff has gone on record discussing the unfit working conditions here. Including Joey. Oh, and how could I forget Miss Vivian?"

Mr. Lawrence dropped his hand holding the cigar down by his side. "You don't know shit about Vivian."

Amelia smirked.

"Oh, but I do. I know all about how before Clark, you did the exact same thing to the previous musician. What was her name? Oh, Bonnie Frank. You and Miss Vivian have this pact in which she provides you with the next big thing. Only this time, with a twist: a spell on the contract for Clark, making him forever tied to the nightclub."

Mr. Lawrence's face flushed crimson. "All right. You've done it. You have my undivided attention. What do you want?"

"End the contract with Clark James. Let him go."

Mr. Lawrence chuckled. "You're cute, but no. That's not happening."

"Fine. Then the story runs," said Amelia.

"So, when are you planning to run this story, Amelia? And is it even approved? You're just an intern. You have no power or pull in the industry."

"Funny you should ask. Because the entire team at the magazine loved it and supported it. In fact, it's already been printed," Amelia stated boldly.

"Come again?" sneered Mr. Lawrence.

"You heard me, Lawrence. It's been printed. Hits the shelves across the country tomorrow morning."

Mr. Lawrence nervously adjusted his necktie.

"You little shit. I NEVER should have trusted you. I did you a favor, you know that?! I hired you, the nobody intern."

Amelia shrugged her shoulders.

"I don't think I'll be a nobody intern after tomorrow. And your entire business? You can say goodbye to that too."

"Get rid of the story, Amelia," Mr. Lawrence demanded as he slowly approached her.

Shaking her head, Amelia replied, "No."

Mr. Lawrence's face was now bright red. With clenched teeth he spewed, "Amelia. Get. Rid. Of. The. Story."

"No, I will not." Amelia crossed her arms. Mr. Lawrence was now just a few feet from her.

He shook his head and laughed.

"You really shouldn't have done this. I am not a person you want to mess with, Amelia."

With that, he launched toward Amelia, his eyes full of fury as his hands reached for Amelia's chest.

Ever so quickly, Amelia slightly stepped to the right, causing Mr. Lawrence to miss her. The swift movement caused him to lose his balance, and he tumbled down the wooden steps. Amelia shuddered at the first thud of Mr. Lawrence's body hitting the steps. As he continued to roll, she quickly turned her head to avoid the sight.

He screamed as his body hit each step until suddenly, it was eerily quiet. Amelia peered over the ledge and saw Mr. Lawrence's limp body in a pool of blood at the bottom of the steps. Placing her trembling hand over her mouth, she covered a silent scream that tried to creep out of her chest.

"Oh, God." She lurched over to keep from fainting. Clark rushed onto the deck.

"Amelia, it's okay." She looked up at him with tears in her eyes. Clark gently squeezed her arm while simultaneously looking down toward Lawrence's body.

"I'll take over from here, okay. Go back to the Sea House and help Joey," Clark demanded.

Amelia nodded and quickly ran off. Clark slowly walked down the steps, keeping his eyes on Mr. Lawrence. When he approached the bottom of the stairs, he grabbed Lawrence by the arms and drug him off the landing onto the sand.

"Ugh," Clark grunted as he drug Lawrene's heavy body through the wet sand and into the ocean. Any minute now the tide would pick up and pull Lawrence's body out to sea. When he got him deep enough, Clark pushed Lawrence's body further out and quickly swam back to the shore.

Exhausted from the haul, he fell onto the wet sand. Waves lapped around Clark's body. He didn't have much time. Exhaling, Clark slowly stood up. It was time to finish the job. The tide began to rush over the beach, allowing Clark to quickly rinse off the pool of blood on the deck. Once the red pools were out of sight, Clark darted back up the stairs to his cottage.

Back inside, he carefully stripped off his wet clothes and laid them in the kitchen sink. Clark pulled on a dry pair of jeans and a t-shirt and grabbed his suitcase and the wet clothes. Clark took a look around the kitchen and then walked out of the cottage for the very last time.

CHAPTER 48

Back at the Sea House, Amelia and Joey poured gasoline all over the dining room, both sweating profusely as they doused everything. Clark burst through the lobby door carrying his wet clothes.

"Joey! Amelia!" he screamed.

Immediately, both stopped pouring gas and looked up at Clark. No words were said, just an eerie silence. Clark nodded his head.

"Clark?" Joey asked.

"He's dead, Joey. Lawrence is dead. The tide has likely carried his body out to sea by now."

Joey let out a deep breath and picked up the gas can.

"Okay, we're ready. Clark, toss your clothes somewhere. And you need to get out of here...now."

Clark threw his clothes on the stage and looked at Joey.

"Okay, it's almost time for the cab to be here," said Clark.

Setting down the gas can, Joey looked at Clark. "You get out of here. And don't ever look back, Clark. Don't even think about coming back to the Sea House."

Clark grabbed Joey and pulled him in for a hug. "Thank you. Thank you."

Joey squeezed Clark one last time and pulled away. "You're welcome. Now go and live *your* life."

Standing in the doorway, Amelia peered back at Joey and Clark. "Guys, the cab is pulling in. It's time to go!"

"Coming," yelled Clark.

He took one last look at Joey and asked, "What about you? You getting out of here too?"

"I'll take care of this. As soon as you guys leave, I'll light the match and scram. Get out of here, man!" Joey screamed.

Clark nodded and quickly dashed out of the dining room. "Thank you, Joey. I'll never forget you!" He quickly made his way to the front entrance.

"You ready?" asked Amelia, as she waited by the door.

"Yes, let's get out of here," Clark said as he grabbed his suitcase and Amelia's hand. They quickly hurried out of the building. Clark opened the back door of the cab for Amelia while taking one last look at the Sea House.

This was it. For the first time in 30 years, Clark was leaving the place. With tears in his eyes, he soaked it all in and then jumped into the taxi.

"Take us to the Pink Flamingo Inn, please," Amelia said.

CHAPTER 49

Present Day

The two pizza boxes sat empty on the dining table. Neal and his grandparents, their bellies full, sat in silence. Neal looked up at the microwave to check the time. Ten o'clock.

Grandad was the first to break the silence. "All these years, Milly. I cannot believe you've kept this story from me all these years."

Nana stacked her plate on top of Neal's and grabbed Grandad's next. "Yes, well, now you guys know. I played a role in both Mr. Lawrence's death and in the disastrous fire at the Sea House."

Grandad leaned back in his chair, crossing his arms over his plump stomach. "Now that I think about it, I remember seeing news footage of the scene. The place was engulfed in flames as the news reporter shared the story."

"Yes, it didn't take long for the media to spread word of the Sea House fire," Nana said as she carried the stack of dirty plates to the kitchen sink.

Neal walked to the fridge and pulled out a chilled bottle of chardonnay. "What did people say? Did an investigation ever take place?"

Nana began to scrub the dishes. "Initially, everyone was shocked. Understandably."

She turned on the tap and rinsed the dishes. "And they did do an investigation, but I believe it lasted only a month or so. No one was ever charged."

Neal took three wine glasses from the kitchen cabinet and began pouring.

"So, what happened to Clark? And what about Joey? Did you ever get in touch with him?"

"With Joey…I…uh, I never got an opportunity to speak with him after that day," said Nana as she dried off the last plate.

"Why not?" asked Grandad.

Nana dried her hands and put the damp kitchen towel on the countertop. Taking a glass of the chardonnay, she returned to her seat at the kitchen table.

"One reason why the investigation didn't last long was because they discovered human remains inside the Sea House after the fire was extinguished," said Nana.

Grandad's mouth dropped. Neal paused mid-step as he walked to the kitchen table with two glasses of wine in hand.

"No, Nana. Not Joey."

Nana took a sip of her wine and placed the glass on the table. She began to gently circle the rim with her fingertip.

"Yes, it was Joey. But back then, there was no such thing as DNA testing. When the police discovered the human remains and what was left of Clark's clothing, it was pretty much a case-closed situation."

Neal took his seat, handing Grandad his glass of wine.

"Oh my goodness. So, the world thought Clark James died in the fire that day. But it was really Joey."

Nana nodded.

"Sadly so. I was devastated when I saw the news. I remember having to just sit down in the middle of what I was doing because I could not believe it. That, obviously, was never part of the plan. He was to start the fire and then get out of the building. Once he was out, he was supposed to phone me at my hotel. But I never got his call."

"Did Clark ever find out, Babes?" asked Grandad.

"Yes, he did. Actually, we were together when the news broke. And I'll never forget that moment in time. Sometimes I still have nightmares in which I'm back in that tiny hotel room with the bright pink floral wallpaper and palm trees. And Clark and I are just sitting there on the bedroom floor in silence. We were completely devastated."

Neal looked at his grandmother with sympathy in his eyes and took a sip from his wine glass.

"Unbelievable. Such a tragic turn of events. And did nobody question Lawrence's whereabouts or discover his body?"

"His body, as far as I know, was never discovered. And he didn't have family nor true friends who really cared about him enough to notice. There were rumors that he had something to do with the fire and then skipped town. But Clark and I were the only ones who knew the truth about that day," said Nana.

"So, if you two escaped the Sea House together, where did Clark James go?" asked Grandad.

Nana sighed. "Geez. You know what? I really got what I had coming for me."

Neal and Grandad exchanged confused looks. "What do you mean, Nana?"

"Call it karma, I guess, for dabbling in Lawrence's games and for playing with Clark's heart. Because those next few days after the fire with Clark were truly something. So magical that I started to think my life could continue with Clark in it. But guess what?"

"What?" asked Grandad, leaning in closer to Nana.

"He left me. And I guess that's what I deserved," Nana said with a sigh.

CHAPTER 50
BIG SUR, CALIFORNIA, 1962

The taxi cab quickly approached the Pink Flamingo Inn. The ride over had been mostly somber. Not much was said between Clark and Amelia. Both were emotionally drained from the events that had just taken place back at the Sea House.

Holding Amelia's hand as he gazed out the window, Clark asked, "Where am I going, Amelia?"

"Right now? You're going back to the Pink Flamingo with me. And the rest we can work out later," Amelia said quietly.

Clark turned his head to look at Amelia. Not saying a word, but gently squeezing her hands three times. "Okay," he whispered.

"I hate to use this phrase, but the world really is your oyster now, Clark. You have so much to see and catch up on," said Amelia.

Clark leaned his head back against the seat and closed his eyes, taking a deep breath. He was trying his best to fight back tears. How crazy that his world had just changed within a few short hours. He was now a free man. Only this time, he was madly in love with someone. Maybe the stars were finally aligning in his favor.

"All right, you two. Here we are, the Pink Flamingo Inn," said the cab driver looking into the rearview mirror at Amelia and Clark.

"Thank you, sir. How much do we owe you?" asked Amelia.

"It will be thirty dollars, miss. For the ride to the Sea House and then back here."

The inn was a tiny L-shaped building with a painted white facade and a dark orange terracotta roof. Pink doors dotted the building, and a variety of colored metal oyster chairs flanked each doorway. The occasional faded surfboard stood tall, leaned against the white exterior. Unlike the Sea House, it did not sit on top of a cliff overlooking the Pacific Ocean. It was closer to the beach, sitting on a smaller bank that featured a small wooden boardwalk from the back of the motel to the beach. A few Monterey cypress trees and other evergreens stood tall over the motel and provided shade from the California sun.

Amelia reached into her silk clutch and pulled out a folded hundred dollar bill. The cab driver pulled up to the front entrance of the motel.

Clark opened his door and jumped out, making his way to the trunk of the cab.

"Sir, thank you so much. Here's a hundred bucks. Could you do me a favor, please?" asked Amelia.

The cab driver turned around in his seat to face Amelia, his bright blue eyes magnified by the square glasses. "Sure, miss."

"Do you recognize the man in the cab with me?" Amelia asked.

The cab driver flashed a smile, revealing a gap between his top front teeth. "Well of course, ma'am. That's Clark James."

Amelia's heart began to stir in her chest. "Yes. Please, sir. Could you keep Clark's whereabouts between us?"

The older gentleman's eyes flashed to the folded hundred dollar bill in Amelia's hand.

He nodded. "Yes, of course. I don't know where Clark James is. He never got into my cab."

Amelia smiled, placing the hundred dollar bill in the man's wrinkled hand. "Ah, thank you so much. You don't know it, but you really are a lifesaver, sir."

The cab driver smiled, nodding his head. "Thank you, miss. You take care now, okay?"

Amelia scooted across the seat to get out of the cab. "Thank you. You too!"

Clark grabbed his suitcase out of the trunk and slammed the yellow door of the cab. Flashing a soft smile, he reached for Amelia's hand. "You lead the way, Amelia."

Amelia smiled and grabbed Clark's hand. "We're just right over there," she said, leading the way. "Right across from the pool!" Amelia pointed to the kidney-shaped pool in the middle of the motel's courtyard. It was surrounded by a chain-link fence. White metal lounge chairs with tufted yellow cushions surrounded the shimmering pool. A few round tables with large yellow-and-white umbrellas made for a perfect seating area along the pool deck.

Amelia picked up her pace, walking across the green courtyard to their room. She pulled out a brass key from her clutch and placed it in the scratched brass keyhole.

"Ah, unlucky room 13," Clark said, pointing to the brass numbers on the door to their room.

Pushing the door open with her hip, Amelia replied, "That's a choice. Some may say it's unlucky. But at this point, Clark, nothing is unlucky."

Clark smiled and walked through the doorway into the colorful motel room. The wooden queen-sized bed had been positioned in the middle of the room, pushed up against a wall. The bedding was simple: a pink quilt and plush white pillows.

"Ah, the musty smell of an old motel room. It's been so long since I've smelled that smell," Clark said, placing his suitcase on the green shag carpet.

"The first of many firsts!" Amelia laughed, closing the door behind her.

"Yes," Clark nodded, looking at Amelia.

"Well, I'm exhausted. Aren't you, Clark?" Amelia asked, placing her clutch on a table in front of the bedroom's window. The California sun peeked through a slit in the closed curtains.

"First..." Clark said, sitting on the end of the bed.

"First, I think I need to sleep. I'm drained. What about you? Care for a nap?" Amelia kicked off her shoes.

"A nap sounds perfect to me."

Clark threw himself across the bed. He patted the empty space next to him.

"Join me, Amelia."

Amelia pulled the curtains completely closed, casting the room into total darkness.

"Okay," she whispered as she fell into bed.

CHAPTER 51

When Clark and Amelia awoke, the sun was just beginning to set.

Clark awoke first, his eyes flashing open as his brain started to replay the daunting moments from earlier that day. Gasping for air, his heart thumped rapidly as Amelia lay asleep with her head on Clark's chest.

Amelia felt the tension in Clark's arms that were wrapped around her. She awoke, her eyelids fluttering open. The room appeared hazy.

"What time is it?" she murmured.

"It's half past seven," Clark said, slowly moving his head on the pillow.

"Oh my goodness. We slept almost the entire day away."

"We have. And I'm suddenly feeling incredibly hungry," Clark said, rubbing his thumb on Amelia's shoulder.

"There's a brochure in the nightstand with some of the nearby restaurants. My favorite is Monty's Pizza Parlor."

"Pizza sounds delicious. Want to call it in? We can have it delivered and then go down to the beach."

Amelia sat up and rubbed her eyes, letting out a yawn. She criss-crossed her legs while reaching over Clark to grab the telephone from the nightstand.

"Well, I do have a very serious question to ask you, Clark."

"And what's that?"

"What does *the* Clark James like on his pizza?" Amelia asked, coiling the faded yellow telephone cord around her index finger.

"Hmm. Gosh, this is pretty serious. I'll eat pretty much any kind of pizza. What do you like, Amelia?"

"Oh, easy. Ham and pineapple," Amelia said, a grin spreading across her face.

"Now, we're talking! The only way to eat pizza!"

"So, it's settled! One large ham-and-pineapple pizza. I'll have the front desk connect me now."

Amelia stretched the phone cord across Clark's legs and over the wrinkled quilt, pressing the phone up to her ear.

"Hi, Sue. It's Amelia. How are you today?"

Clark leaned his head back against the wooden headboard and placed his hands on his lap as he closed his eyes.

"Oh, wonderful. Yes, everything is going great as always. Listen, I'm starving and would love to place an order with Monty's Pizza Parlor." Amelia laughed. "Yes, Sue. I know, I do love that place. Yes. If you could connect me, that would be wonderful."

Clark turned his head toward Amelia, smiling at her. "A Monty's Pizza Parlor regular?"

Amelia nodded, sticking her tongue out at Clark. "Thank you so much, Sue."

She placed the phone on her shoulder, whispering to Clark, "Yes. So, I might be a regular customer at Monty's now."

"Ohh," Clark said, waving his hands in the air sarcastically.

Amelia quickly placed the phone back up to her ear. "Hi. Yes, this is Amelia May. I'd like to place a delivery order, please."

Clark stood up and went to the window, pulling open the thick velvet curtains. The evening light poured into the room. He placed his hands on his hips, taking in the view. The Big Sur sky was orange with hints of pink and a few thick clouds. The breeze from the ocean caused the giant palm trees by the pool to sway. Clark took it all in. This was the first time he'd seen Big Sur from a different perspective in many decades.

"Yes, I'm at the Pink Flamingo Inn. That's correct, you remember. Room 13. Thank you so much. See you soon!" Amelia said, ending the call.

Clark turned to look back at Amelia as she was getting up from the bed.

"Amelia, are we supposed to be hearing from Joey sometime soon?" Clark asked, placing his hands in the pockets of his blue jeans.

Amelia smoothed out the creases in her navy blouse. "Yes, he said he would call as soon as he made it safely to a phone. I'm sure he will call anytime now."

Clark nodded his head. "Okay. I'm just starting to get a little nervous, that's all."

Amelia walked over to Clark, wrapping her arms around his torso. "Hey, it will all be okay. I'm sure Joey is taking care of things. You know, letting the staff know about the fire and stuff."

"True. Guess we just need to be patient and wait until he calls," Clark replied.

"Yeah! Let's make the most of things for now. Why don't we go down to the beach? I can watch for the delivery driver to pull in."

"And what if people notice me on the beach? What do we say?" asked Clark, pulling away from Amelia's embrace.

"Well, lucky for you, Joey and I thought a few things through. Speaking of, I need to give you some things," Amelia said, walking across the room to the closet.

She slid open the closet door and grabbed a black bag from a wooden shelf. Walking back to Clark, Amelia reached into the bag and pulled out a blue ball cap with gold letters stitched across the front. It read "Big Sur."

"A hat to wear for a disguise," Amelia laughed, handing over the cap to Clark.

Clark smiled, admiring the hat..

"Sorry, it's nothing fancy. I bought it at a souvenir shop down the road. But here are some shades to go along with the hat," said Amelia, handing over a pair of sleek black square-rimmed glasses.

Clark placed the cap on his head and then popped on the glasses. He flashed a cool smile. "How do I look? Unrecognizable?"

Amelia chuckled. "Like a normal tourist on vacation now."

She held the bag open, looked inside and then back at Clark.

"What else you got in there?" Clark asked.

"So, this is all for you. This is the money that Lawrence kept from you for years," Amelia said, handing the bag over to Clark.

Clark grabbed the bag from Amelia and looked inside. His eyes scanned the bag, and he noted the wrapped stacks of twenty-dollar bills.

"Holy shit," Clark whispered, running his hands through the bag.

"That's not all of it. There was more, but unfortunately Joey could only grab some of it. But you know you deserve all of this money, Clark."

Clark looked up at Amelia. "I'm not sure what I'm going to do with it, considering I have no game plan nor the faintest idea of what my life is going to look like now."

"And we'll figure all that out, okay? But there is something you should know about the money, Clark." Amelia placed her hand on his arm.

"Okay?"

"Lawrence never actually sent any money to your parents.. He kept it all. And that's why Joey collected as much as he could. Because it's yours. All of it."

Clark placed the bag down by his side, rubbing his forehead with his left hand. "You know, I'm not even surprised. I stayed there for so long. But now..."

"I know, Clark. I know. I'm so sorry, but you're free and out of there."

Suddenly, there was a knock at the door.

"Delivery from Monty's Pizza!"

Amelia smiled at Clark before walking past him to retrieve the pizza. She pulled open the door, letting the orange glow from the sky illuminate the hotel room.

"Good evening, Miss May. Your usual pizza."

The delivery man wore dark bell-bottom jeans and the signature uniform shirt for Monty's Pizza Parlor: a white t-shirt with red bands around the sleeves and *Monty's Pizza Parlor* embroidered in red cursive font across the middle. His shoulder-length brown hair blew in the wind as he held the square pizza box out to Amelia.

"Yes, thank you." Amelia smiled, handing over a wrinkled twenty-dollar bill from her handbag. "And please keep the change."

"Ah, thank you, ma'am," said the man as he gave the pizza box to Amelia.

"Have a good night!" Amelia said, waving to him as she closed the door.

Clark smiled as Amelia turned around to face him. "Wow, you really are a regular. How many times have you ordered from Monty's Pizza Parlor?"

Amelia's cheeks flushed red. "A few times now. That's what happens when you stop spending so much time at the Sea House, I guess."

"Right. Shall we go to the beach?" asked Clark.

"Yes! Let's go!" Amelia said, looping her arm through Clark's as they made their way out of the hotel room.

CHAPTER 52

Over the course of the next few days, Amelia and Clark spent their time together enjoying each other's company. Their mornings started on the beach, soaking up the California sun. Occasionally, they rented surfboards from the front desk of the motel and the two would attempt to surf.

Between surfing and tanning, they would often snack and picnic on the golden sands of the beach with the groceries that Amelia would grab from the local market down the street. The evenings were spent back up at the Pink Flamingo's pool, where Clark and Amelia would each unleash their inner child. There were cannonball contests and sometimes impromptu dance parties when Sue from the front desk let the pair borrow her radio.

The nights were filled with long conversations fueled by cheap wine or beer. Both Amelia and Clark fought exhaustion from the sun just to learn more about each other. Clark shared stories about his time in Paris during the war, and Amelia revealed how eager she was to finally catch her big break in journalism.

But then three days after the fire at the Sea House, the news finally broke about the tragic events. Amelia and Clark had woken up from a late afternoon nap and turned on the television to find a reporter sharing the news.

"A tragic fire struck a Monterey staple earlier this week. The iconic Sea House was apparently engulfed in flames late Monday morning. Fire crew and police arrived at the scene after an emergency call was placed."

Amelia and Clark slowly sat up in the bed, their eyes glued to the television screen.

"The Sea House has been the venue for many famous singers in America including resident performer Clark James. Investigators found human remains in the debris, along with articles of clothing connected to Mr. James."

Amelia grabbed Clark's arm as they slowly turned to each other.

"Clark? Did the reporter just say human remains were found?"

Clark's eyes widened and focused on Amelia's. "That's what I heard too."

Amelia jumped out of bed and threw the covers into the air. She adjusted the TV's volume.

"It's a sad day for not only Big Sur but the world as we mourn the loss of Clark James. May he rest in peace."

Sitting on her knees in front of the television, Amelia covered her face with her hands as realization sat in. That was not Clark in the fire. It was their friend, Joey. The one who was supposed to be calling the Pink Flamingo Inn anytime now to let them know he was safe.

Amelia turned to look back at Clark. He was distraught, his arms folded across his chest as tears began to run down his cheeks. His body began to shake.

Amelia felt the sting of tears on her cheeks.

"I thought he was safe, Amelia," Clark said, looking up at the ceiling.

Amelia wiped her eyes, but tears continued to stream down her face.

"I thought you said he was safe, Amelia."

Amelia inhaled, wiping her cheeks with the back of her hand. "I–I–I thought he was."

Clark slapped his palm against the headboard, the sound echoing through the room.

"DAMN IT! That should be me! Not him. Not Joey."

"I don't know what to say, Clark. I'm as devastated as you are."

Clark jumped out of the bed and began to pace in front of the window.

"He's been dead for the past three days. And here we are. You and I, just fucking around like nothing matters. Surfing the waves. Dancing by the pool. Getting drunk off beer and wine."

"Clark, we didn't know. We–I thought he would be calling us to let us know he was safe," Amelia said with desperation in her voice.

"I should've known this was going to be too good to be true. All of this" Clark said, his face now red from crying.

He forcefully pulled back the curtains from the window, letting the afternoon sun and heat fill the room.

"And damn it, everything was starting to feel perfect. But I somehow keep hurting people in my life, no matter what I do," Clark said, looking out the window.

"Clark, this isn't your fault."

Clark quickly turned around, placing his hands on his hips. "Then whose is it, Amelia?"

"I don't know, Clark. But attempting to blame someone for this isn't going to fix it. We both lost a friend. We're both allowed to be completely devastated by this."

Clark kept his hands on his hips, adjusting his eyes toward his feet. "Yeah, well, I don't know if I can keep doing this."

"Doing what?" Amelia asked, confused.

"THIS! ALL OF THIS. WHAT'S THE PLAN, AMELIA?" Clark yelled, causing the vein on the right side of his neck to bulge.

"I DON'T KNOW! WHY ARE YOU ATTACKING ME ALL OF A SUDDEN?" Amelia screamed back.

"Because. None of this would have happened if you had just left things the way they were."

"Oh, really? Really, Clark?" Amelia asked, crossing her arms. "You were miserable. You hated your life! Lawrence was going to have you killed! You were nothing to him!"

Clark shook his head. He brushed past Amelia and made his way to the door.

"Where are you even going?" Amelia asked, as tears filled her eyes.

"To the beach. I need to clear my head."

"Okay, let me grab my shoes, and I'll–"

"NO, AMELIA. I need to go alone."

Amelia sat on the edge of the bed, defeated. "Clark, what are you saying?"

"I don't know, Amelia. But I need to think about some things." Clark opened the door, letting the breeze flow into the room.

The wind blew Amelia's hair across her face, causing it to stick to the tears on her cheeks until the sudden thud of the door abruptly made the wind stop. Amelia pushed the hair from her face and took a deep breath as she sat alone on the edge of the bed. She had felt this way many times before, all alone in hotel room 13 at the Pink Flamingo Inn. Only this time it seemed worse, as if she knew Clark was right. Perhaps it all was too good to be true.

CHAPTER 53

Present Day

Neal looked at the clock on the microwave. 1:30 am. The adrenaline brought about from Nana's story pumped through his body, forcing the faint feeling of sleepiness away.

"Did Clark come back from the beach?" asked Neal.

Nana nodded. "He did. It was late when he returned. I was already in bed, exhausted from all the tears that I'd cried that afternoon."

Grandad took a sip of the remaining wine in his glass. "And then what, Babes?"

"Well, I pretended to be asleep when he got back, but he woke me up and apologized. He said he was sorry for the things he'd said and how he'd responded, that he needed to think about a lot of things. He said that's why he went for a long beach walk alone."

"Well, I'm sure the news of Joey's death was devastating for both of you. But the guy's entire life had been rocked not once, not twice, but a few times. A long walk is probably the best thing he could have done at that moment," reasoned Neal.

Nana let a soft smile slide across her face. "I would agree with that statement, Neal. When he returned, we discussed our options way into the night. He asked me what I wanted."

"And what did you say?" asked Grandad, resting his chin on his arm.

Nana crossed her arms and leaned back in the kitchen chair. "I said I wanted what we had to work. Because I really wanted to be a part of his life. Although we only were at the Pink Flamingo Inn for a few days, it felt like we had been there much longer. It was the perfect glimpse of what my life with Clark James would be like outside of the Sea House."

Grandad leaned back in his chair, yawning and stretching his arms high above his head. "But it obviously didn't work out. Because...well, here we are, Babes."

"You're right. It didn't work out. After I told Clark that I wanted us to be together, he mentioned the idea of running off to Paris together, that we could start over and leave everything from the Sea House behind."

Neal gathered the empty wine glasses and moved toward the kitchen sink. The fingerprint-smudged glasses clinked as he placed them in the sink, turning on the faucet to wash them.

"And did you go? To Paris?" asked Neal.

"I told him that it was a lovely idea. But ultimately, I had a job to return home to. I mean that really was the whole reason why I went to Big Sur in the first place, to write the article on Clark James. And my career was important to me too."

Neal turned off the water and grabbed a dish towel from the countertop, drying his hands. He took a seat at the kitchen table with his grandparents, noting the clock on the microwave. 2:00 am.

"And how did Clark react to that?" Neal asked.

Nana covered her mouth to hide her yawn. "Ah, well, looking back, I'd say that's probably when he realized it wasn't going to work between us. He agreed that my career was important, and he understood where I was coming from. But he had this look of sadness in his eyes. It was like, 'I can't have you.' Like the universe wasn't wanting us to be together."

Neal yawned, wiping his tired dry eyes. "And that was the last night you two were together, wasn't it?"

Nana slowly nodded her head. "It was. We went to sleep that night. I thought we had cleared the air from the heated discussion earlier that day, but when I woke up the next morning, I felt his side of the bed and he wasn't there. So, I got up and checked the bathroom. Nothing. I was about to see if he was out on the beach when I noticed the note on the little table by the window."

Grandad reached across the table and grabbed Nana's hand.

"And on a notepad from the Pink Flamingo was a brief note Clark had written to me. He explained that what we had was magical but would never work out. He wanted Paris, and I wanted my writing career in LA. And he couldn't dare think about hurting another person in his life again," said Nana somberly.

"Oh, man. I'm so sorry, Nana," Neal said.

Nana held her hands up in surrender. "Oh, Neal. I'm okay. At least I ended up being okay. Of course, at the time, I was devastated. I couldn't believe he was gone. But when I searched the room and couldn't find any remnants of him or his things, it really hit me that Clark James had walked out of my life."

"What a prick. Leaving you like that? Writing a silly little note?" Grandad said, crossing his arms.

"He did what he thought was best at that moment, and that was to run. Because he finally had the chance to."

"So what did you do after that?" asked Neal.

"Well, I did what I had to do. I packed up, checked out of the Pink Flamingo Inn, and I went back to LA. Those first few days after returning from Big Sur were hard. Gosh, they were hard. I had never felt such gut-wrenching heartache.. It was all so new to me. And the only thing I could do to feel even slightly better was to write."

Nana let out a little yawn, continuing her story. "I wrote and I wrote. The little living room in my apartment was just covered in sheets of paper from yellow legal pads. I would write, rip off the page, throw it on the floor, and start again. And I wrote until I felt like I had written the most beautiful piece on Clark James and his life at the Sea House."

"But Milly, why have I never read this story? I don't remember it being published in the magazine."

"That's because it was never published. When I finally returned to the office, I shared the story with my boss and told him all about my time in Big Sur. He knew from the media coverage about the fire and was really concerned about how I was doing. And he agreed that my story on Clark James was compelling, beautiful, and powerful. But it couldn't run."

"What?! Why?" asked Neal.

"Ultimately, the entire story was a huge liability. There was tragedy involved. Nobody had heard of Lawrence's whereabouts, and my boss did not want there to be any connection between the magazine and the events that had taken place at the Sea House. But he kept his promise. He saw that I could write, and he gave me the promotion that I wanted."

"And so you lost Clark, but you got the writing career that you'd always wanted," Grandad said.

"Yes," Nana replied, sleepily nodding her head.

"But you said that you and Clark wrote letters to each other occasionally throughout the years, Nana. When did those start?"

Nana adjusted her glasses. "Well, let's see. When did I get that first letter from Clark? I want to say it was six months later."

Nana paused to let out another yawn and then continued. "It was six months later, that's right. I remember coming home from work, and it was just pouring rain. I went to check my mail. I pulled several envelopes out of the mailbox and saw the postage stamps. "Paris, France." My heart stopped, and I stood there in the rain, staring at them. I couldn't believe my eyes."

Grandad cleared his throat. "And what did they say, the letters? Do you still have them?"

Nana nodded. "The letters are tucked away somewhere in a book in the attic back at home. But yes, I kept them. And I even felt a sense of guilt all these years for keeping them."

"Oh, Milly. That's silly. You shouldn't feel guilty about that," said Grandad, patting her hand.

Nana smiled at Grandad.

"Clark ended up going back to using his given name of Rob. He'd gotten a job working at a cafe in Paris. He was just a normal server with multiple responsibilities. And for the most part, he enjoyed the simple tasks of his ordinary job."

Nana stood up and walked over to the fridge to grab a glass of water.

"I remember reading in that first letter that he was experiencing aging for the first time. I remember finding it comical that someone could be so giddy to discover their first gray hair."

Both Neal and Grandad smiled, letting the sleepiness take over.

"Boys, it's almost three in the morning. My goodness, no wonder we're all so tired. Let's go to bed. We'll continue this discussion over a late breakfast before we head to the airport."

Neal perked up. "The airport. That's right! You guys fly out tomorrow. Well, I mean today."

"I know. It's always so sad saying goodbye to you, my sweet pea. But we'll be back, of course. I'm just glad we booked that later flight out, because phew, we're going to be sleeping in, I can already tell."

"I agree. You two sleep well, okay? I'll see you both in the morning," Neal said, making his way toward the stairs.

"Neal, I think you mean in just a few hours," laughed Grandad.

Moving slowly up the stairs, Neal let out a tired laugh. "Yes, Grandad. See you in a few short hours."

CHAPTER 54

"Neal, wake up, Honey!"

Neal slowly opened his eyes, feeling the morning sunlight hitting his check as he rolled over in the bed. The room appeared blurry as his eyes adjusted.

He heard a knock on his bedroom door.

"Sweet Pea, it's 10:30! We gotta get up and moving!" chirped Nana from the other side of the door.

"Uh, okay. I'll be out in just a second."

"Okay, coffee is poured and breakfast is on the table. Don't be long, okay? We don't have much time before we have to leave for the airport!"

Neal sat up in his bed and grabbed the covers. He ran his hands through his tangled blonde curls and stared out the window. From his bedroom he had excellent views of the Monterey landscape, a blend of luscious green trees and ancient redwoods. In the distance, you could see the deep blue sea resting at the bottom of the hills.

The morning rays shimmered on the blue waters, making the ocean look like a peaceful bathing pool. From any bedroom on the back side of the house, you could see a wider view of what Monterrey had to offer.

The morning views were always his favorite, but the sunsets were just as amazing. While looking out the window this particular morning, he couldn't help but think of Josie and how much she would probably carry on about the views too. Grabbing his iPhone from his nightstand, Neal opened the camera app and snapped a photo of the view.

Neal leaned against the window frame and felt the warmth of the sun hitting his bare chest. He pulled up Josie's contact and typed a message with the photo he'd just taken.

Hi. Woke up to this morning view and couldn't help but think of you.

Neal bit his lower lip in concentration, staring at the message he'd just typed.

"Shit, what am I doing?" he whispered, still staring at his screen.

"NEAL!" Nana's voice echoed up the stairs and through Neal's bedroom door.

Throwing his iPhone onto the bed, Neal picked up a wrinkled black t-shirt off the floor and pulled it on.

"Coming! Sorry!" he yelled, as he flung the bedroom door open and sprinted down the steps.

Rounding into the kitchen, the scent of coffee, fresh cinnamon rolls, and bacon filled the room.

"Good morning!" Neal said, entering the kitchen where his grandparents sat waiting at the kitchen table.

"Mornin', Neal. You finally woke up, I see," Grandad chimed, holding a mug of coffee up in the air.

"Yeah. Guess it's been awhile since I've stayed up until three in the morning."

"Well, us too. But unfortunately when you're older, your body doesn't allow you to sleep in," laughed Nana.

"Very true! Your Nana and I both naturally woke up at seven," Grandad added.

Taking his place at the table, Neal grabbed a fork and got to eating.

"Mm-hmm. Cinnamon rolls! I'm going to have a hard time adjusting to not having breakfast on the table in the mornings."

Nana laughed. "Do you ever cook in this gorgeous kitchen?"

Neal smirked, his mouth full of food.

"Hardly ever. But Josie's favorite meal is breakfast. We used to always cook big breakfasts on Sunday mornings. When we were together, that is."

Grandad put his coffee mug down on the kitchen table. "Well, maybe that's how you get her back. Invite her over for breakfast."

Chasing the bite of cinnamon roll with a gulp of milk, Neal cleared his throat. "Yeah, maybe."

Nana and Grandad quickly flashed each other a look, the kind of look that was their way of acknowledging some progress had been made in Neal's mind in regard to Josie.

"Well, we don't have much time left before we need to get ready to hit the road. Would you all like to hear more about Clark James?" asked Nana.

Neal continued to eat, biting into the crunchy bacon, nodding his head at the same time. Grandad turned his eyes toward Nana, giving her his undivided attention.

"After those first letters, I went through a few different emotions. First, I was just so giddy and happy that he wrote to me. But then I let it linger for a few days and I became angry.

Grandad peered over the top of his glasses.

"How dare he just write me out of the blue and tell me that everything is going so well. Like he didn't have any remorse for leaving me in the middle of the night at the Pink Flamingo Inn."

"He didn't mention anything about that in the letters?" asked Neal.

"Not in the first one, no. The first one was very simple and just updated me on his whereabouts," said Nana, holding her gray coffee mug up to her lips.

"And what did you write back to him, Milly?" asked Grandad.

"Well, I wanted to write, *screw you, mister. Thanks for breaking my heart into a million pieces.* But in the end I couldn't do that. I simply wrote a letter back the way he did, with an update on my life. I let him know that I did, in fact, get the writing promotion I was hoping for and that I was actually doing quite well."

"And the letters continued?" Grandad asked.

"They did. They turned almost into a conversation. But they would be months apart. He would write to me, and a month later, I would respond. Then a few months later, he would write back. We just talked about the everyday things in our lives."

"When was the last time he wrote to you?" asked Neal.

"It was right around the time Daniel and I were getting married, actually. I had told him the news of my relationship, that it was serious. When he wrote back, he told me that he was happy for me. And I think he truly was."

"And what was he up to?" asked Grandad.

"He had moved to the French countryside by then, bought a little house, and was running a farm. He said he'd come to realize it was exactly what he needed in life."

Nana began clearing the table, carrying the dirty dishes to the kitchen sink.

"But after I received that final letter from him, I didn't write to him anymore. And then a few years after Daniel and I married, I received a

THE CLUB BY THE SEA

letter in the mail from someone claiming to be his caregiver. She had discovered my letters to Clark, all of which he'd kept."

Nana began to rinse the dirty dishes in the kitchen sink and placed them in the dishwasher.

"Nana, you don't have to do all that. Please just sit down and enjoy yourself before we have to leave," said Neal, pointing to Nana's seat at the table.

"Oh, it's fine. Enjoy it while it lasts!" replied Nana, looking up from the dishwasher as she loaded the final mug.

"That letter from his caregiver was written to let me know that Clark had passed away in his sleep. He died peacefully. I was obviously heartbroken, but it brought me great peace to know that he got to enjoy his final few years. He'd found a simple life and it ended up being enough for him."

"And you never said anything. You just kept it bottled up inside of you for so long, Milly," said Grandad.

"I just didn't have it in me to explain it all. We'd actually just had our first child when I received the letter from the caregiver. Occasionally, I would let the grief hit me while I was in the shower. The tears would really flow then," Nana said sadly as she returned to the kitchen table.

"Nana, I gotta tell you, I never expected to hear any of this during your visit. But I'm so glad that you finally were able to share this with us. To get it off your chest. Does it feel good to finally speak about it?"

"It does. It's extremely bittersweet. But when we stepped inside the club on the first day of the trip, memories instantly rushed back. I could almost smell the scent of the room when it was packed with people during a sold out show."

"Talk about a full-circle moment," said Grandad.

"No joke! But I think this makes this renovation project even more important to me now. I want to do what's right and bring the venue back to life in memory of Clark...and Joey," said Neal.

"Now that's something I think both of them would've loved," said Nana.

CHAPTER 55

After dropping his grandparents off at the airport, Neal immediately got back to work. The following day, he met Miranda at the club and revealed all of the details he had learned over the past few days.

As they walked the property, Neal revealed the story. On the terrace, Neal told Miranda about the infamous fight between Clark James and his parents. Back in the dining hall, he shared the devastating details of the moments that led to the fire. He and Miranda even searched the property for Clark's cottage and the wooden observation deck.

The stories of Clark James and his grandmother brought a new sense of inspiration to Neal when it came to renovating the space. He decided it needed to be brought back to life and become the high-end place that it once was. While he didn't necessarily see it as a jazz club again, he did, in fact, see it as an upscale dining experience and venue.

After his grandparents' visit, Neal kept in touch weekly to give them updates on the progress of the space. Without revealing too many details, he asked Nana if she would be comfortable sending some of the letters she and Clark had written over the years. After a little hesitation, she eventually agreed and promised to mail him copies of the letters.

One late afternoon, after a full day of meeting with contractors, interior designers, chefs, carpenters, electricians, and plumbers, Neal pulled into the driveway of his house to find a cardboard box at his front door.

Curious, Neal got out of his black Range Rover and walked to the front door, picking up the box. The return address was Tennessee. Ah, here it was, the letters from Nana.

He quickly made his way into the house and used his car key to cut through the tape on the box. Inside the box was a layered stack of multiple envelopes in a variety of sizes and colors. But what really surprised Neal was what he found underneath the letters in the box. Neal pulled a Walkman and headphones from the box and placed them on the counter. He looked in the box and found three cassettes.

"What in the world?" asked Neal as he took the tapes out of the box. Flipping them over, he noticed that each tape was labeled:

The Club by the Sea Part 1
The Club by the Sea Part 2
The Club by the Sea Part 3

Neal hadn't touched a cassette tape since he was a kid. In fact, the last memory he had of a cassette tape was during a visit to Nana and Grandad's house. Flashbacks of scenic drives in Grandad's fun car, a ruby red 1990 Mazda Miata. Neal was always on cassette duty, in charge of swapping out the tapes in the tiny player.

Grabbing the tapes and the Walkman, Neal made his way into the sunroom and took a seat in a chair facing the window. He opened the case labeled *Part 1* and placed it inside the Walkman. He put on the headphones, leaned back, and pressed play.

Static sounded until he heard a man speaking.

"Is this on? Testing. Testing. Ah, it's on."

Neal perked up in his chair, holding the Walkman against his chest.

"This is Clark James in my little home studio. And this is part one of my album, *The Club by the Sea*. This is a collection of songs written about a time period in my life that now feels like a fever dream. These songs are the stories of my career, a rollercoaster of highs and lows and the things I lost to get what I believed was the only important thing in my life. But you see, I was wrong. Because what I thought was the most important thing in my life ended up being a facade. And what truly was the most important thing in my life was a woman named Amelia May. But I let my pride stand in the way of what could've been the best thing to ever happen to me. And so, this is for you, Amelia. The Club by the Sea, the story of you and me."

Neal pressed pause as a shiver went down his spine. Nana didn't mention anything about a secret album being included in the letters. It's one thing to hear the stories from his grandmother but now to hear recordings of Clark James' voice caught Neal completely off guard.

He pressed play. Clark's voice continued.

"Track one: 'Goodbye, Nashville.'" Clark's voice echoed through the headphones.

Neal leaned back and listened as the track began. An acoustic guitar played as Clark's voice sang along, telling the story of a man leaving Nashville to chase his dreams, ultimately ending up in Big Sur, California.

The tracks continued, each one telling the story of Clark's trials and tribulations, each with an underlying theme of loneliness and longing. With track five, titled "A.M. Arrives," the album took a turn.

Neal listened as Clark took an artistic approach on a song with a double meaning. "A.M." meaning the obvious, the initials for his grandmother, Amelia May. But in the track, Clark sang, "But when A.M. arrives, I realize I love her," hinting that perhaps in the morning, he's awakened with the realization that he's in love with Amelia.

Listening to the tape, Neal found himself swaying along with the words of Clark James. He listened to each lyric with great concentration, and when he got to the second tape, he realized that the sun had set hours before. It was almost 9:30 at night. But he couldn't stop listening. He wanted to know more. So, he loaded the second tape into the Walkman and listened to Clark James continue telling his story.

Part two of the album went on to share more details of being in love with Neal's grandmother, with tracks "Big Sur Mornings," "The Only One in a Crowded Room," and "Champagne Nights." One of the more heartbreaking tracks was "Forever 23," a song on which Clark sang about being forever frozen at 23 years of age, having to watch the world move on without him. It was something that he admitted he had become used to, but he couldn't bear it any longer if it meant the one he loved was going to eventually leave him too.

Neal moved inside the kitchen to listen to tape three. Popping open a bottle of beer, Neal placed the Walkman on the island and took a seat on a barstool.

As he continued to listen, he realized that this was the part of the story when Clark was filled with remorse and regret. The first half of the songs continued to tell the love story of him and Amelia. A track named "Pink Flamingo Sky" told the story of magical days in paradise and feeling like there's nothing stopping the two lovers from taking on the world together. But then the tracks took on a different vibe. Clark sang about no longer being with this person and realizing it was a giant mistake.

Neal listened until the wee hours of the morning, feeling the lyrics of each song. Some gave him chills, some made him sway throughout the kitchen and into the living room. On the third tape was a track entitled "Our Friend Joe." The song honored Joey and the friendship that he developed with Clark and Amelia. The album closed with the final song, "Reminders in the A.M." It was the thirtieth song on the album, something that Neal found hard to believe. Thirty songs on one album. That was unheard of in the age of hit singles.

The final track returned to the double meaning of the morning and Amelia's initials. Only this time, Clark sang of how every day the morning brought reminders of the love that he walked away from. The outro of the song was sung in French. "Tu me manques..."

Neal opened his iPhone, searching to translate the French phrase.

"Ah, it means 'I miss you,'" Neal said, staring at his phone.

After completing his listening of the album, Neal couldn't help but take the music of Clark James personally. Not because it was about his grandmother, but because it all kept reminding him of Josie. Did he really want to end up living in this house in Big Sur all alone? Was his career really worth it if it meant being alone, without his one true love?

Neal typed Nana's contact into his iPhone and began typing her a message.

Hey Nana, I thought I would text you since it's so late. Especially your time. I just listened to the tapes you included in the box of letters. This was quite a bombshell, but I think I needed to hear it.

After sending the message, Neal placed the phone on the countertop and took a sip of his beer. He noticed three dots appear almost immediately underneath his message, meaning that Nana was responding. And sure enough, her text soon came through.

Hi, Sweet Pea. I'm still up. Your grandad's snoring is extra loud tonight, so I'm playing crossword puzzles on my iPad. I thought you might like to hear the tapes. Those were included with the letter from Clark's caregiver. He never got around to doing anything with the album, and his caregiver wanted me to have the tapes. I listened to those songs for years and years. Even after you were born. It was my little secret way of keeping Clark alive.

Neal smiled as he read the text from his nana, noticing that the three dots were appearing again directly underneath the message she had just sent.

You know I love your grandfather very much. He's the stability in my life and the one I know I'm supposed to be with forever. You know, he even has a better understanding and love for me after hearing about Clark James. I packed the tapes and letters up when we moved to Tennessee, and I didn't listen to them again. Just felt that it was time. You still have so much time. Don't be like me or Clark. If you love someone deeply, let them know. Even if it ends up hurting you a little bit.

Neal quickly typed into his phone.

I agree. Thank you for sending this to me. Love you, Nana!

And then Neal knew what he needed to do. He pulled up Josie's contact on his phone and began the message that he should've sent months ago.

CHAPTER 56

After a year of vigorous work rehabbing the former Sea House, it was finally opening weekend.

Neal invited his grandparents back to California to attend the opening celebration. And this time he was pulling out all the stops. The opening night of the club was to be a formal affair. Neal arranged for a driver to pick up his grandparents from his house and take them to the event an hour before it was set to start.

When a black Suburban pulled up to the club, Nana and Grandad were greeted by a valet. He held the car door open for them, and there was Neal standing at the entrance of the club.

"Neal!" Nana exclaimed as she slid her way out of the backseat. Her hair appeared more gray than the last time and was now cut into a bob that rested right at her chin. She was wearing a black formal dress with diamond earrings and matching necklace. Grandad was in formal attire as well, sporting a black suit with a bow tie and cummerbund.

While hugging his grandmother and shaking Grandad's hand, Neal said, "Hello you two! And welcome back. I'm so excited to show you both what we've done to the place since you last were here."

Nana clapped her hands in delight..

"Oh, I just can't believe this! It already looks so good just on the outside. A concrete parking lot, new paint and siding, and fresh landscaping. I can tell!"

"Yes, it's definitely been a labor of love. Let's go inside, shall we?" offered Neal.

They walked into the entrance of the building and were greeted in the lobby by a waitstaff in black attire. The lobby remained in the original layout of the Sea House. There was a waiting area with green velvet seating, ornate light fixtures, and a bar with gold accents and stools. On the wall above the green velvet seating was a faded white wallpaper with manuscript writing across it.

Neal looked at Nana, "Do you recognize the wallpaper, Nana?"

Nana pulled out her red-framed reading glasses from her silver clutch and put them on. She walked closer to the wall, analyzing the words that were written across the wallpaper.

"Ah, it's pieces of the letters that Clark and I wrote to each other over the years!"

She continued to take it all in, moving her eyes across the warm lobby.

"Oh wow, Neal. It's stunning! And the photos! Look at that!" squealed Nana, pointing to enlarged vintage photos of the Sea House in gold frames. She grabbed Grandad's hand and led him over to a wall that featured a gallery collection of the vintage photos. There were photos of the exterior of the Sea House, guests partying, shows, Clark James, and a photo of the younger version of Amelia with Clark James out on the terrace.

"Look, Babes, it's you," said Grandad while pointing at the photo. Nana excitedly handed her iPhone to Grandad. "Oh, Daniel, take my photo!"

Neal laughed and walked up to his grandparents with two glasses of champagne.

"Let's go see the dining hall now."

Following with champagne in tow, Neal pushed through a velvet curtain entrance that led into the dining hall. Although the interior decor and design was more modern now, Nana felt like she was almost walking back in time. The tables had fresh white linens and perfectly placed table settings. Candles illuminated the center of each table. The booths by the front of the stage had been restored and featured the same green velvet upholstery as the ones in the lobby. The hardwood floors shined with new life. The picturesque windows had new glass and automatic shades.

"Holy shit, Neal. This place is the real deal. I don't see a single graffiti drawing in sight," laughed Grandad.

"Like I said, Grandad, it's been a labor of love. It's come a long way since you both were last here. "

Nana led the way from the dining room out to the terrace. It was as if her body naturally knew what to do and where to go. Outside, the terrace did not disappoint. A bar had been built with blue mosaic tiles glistening in the light. Round iron tables with giant white umbrellas aligned the terrace. Terracotta pots with lemon trees were tucked between tables, giving the terrace a European feel.

"Absolutely stunning. It's just all so amazing, Neal!" said Nana facing the bar. She noticed the back of a lady standing at the bar with a glass of champagne. The woman's brown wavy hair gently flowed with the breeze off the sea. She wore a light blue sleeveless dress that framed her hips and fluttered in the wind.

The woman turned around at the sound of Nana's voice.

"Nana! I knew I recognized that voice!" The woman smiled brightly.

"Aw, Josie! Come here, sweet girl!" Nana laughed, running up to Josie.

Josie placed her glass of champagne on the table beside her and held her arms out wide to embrace Nana.

"Hi, Nana. Do you love it? The space?"

Nana pulled back from Josie's embrace, smiling. "Oh, it's incredible. All of it. Neal really did an unbelievable job with this one."

"He did!" Josie said, noticing Neal and Grandad approaching.

Neal grabbed Josie's hand and gave her a kiss on the cheek.

"I see you found your way out to the terrace," Neal said, smiling at Josie.

"I sure did. And I found the champagne too! I had to come out and experience it after hearing the incredible stories of you, Amelia."

Nana's cheeks blushed. "Yes, it was so surreal being back here when Neal brought us the first time. But now with it being finished, it's like I'm back all over again. Looking at you standing there at the bar, I thought I was looking at my younger self!"

Josie laughed. "Well, that is an honor then. Has Neal shown you the front yet?"

Nana looked at Neal, shaking her head.

"I haven't yet. But why don't we all go to the front? I want to reveal the new sign and name," Neal said, leading the way, still holding hands with Josie.

They wove their way through the perfectly placed tables to the front parking lot. At the entrance of the parking lot stood a tall sign that was draped in a large white cloth. Neal walked his grandparents over to it.

"When we started the renovations, we knew it needed a new name, a new story. But I wanted to really honor the history of the place at the same time," said Neal.

Nana nodded while taking a sip of her champagne.

"After you shared your story with us, I felt so inspired by everything you had told us. And I felt like that story needed to be conveyed in the design of the place. Especially in the name."

Nana looked at Grandad and then at Neal.

"And what's the name? Do you know, Daniel?"

Grandad shrugged and smiled. "Babes, I have no idea!"

"Josie?" Nana asked with humor in her voice.

"I don't know. Maybe. Why don't we let Neal reveal it," Josie said, placing her arm around Nana's back.

Neal walked over to the sign and grabbed ahold of the cloth. Smiling, he quickly pulled the sheet off to reveal a new neon sign. Amelia & Clark's, it read.

"Welcome to Amelia and Clark's, Nana!" said Neal.

"Oh my word!" Nana gasped and covered her mouth with her hand. Grandad laughed and wrapped his arm around her.

"This is just...what a sweet thing to do," said Nana.

Neal walked over to his grandparents, pulling them both in for a hug.

"Like I said, I wanted to honor the history of this place, especially since you never got to tell the story of you and Clark James. And now it lives on."

"It certainly does, Neal," Nana said.

She stood between Neal and Grandad and looped her arms through theirs.

"Now, let's go, boys. And Josie?"

Josie brushed her hair back behind her ears. "Yes?"

"I'm so glad you're here. This makes the night even better."

Josie smiled, giving Nana's shoulder a gentle squeeze. "I'm so glad to be here too. And I want to thank you for sharing your story with Neal. He shared some details with me on the phone. And I knew that

I needed to know more, but he only promised to share more if it was in person."

"Smart man! Well played!" Grandad said, gently punch Neal's shoulder.

"Thanks Grandad. Josie came up for a weekend, and I brought her here to the space and told her more of the story. In fact, it was her idea to use the photos and letters to decorate the space."

"Josie, that is so kind of you! I knew the minute I met you, you were a good one. Daniel and I view you as family. We always have, and we always will," said Nana.

"Same to you all. You're very special to Neal and that means you're special to me too."

Nana let out a happy laugh, grabbing ahold of Grandad's hand. "Well, shall we celebrate?"

"Yes! Tonight we listen to all the jazz and drink all the champagne!" Neal said, grabbing Josie's hand.

"Hear, hear!" Grandad chimed.

With that, the four made their way into Amelia & Clark's for a night of celebration.

THANK YOU

They say it takes a village... and boy, am I grateful for mine. This book would not have been possible without the love and support of so many people in my life. The smallest way I can ever repay them is by permanently putting my gratitude in print.

My Board

Throughout all of my endeavors, I've been blessed with friends we've coined as "The Board." Katherine, Mollie, and Jenky have supported me every step of the way in my career. Thank you all for always listening to my crazy ideas and for not only supporting them but also for being that extra boost of ambition I needed to get to the finish line.

Hoskins in the Flat

When I started writing *The Club by the Sea*, I needed a place to retreat. A space that would provide the clarity needed to hunker down and focus on this make-believe world. Hoskins in the Flat was that space for me. For weeks, I would show up and sit at the little table in the front window. The ladies of Hoskins in the Flat never tired of me and were always the kindest hosts. I cannot wait to return to that spot in the window one day for another book. Once you visit their shop, you'll understand why it was the perfect escape. hoskinsintheflat.com

Terri Gilbert

I don't think we ever truly realize the impact of our teachers until we are well into our adult lives. Terri Gilbert, one of my high school English teachers, is a perfect example. Thanks to her, I know how to write a good paper to this day. Ten years after I graduated high school, Terri reached out to me about a book she was about to publish, asking if I would be interested in helping with her headshots and website. I happily said yes, and she even agreed to read multiple drafts of *The Club by the Sea*. Her support, advice, and feedback played a valuable role in the making of this novel. Check out her novel, *The House at Blackwater Pond*, at terrigilbertauthor.com.

Tuyen Ho

Tuyen Ho with Bedesignerly was the mastermind behind the cover of this novel. Our paths crossed in 2023 when I owned a bookstore in my hometown of Clinton, Tennessee. Tuyen had just published a children's book, *I Want to Be a French Fry*, and at an author event, we discussed the creativity behind her design work. When it came time to figure out the look of this novel, I knew I wanted her to design it. I'm so happy she said yes and even took the time to read the entire novel to craft the perfect cover. Check out more of her work at bedesignerly.com.

Criston Bishop

One day, while at Hoskins in the Flat, Criston got volunteered to become the editor of my novel. It's funny how the universe works sometimes. I wrote most of this book at Hoskins in the Flat before

Criston started working there. When I casually mentioned the book to her, I learned she was an editor—the final piece I needed before publishing. Criston, thank you for taking time out of your schedule on short notice to edit this book. I appreciate you so much!

My Family

Everyone says they have the best family... but I'm pretty certain I actually do. I keep them on their toes endlessly with my crazy ideas and projects, yet they've always loved and supported each one, even when things didn't always work out. My mom and Aunt Hope are my biggest supporters in life, and I don't think I could ever thank them enough. My grandparents, the real Nana and Grandad, were the inspiration for the grandparents in this novel. With every scene I wrote, I smiled or laughed because it was so them. Thank you a million times.

My Beta Readers

Thank you to the following people who kindly said yes to reading *The Club by the Sea* before it went out into the world. Your feedback and support meant everything to me: Katherine Birkbeck, Callie Archer, Julie Swisher, Taylor Payne, Kennedy Blair, and Molly Campbell.

YOU

Lastly, thank you so much to the readers who purchased a copy of this novel. I never dreamed in a million years that I would see my work in print and in the hands of others. Your support and love mean so much to me. I hope you enjoyed it.

www.ingramcontent.com/pod-product-compliance
Lightning Source LLC
LaVergne TN
LVHW091712070526
838199LV00050B/2370